Fiddle and Fire

HEARTS OF GOLD
BOOK TWO

ARIELLA TALIX

Ebook ISBN: 979-8-9856766-7-9

Paperback ISBN: 979-8-9856766-8-6

Hardcover ISBN: 979-8-3919145-4-9

Cover Design by Dar Albert, Wicked Smart Designs

Western classical players sometimes use "fiddle" as an affectionate term for the violin, that intimate companion and workmate.
—Gordon Swift, *Is That a Violin or a Fiddle?*

Music is often the spark that lights the fire of the soul.
—Jeffrey Fry

One

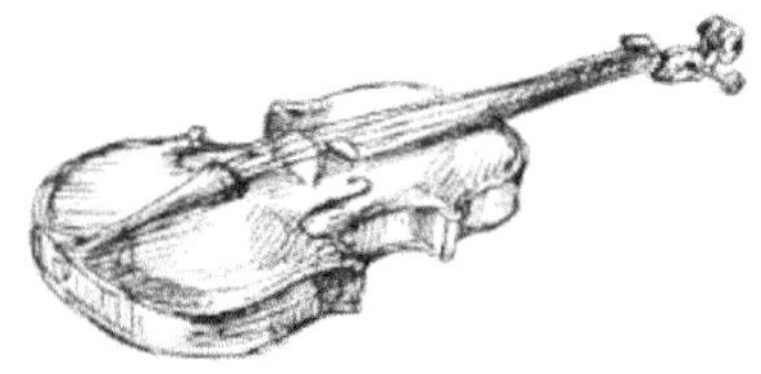

"Fire!"

The dreaded word echoed through the streets of San Francisco that foggy morning. It was pandemonium as people ran both toward and away from the blaze, and bells clanged in the closest fire companies.

Isaac, Walter, and the other volunteer firemen dropped everything and grabbed the hand-drawn firetruck. As quickly as possible, they dragged the heavily loaded cart full of water and equipment up and down the steep city streets. Other men grabbed a ladder loaded with water-filled buckets hanging from it by hooks. It took four men to carry it the way pall-bearers hoist and move a coffin.

The Aylesbury Fire Company's two Dalmatians, Ember and Cinder, ran ahead of the firemen. The dogs barked a warning, letting people know that firefighters were on the way and the street needed to be cleared. Firefighters also shouted at pedestrians to move and hoped fervently they could make it in time to douse the flames before another major fire destroyed the city. That kind of catastrophic destruction happened all too frequently in San Francisco.

"Thank heaven, this one wasn't too big," Walter sighed as they trudged back up the hill to their department.

"Yes. No injuries either!" Isaac agreed. "Not like the one that broke out last May when so many people were hurt, and it burned down that whole block. A terrible thing." He shook his head sadly, remembering the event. As they neared the front of their building, he grasped Walter's arm to halt him for a moment. "I never get tired of looking at this, Walter. You outdid yourself with the design. We're the envy of all the firemen in the city with this place."

Walter had worked back in Philadelphia as an architect, but the stifling job left him unfulfilled and ready to move on to something better out west. He'd quit his job after refusing to cut corners and design shoddy buildings—something that had been a problem for his employer... who was also his father.

So Walter severed ties with the man who'd tried to control his every move. His father was strict and humorless, never showing any pride in his son's work or affection for him. His mother had been better, but she'd long since passed away. At least, Walter reasoned, they'd seen to his education, and Walter genuinely loved architecture.

Restless and young, he had saved enough money to take off on an adventure to find something that would inspire him. A small inheritance from his grandfather also helped.

Walter smiled graciously. "Yes, well, I'm sure the competition between the fire companies will continue even if our building is superior. There are so many egos involved, and with most of the city acting as if we're almost celebrities… Except you, of course. You're an actual celebrity, I suppose."

Isaac snorted. "Just because of my fiddling? Hardly. When we play, they're probably all coming to gawk at Adeline." Isaac performed with Adeline Hart Dawson-Langley, a beautiful and exceptionally talented pianist. When she'd arrived in San Francisco, the ratio of men to women was roughly ten to one, and although the odds were gradually evening out, women were still very much in the minority.

The firefighters stowed their gear carefully as Walter argued, "You're selling yourself short. I see how the ladies look at you when you play. And some of the men too."

Isaac shrugged. He'd played the violin since he was a small boy. His parents had encouraged it, deciding he needed an activity that would help him use up some of his excess energy. Luckily for everyone, music fascinated him.

Now that he was grown, there was nothing small about Isaac. He was a giant of a man at over six feet tall with muscles honed from years of heavy, backbreaking work. He and his partners had mined for gold before and during the California Gold Rush, made a substantial fortune for themselves, and then built The Discovery—a successful hotel and casino. Eventually, they formed a building company Walter and Isaac ran with Jasper and Royal—who, with their wife Adeline, were their best friends in the world. Isaac and Adeline also gave music lessons and recitals together at the National Theatre.

Isaac was not only a gifted and proficient musician, but he also handcrafted beautiful instruments. And because the demand for that in San Francisco was limited, he also crafted exquisite wooden furniture and finish carpentry. With all of the building going on in the city at that time, their company Roja Wais was tremendously busy and sought-after.

Isaac was one of the busiest men in San Francisco, being a volunteer fireman, a carpenter, instrument maker, music teacher, and practicing musician. He wouldn't have it any other way, however, as his exuberant nature and boundless energy needed plenty of outlets. His parents had been right to channel his high spirits into music.

Walter, on the other hand, was quite content to plan and design buildings and homes for the men of Roja Wais to build, and when he wasn't helping put out fires or drawing up architectural plans, he had his nose in a book. Walter was well-read on a staggering array of topics; he seemed some-times like a walking library. He also had a golden tongue and loved to tell stories.

Although only a few years older, Walter sometimes felt he needed to look after Isaac to make sure the younger man was getting enough food and rest, but he kept that to himself and did it unobtrusively.

"You know, the people who are moving into the new house we just built ought to be arriving in a few days," he pointed out to Isaac. Their friend, Doc Louis Montrachet, had distant acquaintances who planned to send their son to San Francisco from France and who needed to have a house built for him. It took a year for the necessary letters to go back and forth to seal the deal.

"Yes, I'm aware. I'm actually heading over there now because I still need to do some finish work in the dining room. It's the one room that's not completed." He looked down at his sooty clothes, soiled from the fire they'd just put out. He was sweaty and streaked with ash. "I guess it doesn't matter what I look like if I'm going to go make a mess of myself over there anyway. I'm just going to grab a quick bite, and I'll see you later. Adeline and I have lessons scheduled this afternoon, so I'll need to hurry if I want to accomplish anything." He scarpered off to the kitchen, hoping to find the chef in an amiable enough mood to offer him something in a rush.

Walter decided he'd clean up and relax for a few minutes with a new book he'd just found about electricity. It sounded like magic to him, and he could certainly see the potential value of it. After that, he thought he'd make some headway on the new building plan he needed to draw up.

Walter and Isaac had recently moved out of The Discovery —thus giving more space to the hotel for guests—and into their exquisite firehouse. This fire department was known as Aylesbury Fire Company because of the fancy top hats they sported during the formal dress parades that happened at various times throughout the year. Each firehouse had its own personality, and theirs was basically a fine gentlemen's club. They had a highly trained chef who kept them fed with nothing but the freshest and finest foods, and they constantly stocked the best spirits and cigars they could get their hands on. Unlike the blue-collar firemen of the eastern states who had a well-deserved reputation for violence, San Franciscan firemen were not only local heroes, but they were also considered gentlemen with fine taste. They may have felt competitive about getting to a fire before another company, but in the enlightened age of 1855, they didn't do anything about it other than brag.

Ensconced in a comfortable chair by a sunny window—now that the morning fog had burnt off—Walter smiled fondly as he watched Isaac, his favorite person on earth, rush out of the building and off to take care of business.

Catching Walter's smile, another fireman named Richard, who was also relaxing with a book, asked, "You've known him long?" Ember and Cinder lay sprawled at his feet. Richard had trained the young dogs since they were puppies, and as much as they enjoyed the company of all the men, they were completely devoted to him.

Walter answered with a smile, "Several years now. We met back east by accident, and we've been best friends ever since that moment." Walter got a faraway look on his face when he added, "Traveling across country together and then working side-by-side every day definitely forms a bond. And Isaac isn't just a good man. He's the best. He's also the most talented person I know."

"How'd you meet him by accident?"

Walter closed his book and laughed. He loved to tell this story. Actually, Walter loved to tell *any* story, but this was one of his favorites. "I was driving my wagon down a Pittsburgh city street when all of a sudden, this enormous young blond fellow flew out of a building, all wide-eyed. He flung himself into the back of my wagon, hunkered down out of sight, and begged me to get out of there as fast as possible. I'd have been worried that he was trying to rob me or something, but his arms were full of what looked like a heavy-as-blazes pack of tools and—of all things—a violin case. He looked so sincere when he begged me—" Walter deepened his voice in an imitation of Isaac, "'Please, mister! I swear I'm no thief, but I need to get out of here!' It was then that I spied another older fellow come barreling out behind him with a shotgun. The man seemed to be trying to run and load the gun at the same time, and then he tripped over his own clumsy feet. Not wanting to be shot by the careless fool, I coaxed my team into a speedier gait—but not so fast as to draw undue attention to ourselves, mind you—and figured I'd find out what all the fracas was about when we were out of range of that buffoon with the buckshot. We made our way as quickly as was prudent straight out of town.

"I finally let the horses have a rest in a nice shady area a far piece out of the city where they could get a drink and graze a while. I can't tell you how curious I was to find out whether or not I was harboring a criminal, but my gut instinct told me it was something else that made that big, young man bolt that way. He had too honest of a face to be a thief or a killer, and he was barely out of boyhood back then."

Richard laughed then and observed, "Apparently, you have a good eye for character. I don't see any evidence that he slit your throat or shot you."

"Isaac is the kind of man who's big and strong enough to tear someone limb from limb. He does have a temper that he normally keeps locked down, but when he's feeling emotional, he'd rather pound nails into wood or rip things up with that fiddle of his than do actual bodily harm to anyone. He pours more passion into his music than you could even imagine. Being a firefighter is perfect for him because he wants to save the world, but I always worry he'll hurt his hands and not be able to play anymore." Walter sighed. "That would be such a loss." Walter fixed his gaze on the window and ruminated.

"So, why was he running?"

Walter blinked. "Oh, sorry. I got diverted there for a moment, woolgathering about his music. Yes, well, he was running from a furious father, as it turns out."

Richard smirked and nodded. "Did he leave behind a bastard?"

"Oh, no! Nothing like that. He was an innocent victim of circumstance. The daughter of the man he was apprenticed to was apparently quite taken with Isaac and caused the whole thing. She actually hoisted her skirt, jumped onto Isaac's lap, and wrapped her arms around him right when she knew her father would see them. She'd hinted to Isaac on more than one occasion that she'd like to marry him, but Isaac had no interest in losing his apprenticeship or in marrying her. He thought she was pretty, but also a scheming little trouble-maker, and obviously, he was right." Walter chuckled and shook his head. "Her antics and her flirting just got worse and worse until this time, she plastered a kiss on his lips and tried to make it look like they were in a compromised posi-tion so her father would force Isaac to marry her. Isaac heard her father coming, dumped her off his lap, grabbed his tools and violin, and skedaddled out of there like the devil himself was after him. He didn't want anything to do with either of them after that."

"Well, I'll be. Did he ever see her again?"

"Nope. As soon as I realized he was serious, we just kept heading west. He said his apprenticeship was nearly finished anyway, and he was ready to move on. We hit it off famously from the very start, so I told him about my plans to keep trav-eling and meet up eventually with a wagon train in Missouri. That was fine with him, and the rest is history." Walter thought a moment and then added, "Isaac is such a talented woodworker; I'm sure he had to have been better at it than his employer at that point. I wager that the man was trying to force him back to work by scaring him rather than trying to run him off. For all I know, he might have put his daughter up to it, was using her as bait to better his own business by keeping Isaac around permanently. He's certainly been an outstanding part of our building company. No one can beat his carpentry skills."

"What did Isaac's father say about him leaving his apprenticeship? He must have been disappointed."

Walter looked sad then and got that faraway look again. "Isaac was on his own. His parents perished in a house fire, and he ended up finding his own apprenticeship. He was not at home when the fire happened because he was off fiddling for some folks, and it was a dreadful shock for him to come back to, I can tell you that. He had no siblings, and his parents were older. I guess they were pretty close. He was so shaken up about it he could barely even stand to look at a campfire for the longest time. It was when we arrived in San Francisco that he faced his fears and began fighting fires. He says it's his way of making sure no other families suffer the way his did."

"That's quite a story," Richard exclaimed softly. He reached down and petted the dogs thoughtfully. "Just goes to show how little we know about people we see every day."

Just then, they heard a bell chime, signaling that their noon meal was ready. "Let's eat. I'm starved," Walter declared.

Two

Isaac was completely engrossed in his work. He loved wood. He loved the smell of it, the textures of it, and the rich colors when it was stained. He knew instinctively what particular wood would work best for what project, and he was known to set aside certain pieces for the instruments he crafted. Some of the wood seemed to him to resonate in his hands, and he could imagine the sounds that would come out of the violin or cello he would make.

Other pieces spoke to him in ways that gave him creative ideas for furniture. He found burl wood especially beautiful and constantly looked for shapes and patterns he could make into something magnificent. The vast number of ships that were abandoned in the San Francisco harbor during the gold rush offered him a wonderful supply of wood to work with. He often made trips to the waterfront to scavenge for the best pieces before the ships either sank or became repurposed into shoreline buildings.

It was no wonder that he was lost in his creative process when a voice broke into his reverie. He'd been carving an ornate piece of trim he planned to use on the ceiling of the dining room he was finishing. He'd been right not to bother changing his clothes as he was liberally flaked with sawdust. It was in his hair and all over his body. Two of his workers were likewise involved.

"*Il y a quelqu'un ici?*" a voice called out from the front door. A dapper, well-dressed man appeared a moment later, having followed the noise into the dining room. "*Eh, bien, bonjour.* I am Pascal de Massey, and I am here to take possession of my new home. Can someone help me? We have just arrived." Just then, there was a huge scraping thud behind him as some rough-looking men crashed a large trunk into something. "*Mon Dieu!* Be careful with my things!" he cried.

Ignoring de Massey, Isaac stomped toward the workers and scowled at the huge scratch they'd created in his beautiful carved door. He knew immediately how many hours it would take him to repair it. He swore loudly and crudely just as a woman started up the stairs to the front porch.

She gasped at his language and then glared at him. At the same time, she appeared to be taking him in and appreciating his overall stature. Her face morphed from one emotion into the next as her frown cleared, her eyes dilated on a sharp intake of breath, and then she pursed her lips and scowled again.

As angry as he was over the clumsy movers' accident,

Isaac had an immediate appreciation for this woman. Despite her glowering at him and her flared nostrils, she was something to behold. Slender and golden-haired, she looked delicate enough to blow away in a strong gust of wind. She had a tiny waist that Isaac had the sudden desire to encircle with his hands, and a pair of shapely… he quickly raised his eyes back to her face. "Afternoon, ma'am," he said with a wink. "I'm Isaac Stark from the Roja Wais Building Company."

"Indeed," she countered with no enthusiasm whatsoever. She tried to step past Isaac into the house and, at the same time, avoid touching his layer of sawdust with her lovely dove-gray traveling ensemble. She wrinkled up her nose slightly as she swept past, no doubt offended by his sweaty, sawdusty, smoke-filled aura.

"And you would be?" Isaac reached forward as if to take her hand, and she shrunk back. He noticed this and looked down at his own filthy hand. "Oh, sorry. I've been working since before dawn, and I'm a little soiled, I suppose, what with the fire and all."

Pascal overheard that comment and rushed to Isaac with fear in his eyes. "Was there a fire in the house? Is it safe for Suzette and me to move in?"

"No, sir. Your house is fine. We were putting out a fire elsewhere. The only work left is the dining room," he gestured to the door, "and now this." He glared at the extra work again. "We weren't actually expecting you for a couple more days, but don't you worry. You and your wife will be comfortable and safe, and we'll try to get this work done as quickly as possible."

"Suzette is not my wife. She is my sister." He gave a nasty smirk and added, "She only accompanied me at the last minute."

Isaac's eyes slid involuntarily to Suzette, and his face had a hungry look that came and left in a flash. She sniffed and gave him a regal glare, and Isaac stifled a frown. She might be beautiful, but he hadn't made a very favorable impression on her, it seemed. He could barely blame her as he looked down at his sloppy work attire. He hoped he didn't smell too awful, but in reality, he was confident that he did.

Suzette straightened her spine to an even more rigid degree as she tried and failed to look down her nose at the man who towered over her. "I hope you'll be quick with the rest of the work. Pascal and I do not wish to be annoyed by workmen coming and going. I have a staff to hire and like my peace and quiet so I can practice."

It was then that Isaac noticed the very old and worn violin case she held tightly in her grasp. His eyes and interest in her flared again. "You play?" he asked almost reverently.

"Yes, of course," she said as she swept past him. "I just hope there is someone in this god-forsaken territory who might appreciate it."

"Oh, there certainly is," he muttered to himself as he watched her glide into the house, taking in her surroundings. More audibly, he offered, "I can give you a tour of the house and point out some of Walter's innovations if you'd like."

She turned and faced him, "That won't be necessary. I can see for myself."

Pascal broke into the conversation and asked Isaac, "Can

you get a message to Walter James or Jasper Langley, please? Let them know we're here, and I can pay the balance we owe later today if they'd like."

Chuckling to himself and thinking that he'd be just as able to accept payment as he was a full partner in the company, Isaac decided Walter would enjoy showing off the house himself. "Yes, I can get word to them and have them over here right away if you'd like."

At that point, what looked like an army of men arrived with more trunks and large pieces of furniture that they'd undoubtedly unloaded from the de Masseys' ship. Isaac stepped out of the way and headed back into the dining room. The door repair could wait, but he needed to get the other work done soon. He immediately dispatched one of his helpers to head back to the fire company to get Walter and to tell him that their clients had arrived early. He then sent the other worker to Jasper's house to alert him as well. Neither messenger had far to go.

Seeing that Pascal had followed him, Isaac regarded him and spoke up. "If you don't mind, I would suggest the sitting room just through there for your sister's practicing." He indicated the hallway with his large, calloused hand. "It's nice and sunny and has excellent acoustics. I would tell her myself, but I am afraid my appearance has frightened her off."

"Acoustics," Pascal said in a flat, bored voice.

"Yes, the quality of the sound will be excellent in that room, I'm certain. Please let her know."

"Yes, right. I wonder where she's gone off to." Pascal sauntered away like a man without a care in the world.

Isaac doubted he would pass along the message. A shame, that was. But then he heard Pascal raise his voice as he ascended the staircase. "Suzette, that worker Ichabod—or whatever his name is—says to use the parlor to the right of the foyer. He says your scratches on that violin of yours have a better chance of sounding decent if you stay in there to play! I hope it has a thick door."

Isaac could hear the man laughing at his own rude joke. Shaking his head, he got back to work and tried to ignore the men crashing through the house with furniture and trunks. *Are they all drunk this early in the day? I hope I don't have to repair the entire house when they're done.*

About half an hour later, Suzette stomped into the dining room and straight up to Isaac, who was picking up his tools to leave. Her face was flushed, but she had removed her jacket, and he was able to get an even better look at her shapely little body in a modest white blouse. Again, he had to force himself to look at her face, but the look of anger and frustration in her eyes was something to behold. Something about it made his blood heat up and his body react.

"Something wrong with the house, ma'am?" he asked as calmly as possible.

"Not at all. The house is perfectly adequate. I am appalled at your supposition, however, that I make terrible scratching noises on my violin! I will have you know that I have had the great pleasure and honor to have been a student of the great

Paganini himself! Not that you probably know who he was. I am an accomplished musician!"

Isaac felt the need to squelch a smile. He loved her fury. She looked so bottled up and straight-laced, but there was an inferno in that woman. He could smell it boiling.

And he wanted it.

His hands itched to loosen her hair at that very moment and mess her up. He wanted to debauch every inch of her. He wanted to feast on that mouth and quiet her with deep kisses.

"Why are you staring at me that way? Are you not going to apologize for your rudeness?"

"You seem to have pegged me for something I am not, ma'am. I reserve the right to form an opinion about your talent only *after* I've heard you play. I merely suggest that the room through there would be an enjoyable place for you to practice. It's sunny in there on most days, and—as I explained to your brother—has the best acoustics in the house."

Suzette's brow furrowed slightly at his words, but she did not apologize. She just looked confused.

Softly, Isaac added, "I think your brother was having a little sport with you. I'm sure your playing is more than adequate."

"Adequate?! I have played with…"

"Yes, the great Paganini. So, I heard. Very impressive, although I've also heard he was not the best teacher of violin virtuosity because his heart was never in it. He just did it for the money. His great talent lay in his playing and his compositions."

"What would you know?" Suzette huffed indignantly.

Isaac smiled at her with his eyes burning and gave a little shrug. "I know that you must have been just a little girl when you studied with him. Now, excuse me, ma'am, I have another appointment and must leave immediately."

"You're going to leave this woodwork in a mess? How dare you? We need you and the other men finished and out of here so we can get on with moving in."

"Ma'am, you're earlier than we expected, and the work will be finished by the appointed date, of that you can be certain. And I will be out of your way, I promise. But, for now, I have an important engagement." *I'd sure rather stay here and pester you, though,* he thought as he strode out the door. *I've never seen anything like her. I wonder if she can really play or if she's just as full of herself as her brother. That man looks like he could be trouble.*

As Isaac started to make his way down the front steps, he confronted Walter coming up. Walter, as usual, looked delighted to see Isaac and gave his best friend a blindingly happy smile. Isaac responded in kind and said cryptically with a soft laugh, "Just you wait until you meet our new neighbors. I have to hurry and get cleaned up so Addie and I can work with the students on their upcoming concert. See you at dinner tonight. They're expecting us." He clapped Walter on the back as they passed, and Walter turned slightly to watch Isaac stride away in a rush.

Three

Walter paused at the front door. He was accustomed to coming and going as he needed when Roja Wais had a project going on, but it felt wrong to do so now that the owners were present. Still, the door was wide open to accommodate the noisy movers, so he shrugged and wandered into the foyer.

Once inside, he nearly collided with a trim little woman whose back was to him. He smelled something faint but lovely that reminded him of the lilacs growing around his parents' house a lifetime ago and beheld a head of barely contained curls so shiny and bright, they looked like spun gold. Instantly, he wanted to touch this creature, and he gave a huge intake of breath, gulping down her scent. "Pardon me, miss," he choked out. "I'm Walter James from Roja Wais."

Suzette swung around with wide eyes and took in the sight of the first true gentleman she'd seen since disembarking this morning. A tall, lean man with a kind face stood staring at her. He had wavy brown hair that flopped engagingly over his high forehead, wore spectacles, and had a rather professorial look to him. She was instantly intrigued and pleased with someone who had such impeccable posture, dress, and obvious manners. He was nothing like the rough know-it-all who'd just left. That other man had ignited a hunger and a fury in her that she needed to obliterate before it consumed her, but this man exuded peacefulness that made her wish to rub up against him like a cat so he could stroke her. She wanted to listen to his deep voice forever telling her that this new life of hers in this strange city was going to be a good one.

Blushing, she smiled politely. *"Bonjour, monsieur.* I am Suzette de Massey, and my brother Pascal is around here somewhere. I know he has business to attend to with you. I would offer you a seat, but I am not sure where one is at the moment. I'll just go now and try to locate my brother."

They both heard another loud crash coming from upstairs and some colorful cursing. Suzette's face flamed scarlet. She ducked her head, and before Walter could say a thing, she scooted off in search of Pascal.

Walter decided to take a look around. He hadn't been in the house for a few days, and he was curious to see how far along they were on the finishing touches. Spying the ongoing work in the dining room, Walter headed that way and laughed to himself as the other two workers entered the room to get back to work. "Leave it to Isaac to go above and beyond. This is fine work, men. Thank you. You'll see a bonus in your pay for this."

They smiled and extended their thanks. Both men, Walter knew, worked well with Isaac. He pushed hard, expected exceptional work, and had wonderful ideas, and these two were the cream of the crop as far as woodworkers went in San Francisco. The city was still so new, and there were properties being built to accommodate the huge influx of newcomers. There were countless opportunities for workers who wanted to make something of themselves, and Walter had no doubt that these two men would excel. Roja Wais just had to keep them busy and well-paid, so they didn't jump ship and go work for someone else.

He heard footsteps behind him and swung around. A handsome, fair-haired young man who looked a lot like Suzette wandered in, yawning and rubbing his eye. He looked like he'd just woken up from a nap, and Walter wondered where he'd located a bed during this stage of moving in. Then Walter got a faint whiff of alcohol and formed an instant opinion of the young man. Indolent.

Walter extended his hand. "Good afternoon, sir. I'm Walter James from Roja Wais. Welcome to San Francisco. I hope the house and the city agree with you."

Pascal took Walter's firm grip with an astonishingly limp and smooth hand. "Pascal de Massey. *Enchanté.* The house is fine, and I have not seen much of San Francisco yet other than the congested harbor and the hilly streets we had to take to get here. So, we shall see." He exuded an air of boredom and didn't quite meet Walter's gaze as he added, "I just hope there is something to *do* around here."

Forging ahead as if Pascal were completely overwhelmed with the beauty of his new home, Walter offered, "May I show you and your sister around and point out some of the innovations we've included in the house?"

"I am sure that will not be necessary," Pascal drawled. "We lived in a chateau in France that makes this look like a stable." Then he finally looked at Walter, who'd gasped at the insult. "Do not look so crestfallen, dear man. Suzette and I have no need of a damned chateau, we just need a roof over our heads that is reasonably comfortable. This might be a palace by San Francisco standards; I have no idea, actually."

Just then, another familiar voice broke into their so-called conversation. Jasper, another partner from Roja Wais, walked through the open door and cheerfully exclaimed, "Mr. de Massey! Welcome to San Francisco. I'm Jasper Langley. I trust you're finding the house to your liking?"

Pascal gave a bored shrug and asked, "Is there any gaming in this city?"

Jasper gave the man a calculating look and answered, "Indeed, sir, there is plenty of it. I might recommend you stay away from some of the seedier locations if you don't want your throat slit, however. Avoid the area known as Sydney-Town if you value your life. You'd no doubt be the most comfortable in The Discovery's casino, where you'll be safe. In fact, I have business there this afternoon and can show you the way up just as soon as we settle your account." Walter bit back a smile, knowing what Jasper was thinking—if the man gambled, he didn't want Pascal to fritter away their final fee before they ever saw it. Jasper looked at Pascal expectantly.

"Yes, of course," Pascal drawled as if the matter of money were of little consequence. In any case, he settled up his account with Jasper and Walter with no delay. During the entire transaction, Walter kept craning his neck around, hoping to get another glance of that exquisite little Suzette. She was really something. Sadly, she did not reappear.

With the payment made, Walter took his leave to get back to the architectural design he needed to complete, and Jasper left with a more cheerful-looking Pascal. The Frenchman seemed much more pleased now that he had the promise of some good whiskey and cards in his near future. He hadn't bothered to tell Suzette where he was going, Jasper noted.

Suzette, however, was well aware of her brother's intentions. He planned to leave her to sort out the movers and would probably stumble home sometime well past midnight. Sighing, she thought, *He'd just be in the way, most likely.* She certainly had enjoyed listening to the timbre of that man Walter's voice from where she'd stood out of eyesight part of the way up the stairs, but she knew it was not her place to interfere while men were conducting business. Her parents had drummed that notion into her enough times. Pascal would manage the money, and she would manage the household—that is unless she found a man of her own—if that were even possible. She wondered if, in this new life of hers, she even wanted to cede any authority over herself to a husband the way her mother had done. *I hope it is different here, and I hope I can escape my past enough to make a future for myself.*

A flash of that other, rougher, confusing man burst into her thoughts. He'd said his name was Isaac Stark, and she wondered whether he was as domineering as she imagined. She shook herself and went to look for workers to direct and possibly a trunk to empty and sort out. She would not let herself think about a man so obviously beneath her station, no matter how impressive he looked. Her parents would be shocked she would even consider such a man.

Suzette stifled the tiny voice in her head that asked whether that might not be a good thing; after all, she had come so far, traveled so long, to build the life she wanted. Would she really be serving herself by bringing the traditions and rules of France all the way here with her? Certainly Pascal felt no need to meet her parents' standard of behavior. Why should she?

Just then, a group of men arrived with more furniture from the ship, and she needed to direct their efforts.

Four

Over the next several days, Isaac showed up to work at the de Masseys' new house. He was pleased to see that it was taking shape nicely—not only because of the pride he took in his work, but for Suzette, who he couldn't seem to get off his mind.

Suzette had unpacked some lovely pieces they'd shipped from France, but the rooms were still sparsely furnished. Isaac found himself wondering where he would place things in this beautiful room.

The woman in question appeared and disappeared frustratingly quickly throughout the day while he worked. Judging from the parade of people in and out of the house, she was conducting interviews for a household staff. The candidates appeared to him to be fairly disgruntled as they left, so he assumed she was not having very good luck.

He saw even less of Pascal except for one time early in the

morning while Isaac was out on the front porch fixing the scratched finish of the door. Pascal stumbled up the steps smelling of cigars and spirits after what was apparently a night of overindulgence. Isaac politely stuck out his hand and said in a cheerful voice, "Good morning, Mr. de Massey."

Ignoring Isaac's hand, Pascal swayed and leaned over the handrail where he puked. Then he mumbled something unintelligible and staggered toward the doorway.

Isaac wondered how the man had managed to find his way home… and how Suzette could stand to live with a man who behaved like that. Shaking his head in disgust, he got back to work as Pascal disappeared into the house.

One day, Isaac was getting ready to leave for the afternoon lessons he gave at Adeline's house when he caught sight of Suzette standing in the parlor he'd recommended for her practicing. He'd yet to hear any music from her, so he figured she must play when she was alone and wanted her privacy. On this day, she had such an unhappy expression on her face as she stared out the window, he wanted to capture her in his arms and make her worries disappear. Without thinking about it too much, he approached her.

"Ma'am," he addressed her softly. Her head snapped toward him, and her eyes went wide. "Is there anything I can do to help you? You seem troubled, and I'm sure all of this uproar of moving has been a difficult adjustment for you."

Temper flared behind Suzette's eyes. She opened her mouth, ready to put him in his place, but the caustic words stuck somewhere in her throat and wouldn't come out. Instead, she just sighed and then tried to stiffen her posture and look unaffected either by his kindness or by his virile magnificence. The truth was, she was hungry, bone-tired, angry with Pascal for his immaturity—not that it was a surprise—and desperately lonely. "Thank you. I do not need any assistance." She perused his appearance and noted to herself that he was cleaner than he had been that first morning when they arrived. He no longer smelled of smoke and soot, although he still appeared to be a common laborer in his plain work clothes.

Isaac stood his ground and narrowed his eyes at her thoughtfully. After a moment, he offered, "My friend Adeline might be someone you'd enjoy meeting. And one of her closest friends is a Frenchwoman. I'm sure they'd love to welcome you to the neighborhood. I'll let Addie know this afternoon. You need some women friends, and they're still pretty scarce in this city, though nothing like when I first got here." Before Suzette could protest or agree, he strolled out the front door, whistling a bawdy dancehall tune.

Suzette stared after Isaac. *That was particularly thoughtful of the man, but I wonder what sort of women he knows. I have heard many of the Frenchwomen here are prostitutes.* She shuddered. *I certainly do not need to make their acquaintance if that is so.*

THE NEXT MORNING, HOWEVER, SUZETTE WAS NONPLUSSED TO BE called upon by two of the most beautifully dressed women she'd seen outside of Paris. And not only were they dressed impeccably, they were both incredibly attractive and refined. Her notion that Isaac's acquaintances were possibly ladies of the evening was dashed to bits as soon as the younger woman announced, "Good morning. I'm Adeline Hart Dawson-Langley. We are delighted to welcome you to San Francisco and apologize for not coming sooner. We thought it prudent to let you settle in for a few days before descending on you like a swarm of locusts." Adeline smiled sweetly with a soft laugh. "It was my husband Jasper who met you the day you arrived. If you recall, he and Walter James came by to finalize payment with your brother. And this is my dear friend Madame Marguerite Beaufort, who has an absolutely booming dress design business that is unparalleled—probably in the whole country. You'll definitely want to have her as a friend."

After receiving kisses on both cheeks and a rapid greeting in French from Marguerite, Suzette replied, "Please, come in, and I shall attempt to make us some tea. We can sit in the parlor over this way, although I am afraid we're still a little short of furniture."

"Oh, don't trouble yourself with tea. I know you must be busy, and we just wanted to have a quick visit with you. Have you spoken to Isaac about furniture?" Adeline asked, glancing around.

Blinking, Suzette replied, "Why?"

Marguerite and Adeline shared a look, and Marguerite turned to Suzette. "Isaac is the most sought-after furniture designer in the city. He creates works of art! The armoire he designed for me is as fine or finer than anything new I could have found in France."

Suzette thought to herself, *That man himself is a work of art.* But she said nothing as she raised her eyebrows in surprise.

"You must speak to him. I know he has a backlog of requests because of all of the home building they're doing right now, but he loves his work so much, he might be persuaded to put you ahead of the pack," Adeline said as she shrewdly observed the slight blush that had suddenly bloomed in Suzette's cheeks at the mention of Isaac's name. "And I might add that aside from my husbands, Isaac is my oldest and closest friend here in California. I can personally attest to his reliability and artistry."

Blinking as she tried to process all this new information, Suzette answered merely, "Oh!" Surprised that a fine lady like Adeline would consider calling a worker like Isaac a friend, she added to herself, *Worker or no, I would not mind having him around to look at a while longer. He is quite decorative.* Then she took a moment to ponder what Adeline had just said and considered it sad that someone so young had already lost a husband and remarried. She had, after all, mentioned husbands, plural. There must have been a death.

"In any case, we also came to extend an invitation to the two of you to come and dine with us at Hart House." She extended her hand, holding out a delicate calling card. "The address is on this, and it's only a short walk to the north on the opposite side of the street right here on Rincon Hill. You can't miss it. May we expect you this Friday evening at seven o'clock? We'll have some of our dearest friends there, and I'm sure they'll enjoy meeting you. It will be a casual get-together, so don't worry about dressing formally. The children will be underfoot too, no doubt. It's always a bit chaotic at Hart House."

Adeline's warmth and her welcoming attitude suddenly made Suzette's eyes fill with tears. She fought to hold them back as she answered, "I would be delighted to join you, and I will certainly extend the invitation to my brother Pascal as well, though I can scarcely guess what he may have already planned for the evening. I shall do my best to bring him along. Thank you, Mrs. Dawson-Langley."

Adeline gave her a blinding smile and said, "Please, call me Adeline. We San Franciscans are a relaxed bunch. So, we look forward to seeing you then."

"Yes, of course. *Merci beaucoup!*" Suzette suddenly realized she wasn't ready for these lovely women to leave her house as it was such a comfort to be in their company, so she asked, "I wonder if either of you has any ideas for how I might employ a housekeeper and a cook? I have had terrible luck so far, and this house is too large for me to handle on my own. I am also a disaster in the kitchen, it seems."

Adeline looked sympathetic while Marguerite suddenly brightened up like a Fourth of July sparkler. "*Mais oui!* You may be the answer to my prayers, and this would help me out as well," she exclaimed. "I have two young ladies—sisters— who were sent to me from France in hopes of finding them employment. They are both polite and intelligent, but they are only adequate with a needle. I need talented seamstresses, not domestics, and I have kept them on only out of loyalty and to keep them out of the brothels. I shall send them over to you immediately." She smiled brightly at Suzette's startled expression and added, "It's settled then. They can move out of my rather crowded space and into your servants' quarters today."

Suzette stammered, "I…"

"No need to thank me. We are doing each other a great service. You will not be sorry. They are lovely girls, and I just hope they do not marry and leave you suddenly. That has a way of happening in this city all too often, especially with good help. You will want to compensate them generously. There is such a shortage of women in San Francisco, they are sought after like rare gems."

"Yes, well, please send them by, and we shall see." Looking around and pondering why her house seemed so strangely quiet, she blurted out, "I wonder where Isaac is this morning."

"Didn't he tell you he was finished?" Adeline asked. "That man has his mind on too many things, I believe. I shall have to chastise him and let him know that you're in dire need of his services still, and he should not have abandoned you!" She laughed to soften her words. "Or perhaps I should leave that to you for when you see him next."

Suzette's eyebrows furrowed slightly as she wondered how she could see Isaac to ask him and was still reeling at the way these women had come in and rearranged her life with a velvet hammer. Obviously, they meant well, but she wanted to make her own decisions. She'd been pushed around her whole life by her father and older brothers, and it was time she demonstrated her own competence.

Still, the fact that they had swooped in to welcome her and assist her warmed her heart more than irritated her.

For the next hour or so after her company left, Suzette wandered through her house, making an inventory of things she needed. A table here, a chair there… the list went on and on. *Surely,* she thought, *there must be a place I can purchase some of what we need so I will not have to rely on Isaac for everything.* And then she heard the front bell ring.

Rushing to answer, Suzette straightened her clothing and pushed a stray curl out of her face, hoping to open the door to the man who'd invaded her thoughts all too often. She was surprised to find, however, two young women in the company of none other than Walter James.

"Good afternoon, Miss de Massey." He greeted her with a broad smile, as she thought again of what a handsome gentleman he seemed to be. "I heard from Adeline and Madame Beaufort that you were in need of these ladies' help, so I took it upon myself to escort them over here. And I'll admit, I wanted to check on how you were settling in now that the work is done."

Suzette gave him a bright smile and answered, "I seem to be rich with callers today. Thank you. Please, everyone, come in." It seemed that Walter could at least temporarily dispel any thoughts she had about Isaac. The man was delightful, and she wanted to get to know him better.

Walter indicated the woman on his left. "This is Delphine, who is to work for you in the kitchen, and this," he indicated the other, slightly younger one, "is Fabienne, who will keep your house in tip-top shape, I'm told."

After a brief conversation with the sisters in French, Suzette was pleased with their manners and experience. Noting that they both held valises, she excused herself from Walter and showed them to their new quarters. They would be sharing a bright apartment off the kitchen, and the ladies seemed enchanted with it. Suzette had a good feeling about this at last. Leaving them to settle in, she went back and found Walter studying the dining room ceiling.

"He did a grand job, as usual," Walter said cheerfully. "The man is a true artist."

"Indeed," she agreed, knowing "he" meant Isaac.

Walter looked directly at Suzette then and blurted out, "Pardon my straightforwardness, but I wonder if I might ask you to accompany me to what will be an exceptionally entertaining concert next week at the National Theatre. It will be a week from Saturday, and I already have tickets." He appeared charmingly flustered as the tips of his ears and his cheeks turned pink.

"Oh! Well, I do love music," she replied with a sweet smile. "Thank you, Mr. James. That sounds lovely, and I should very much enjoy learning about what San Francisco has to offer in the way of entertainment." Privately she thought it might be rather bleak after what she was used to in Europe, but it was better than sitting around worrying about what trouble her brother was getting himself into.

Walter laughed. "Not *all* of San Francisco's entertainment is quite fit for a lady such as yourself, ma'am, but I guarantee this will be suitable." He acted then as if he didn't know what to do with himself for a moment, so he looked back up at the ceiling again and sighed fondly, "That Isaac. Truly a genius." Gathering himself again, he addressed her and said, "I understand from Adeline that you'll be there for Friday night supper at Hart House. Come hungry! Their chef is one-of-a-kind. I look forward to seeing you there." His eyes seemed to twinkle behind his spectacles.

As he looked down at her, that lock of hair she found so sweetly adorable fell across his forehead, and Suzette had the sudden urge to run her fingers through his waves. They looked so soft and silky. *Where did that thought come from?* she wondered. "I would not miss it," she said cheerfully. The notion of spending more time with Walter delighted her.

"Fine, well, I'll be seeing you on Friday then, and please call me Walter."

"Thank you, Walter, and please call me Suzette."

"A beautiful name for an enchanting lady," he said with another blush, and then most uncharacteristically stumbled over his own feet as he stepped out the front door.

Suzette stood staring at the closed door for longer than she realized until she heard Delphine ask, "Pardon me. I have had a look in the kitchen, and I think Fabienne and I need to do some shopping for provisions."

And thus began a very successful business arrangement between Suzette and her lovely new household staff. That they were also French and understood exactly her needs was a huge plus in her thinking. She hoped they would stick around for a long, long time.

This had certainly been an illuminating and eventful day. Now… where was that confounded brother of hers?

Although grossly ill-equipped, Pascal was expected to find something to do to make his own way for once. Their father had provided an allowance for them to live on, but Suzette fervently hoped Pascal would not gamble it away. He needed a few investments or a job to bring in some income, but corralling him into figuring that out might prove to be an impossible task. San Francisco was considered the land of opportunity, both because of the recent gold rush as well as its status as a boom town, and people around the world knew that the possibilities for advancement were plentiful. One just needed some gumption and the intelligence to ferret them out. She worried that Pascal had neither. But he certainly loved his drink and his cards.

As the second son, Pascal was not ever going to inherit any land from their father. All of that would go to his elder brother. After hearing all of the news about the gold rush in San Francisco, their father had unilaterally decided Pascal needed to make his fortune in that city. Even if the gold supply was exhausted, he'd been convinced there were plenty of opportunities for his son. So, without much further discussion, plans were made to ship Pascal off to California.

Five

On Friday evening, Suzette and Pascal rang the bell at Hart House promptly at seven. Pascal was sober, much to Suzette's relief, and appeared to be in an amenable mood for a change. Jasper—looking a little ruffled with his shirttail partially out and his hair mussed—opened the front door with a darling little girl in his arms. She looked like a tiny female version of him with black hair and startling blue eyes.

"Welcome! So glad you could join us," he greeted them happily. "This is my daughter Marigold. Can you tell our guests 'Good evening,' Marigold?"

The little girl giggled and reached out to Suzette, saying, "Pretty! Carry me!"

Suzette, who had little experience with toddlers, was both charmed and frightened by the possibility of dropping her as Jasper deposited the bundle into her arms with a friendly laugh.

"She's like her mother. Knows just what she wants," he told them. "Now, please come in and meet the family."

Suzette could hear lots of male laughter coming from the parlor. She did not expect to see, Isaac and another tall, blond man sprawled on the beautiful Oriental rug, playing with two identical little blond baby boys. The babies were giggling, and the men were laughing. It was such a happy, domestic sight—and one her family had never experienced— she was nearly knocked over by the sheer beauty of it. Both men were in shirtsleeves, looking casual and comfortable as the babies clambered all over them.

Immediately Marigold squirmed out of Suzette's arms and jumped onto Isaac's back, hollering, "Horsey ride, Unkie Zac! Fast! Papa Roy, watch me!"

Isaac accommodated the demanding little one and raised up onto his hands and knees, commanding, "Hold on tight. Here we go!" He slowly crawled across the floor, looking utterly ridiculous and sublimely happy.

Just then, Adeline entered the room behind them, saying, "I see Marigold has already monopolized everyone. I warned you it would be a casual evening!" She burst out laughing as Ernie—one of the twins—pulled on Royal's earlobe while Augie tried to grab one of his shirt buttons. "My children seem to act more like puppies than people around these two." She gave them a loving, fake stern look. "I know you know Isaac, and may I also introduce you to my husband Royal."

Royal laughed, saying from the floor, "Pleased to meet

you. Sorry I can't get up right now." He wiped a splotch of drool off of his cheek.

"Yes, um… hello!" She looked questioningly at Adeline, then Jasper, then Royal, and back to Adeline. "I thought you said…?"

"Yes, Jasper is my husband, and Royal is as well. We're not all that unusual in this city, believe it or not."

It was then that Suzette noticed the obvious resemblance of the twins to Royal.

The bell rang again, and Jasper went to answer it. Suzette could hear him say, "Mother! Father! So happy you could make it. Come in and meet our new neighbors. Oh, and I see Séamus and Timothy right behind you. Has anyone seen Walter yet?"

On and on, people kept entering the house. Suzette recognized Marguerite Beaufort, who arrived on the arm of a rather amused-looking Frenchman they all called Doc Louis. A lovely American woman named Olivia arrived, along with her stuffy, starched banker husband, who was clearly besotted with his wife, and finally, Walter swept in with a bouquet of flowers he handed to Adeline—who accepted them graciously and kissed Walter's cheek. His ears went pink.

After a pair of nannies whisked the children upstairs, Adeline sat Pascal next to Marguerite in the dining room. She proceeded to charm the daylights out of him.

Pascal tried and tried to flirt with Marguerite, but each time he said something mildly suggestive, Doc Louis glowered at him. A few times, Doc Louis put his arm around

Marguerite and once even kissed her on her neck. Adeline looked at Royal and Jasper and laughed quietly at their antics. She knew her friend was eating up the attention. Marguerite Beaufort was a born flirt.

Adeline situated Suzette between Isaac and Walter. Walter immediately pulled out her chair and took Suzette's napkin and put it in her lap with a flourish. Isaac, however, simply seemed to take up too much room and kept touching her with his leg or his arm. Suzette wondered if he was doing it on purpose or just needed more area to maneuver. There were, after all, several people taking up space around the table, and he was a large man. Each time he accidentally brushed against her, she felt heat emanating from his body. Then he seemed to lay his long leg against hers, and she was afraid to scoot away and look too obvious to everyone at the table. At least, that's what she told herself. She actually loved the feel of his hard, muscled leg, even though he was speaking to Jasper's parents and not to her most of the time.

Determined to think of anything but him, she turned her body away, trying to concentrate on what Walter had to say. But no matter how hard she tried, Isaac seemed to invade her senses. Instead of being covered in sawdust for once, he was dressed neatly and smelled faintly of soap. His hair was combed, and he looked dashing in his white shirt with the sleeves rolled up. By contrast, Walter wore a suit and looked distinguished, and he carried on entertaining her throughout the meal. He was presently relaying a story about crossing from Nevada to California through the snow-covered Sierras. Apparently, it had been a harrowing adventure for the men.

"I hope that I shall never be that cold or that hungry again in my life," Walter said firmly. "I was sorely tempted to eat one of the books I had tucked inside my clothing. However, they served to insulate me. I decided I would freeze before starving, so I left them in place."

Laughter and conversation flowed around her in both French and English so fast that Suzette was becoming confused. As interested as she was in what Walter had to say, she stopped asking him questions for a while and just observed the dynamics around the table. Jasper and Royal were both solicitous and affectionate with Adeline. She'd like to know more about that. She watched her brother's frustration grow across from her as Marguerite turned away from him and paid more attention to her escort Doc Louis.

Trying not to seem obvious about staring, Suzette noticed something odd. The two Irishmen, Séamus and Timothy, were studying her brother carefully and whispering something to each other. The ginger one narrowed his eyes at Pascal briefly and then nodded almost imperceptibly at the dark-haired one. Had Pascal met them before? Had he angered them in some way? Pascal seemed to avoid looking at them, which to her mind indicated that there was almost certainly something there. She wondered how she'd get to the bottom of it, but the two Irishmen were too far down the table for her to comfortably converse with them. She hoped she could get some information out of Pascal later.

Unfortunately, just as they were finishing their dessert and coffee, Pascal stood and tried to look as contrite as possible when he announced, "I am sorry to say, I have another engagement tonight. This has been a most enjoyable evening and a splendid meal, but I must leave now. Thank you for graciously including us." He turned to Suzette then and ordered, "Come with me now so I can escort you home."

"That won't be necessary," Walter said smoothly. "I'll be happy to see that your sister gets home safely if it suits her." He looked at Suzette questioningly.

"Yes, thank you, Walter. I find that I am not at all ready to leave such pleasant company."

Walter's face relaxed into a charming smile, and she felt that same sense of peace wash over her once more; but at the same time, Isaac's leg pressed harder against her other side. This time, her head whipped around so she could stare at him. His look was of nonchalance and innocence, and then he turned away to ask Adeline something about her piano.

"I've been promised that the loose pedal will be fixed tomorrow," she answered. "It's a pity we won't be able to have any music tonight."

"Want me to look at it?" Isaac asked.

"No, you enjoy your evening, Isaac. You work too hard as it is."

"It's no trouble," he insisted. He stood from the table, and Suzette instantly felt the loss of his strong presence next to her. She missed his heat and the sound of his voice.

Isaac sauntered away into another room, and both Suzette and Walter watched him leave. Adeline noted the identical looks on their faces as Isaac departed. It was unmistakable desire. *Fascinating,* she thought. She couldn't wait to discuss this with Marguerite.

A few moments later, Isaac returned, looking wistful. "I'll need some special tools for that job, and I don't have anything here. Sorry, Addie."

"No matter. As I said, enjoy yourself tonight, and I'll have it looked at tomorrow by the piano tuner."

ONCE THEY WERE ALL SEATED AGAIN IN THE MAIN PARLOR AND brandy and sherry had been served, it was Isaac who spoke up loudly enough to capture everyone's attention. "Did you all know," he said, looking around, "that we have another musician in our midst?"

His question was met with inquisitive looks and answers of "Really? How lovely," from the guests.

"Miss, er... Mademoiselle de Massey not only plays the violin, but she has also studied with the great Paganini himself!" he bragged for her. He also had a mischievous look on his face. "I don't want to put her on the spot, but perhaps she would like to play for us sometime. I know I'd be delighted to hear her."

Walter, who had captured the seat next to Suzette on the settee, looked enthusiastic. "Why, that's a marvelous idea. We are all music lovers here; you'll soon find out. We'd enjoy hearing you play."

"Should I fetch one of the spare student violins?" Adeline asked.

Suzette turned scarlet and stammered, "Oh, no, please. Do not get a violin." She doubted anything a student instrument could produce would sound very good to her well-trained ear anyway. "I have a very special one of my own, and I have not played any other violin for most of my life. It's like an extension of me, you know. Perhaps another time. I could invite you all to my house. I can prepare something to perform that way." Then, hoping to get the attention off of herself, she said, "I understand there will be a recital in a few days at the National Theatre. Walter has asked to accompany me, and I am looking forward to experiencing the local talent."

Isaac gave a small snort, and Adeline spoke up graciously, "That's lovely. I hope we meet your standards of excellence. I'm sure that in France you heard some wonderful concerts." She turned to the nanny then, who needed to interrupt her with a report about the children.

Suzette wondered at the slight chill of frostiness in Adeline's tone, even though she was unfailingly polite in what she'd said. She guessed Adeline was defensive about San Francisco and its citizens. *I hope whatever the program is, it's not too uncivilized. Heaven only knows what kind of music will be played.*

Suzette looked at Isaac then, hoping somewhere deep down in the bottom of her heart she would be able to detect a bit of jealousy in him over the news that Walter would be her escort to the theater. To her surprise, he looked at her with amusement and some other emotion she could not readily identify. Then she saw him catch Walter's gaze and saw him nod almost imperceptibly with a warm smile. This reaction was not what she'd expected to stir up… not at all.

Later, however, as Walter tucked her hand in his arm and set off to walk her home, Suzette was startled to see Isaac take up the space on her other side. She looked at him questioningly.

"Walter and I both live at the Aylesbury Fire Company, and it's just a short way past your house. Not far at all. We're all going the same way at the same time, so I thought I'd also escort you home." He then took her other hand and tucked it into the crook of his elbow the same way Walter had done—with one great exception. She could feel the warm skin of his bare arm where his shirt was shoved up. He had not thought to do up his sleeve button and cover himself. Suzette immediately felt electrified by the heat and swallowed back a gasp at the feel of his steely muscles. She should have worn gloves, but it was just too hot for that. Prior to this, she'd only felt a man's hand—never another part of his body. It was thrilling. The men both seemed nonchalant about it, however. Off they went at a leisurely pace. *San Francisco will take some getting used to*, she thought.

Once they all reached Suzette's door, there was no awkwardness. The men smiled at her, and Walter said, "I look forward to seeing you next Saturday. I will call for you at half past six, and that will give us plenty of time to get to the theater." He tipped his hat and said, "Good night, Suzette."

Isaac then spoke up—was he smug? She wondered. "*I'll see you on Monday morning, and we can discuss your furniture needs then. Is eight o'clock too early to call?*"

"Oh, I see that you have spoken to Adeline about my lack of furniture."

Isaac huffed out a small laugh. "It was pretty obvious, Suzette. I've been in your house and wonder what you sit on most of the time. So, eight?"

"Eight suits me just fine. Thank you. And thank you both for seeing me to my door." *When did Isaac start calling me Suzette? I do not remember encouraging that.*

She took her leave then, but once inside, she rushed to the window and pulled aside the curtain to look out at them. Walter slung an arm around Isaac's shoulders in an affectionate way that touched her. And confused her a bit. He dropped it as they made their way up the street.

Six

Suzette dressed carefully early Monday morning and then asked herself why she had butterflies in her tummy. *It's just Isaac,* she told herself over and over. *I've seen him many times in my house.* But the phantom sensation of his strong thigh pressed against hers and the feel of his muscled bare arm would not go away.

At eight o'clock exactly, she heard a firm knock at the front door and sent Fabienne to answer it while she nonchalantly—she hoped—sipped her morning coffee in what she thought of now as Isaac's dining room. In front of her, she had a list of items she felt she needed.

When Isaac entered her space, it was as if he took up all of the air, and she couldn't breathe properly for a moment. Although clearly dressed for work, his clothes were freshly laundered, and he smelled faintly of soap and polished boot leather. She drew in a deep breath, surprised by the sudden desire to have him wrap those strong arms around her. She could not help the blush that stained her cheeks.

"Good morning, Suzette. Are you well? You seem a bit feverish," Isaac pointed out with a cocky smile.

"Perhaps the coffee is too hot."

"I like it hot. May I join you in a cup?" He raised his eyebrows slightly.

She cleared her throat delicately and willed her flaming cheeks to behave. "Yes, of course." She rang a small bell and fired off some orders to Delphine in rapid French. Delphine quickly brought a cup and set a plate of freshly baked croissants and a pot of jam down on the table.

"Please, help yourself, Isaac. I am sure a man such as you has a big appetite."

"Normally, yes, but our chef at Aylesbury Company feeds us extremely well, and I've just finished breakfast. You might want to come and dine with us one evening," he said with a congenial smile. "Our chef is recognized in San Francisco as one of the finest."

"Do you and Walter not live in a firehouse?" she asked with a surprised look.

He chuckled. "Yes, but you've never seen anything like this, I would assume. It's not just a bunch of sweaty men who smell like smoke living like bachelors. It's more of a gentlemen's club atmosphere. Our library, for instance, is incredible. It's a very pleasant place to live. For now, anyway."

"Do you have plans to move into a house?"

Isaac shrugged slightly. "We'll see." He smiled and looked her in the eye. "Do you have a list for me there?"

Caught in his gaze, Suzette took a moment before his question penetrated her awareness. When she realized he was waiting for her to answer, she blushed even harder. "Excuse me. What did you ask?"

"Your list. I came to discuss the furniture you'll be needing in the house." He said it slowly and clearly as if speaking to a child and then took a swallow of coffee.

"Of course. Ahem. Yes. This is the list of things I would like you to make." She slid the paper over to him.

Isaac looked at it and laughed.

"Is it too much?"

"Well, I truly have no idea. It's all in French, so it could be anything from a writing desk to an elephant cage, and I'd never know. Shall we try again in English this time?"

Gasping, Suzette apologized. "I forgot. I made several lists, adding things as they came to me, and then I made this one sorting it according to importance. I was concentrating so hard; I forgot my English. I am so sorry."

Isaac scooted his chair closer so they could peruse the list together, and she translated what she'd written. Sitting so close, however, Isaac became caught up in her faint lilac scent and stopped listening. Finally, he realized she was looking at him for direction. "Sorry, I do not know the name for *une crédence.*"

Isaac had a fairly decent idea of what she meant but asked anyway, "What is the purpose of this piece you want?"

"It would hold dishes." She put her hand out to the side. "About this high. It would go against that wall over there."

She indicated the opposite wall. "And it ought to look compatible with the existing table."

"I think you mean a sideboard. Some folks call it a credenza."

"Ah, yes. Can you make one?"

Isaac scoffed. "Is this the extent of your list?"

Suzette blinked in surprise. "Yes, for now."

Isaac gulped the rest of his coffee, rose suddenly, and announced, "I will be back on Friday with drawings and prices."

"That's all?"

He looked at her with amusement. "What else do you want from me, Suzette?" His eyes seemed to burn into her. Even though they were fixed on her face, she had the sensation of being undressed by them.

She cleared her throat. "I do not need anything else, Isaac, at the moment."

"Good. We'll figure out what else you need from me later then."

She had the definite sensation he was referring to something that had nothing to do with woodwork, and that caused her face to flame again.

"Maybe," he added, "you need to drink cooler beverages." He grinned again. "I shall see you Friday morning at around ten." And with that, he nodded politely and left.

WHEN FRIDAY MORNING ARRIVED, SUZETTE DISCOVERED SHE could not sleep past pre-dawn, so she told herself to get up and do something useful or relaxing to calm her nerves. Once again, she tried to tell herself not to get into an uproar just because Isaac was due to arrive in a few hours. So, she dressed, had a quick breakfast, and headed to the parlor, where she intended to calm her nerves by practicing the violin. That worked so well she lost herself in her music and jumped about a foot when Isaac strode into the room with a frown on his face.

"Isaac! You startled me! I did not hear you knock."

"I know. Delphine let me in. May I see your violin, please?"

Taken aback by his odd question, Suzette reacted before thinking and passed the instrument to him. She watched as his expression morphed from concern to excitement and back to concern within seconds.

Isaac's eyes snapped to hers, as he exclaimed, "It's a Stradivarius! But did you know it's cracked? The sound would be so much better if you had it repaired."

"What? It cannot be damaged… unless… oh, those blasted men who moved the furniture into the house. They kept crashing into everything, and I thought I had it carefully protected in its case, but now I remember thinking it was not in the same place as I left it in my room upstairs. Someone must have knocked it over when I was not looking. I could kick myself!"

"Show me the case," Isaac demanded, still holding the instrument.

Suzette presented the case to him, and he carefully set the violin inside. He closed the lid and flipped the case over. She gasped to see its back. *"Mon Dieu!"* she gasped. There was a sizable dent in it.

"Didn't you hear the odd vibration?"

Suzette sighed and answered, "I heard something was off, but I just kept telling myself to practice harder. What can I do? This is a very valuable instrument."

Isaac gave her what he hoped was a reassuring smile and said, "Don't worry, I can fix it. No charge."

Stepping back, Suzette exclaimed, "I should probably send this back to a luthier in France! What do you know about repairing a violin such as this?"

"I assure you I can handle it. I make violins, you know. And it may be a special one, but I'm confident I will be able to manage. The crack is there, but it's not significant damage."

Taking a deep breath, Suzette conceded, "I will think about it. In the meantime, I shall send a letter to France and see…" She trailed off, and she noticed the look on his face. He looked put out and, at the same time, rather amused. "What?" she asked.

"I guarantee you won't find a better instrument maker, even in France."

"Are you always so arrogant, Isaac?"

"When I'm confident in my worth, there is no reason not to be. But write your letter and ask if anyone has a recommendation for someone to repair it in California, or anywhere in North America for that matter. Then consider how confident you'd be letting this out of your hands to make the trip back to Europe unattended, and how sure you are that you would ever get it back again in better shape than it's in right now. This violin is worth thousands of dollars, and it would have to pass through many hands to reach its destination. Unless… are you planning a trip back home to France soon?"

"No," she said, lowering her gaze. "This is my home now —for better or worse." She considered her brother's lack of enthusiasm for finding employment and grimaced inwardly. Then she thought of her own reason for being so far away from France and suppressed a shudder.

Relieved that she was planning to stay in San Francisco but frustrated by her lack of trust, Isaac said, "You think about how long you want to wait until that crack gets bigger and completely ruins the instrument—which would be a shame. And I won't bother you again until you ask me to fix it. If you choose to do so, it would be my honor to work on such a violin." He set it down and pulled some papers out of a satchel he'd carried in. "In the meantime, let's look at the furniture ideas I have for you. My crew is ready to get started immediate-ly." He didn't tell her he was paying them a premium to hurry up and accommodate a lovely woman he wanted to please.

Although she'd seen the beautiful work he'd done on her house, and she had Adeline's assurance that Isaac was an incredible craftsman, the exquisite plans he showed her were so detailed and completely on-point for what she wanted, she was still amazed. "Isaac, these drawings are incredible. The plans are perfect."

"Thank you." She looked up and realized his eyes were

locked onto her. He was not looking at his drawings. "I enjoy beautiful things," he said softly.

Suzette gave a sharp intake of breath and returned his stare. They seemed to lose some of the distance between them as if they longed to kiss—until they were rudely interrupted by Pascal.

Her brother sauntered in and smirked. "Has my sister been annoying you with her so-called music?" Pascal asked in a petulant tone. He'd been sent home early from his gaming the night before when he'd started a quarrel with a regular at the casino, so he was less hungover than usual.

"Good morning, brother. I am surprised to see you up and about before noon. Are you well?" she asked, ignoring his insult.

Pascal shrugged.

Isaac frowned and answered the man's insolent question, "Your sister only played a few bars that I heard, and *she* was not scratching at all. Her violin has taken some damage, though, and perhaps your highly-trained ear picked up on the finer details of the sound that the Strad itself was not accomplishing at this time."

"Damage, you say?" For once, Pascal looked genuinely concerned for something other than his own amusement. "Can it be repaired? Will it lose value?"

"In its present state, it's worth less than if a qualified luthier worked on it, definitely. Once it's fixed, it will be fine both in quality and value."

Pascal glared at his sister and ordered, "You had better

find someone to fix that thing right away." And he wandered away.

Strange man, Isaac thought. To Suzette, he said, "I'll see you soon. I need to get back to work." And he was gone.

Suzette had the sensation that all of the light and color departed the room with Isaac. *I shall speak to Adeline about his claim to know all about violins. She did not seem too anxious to have him fiddle with her piano pedal, although she did say she preferred that he enjoy his evening rather than work. She also mentioned that a piano tuner was coming. Still, she claims to know him quite well. Perhaps she will be at the National Theatre tomorrow night.* A slight thrill went through Suzette as she thought about spending time with Walter. *That man has the best manners and is so handsome and well-educated. The gentlemen of San Francisco are definitely interesting and a most pleasant surprise. Or… at least two of them are. What has come over me?*

The next evening, Suzette donned her favorite gown, hoping she would not upstage the ladies of San Francisco too badly, but she wanted to look her best for Walter. Just thinking about him gave her a case of butterflies. He'd sent a messenger letting her know that he would be by with a carriage for their ride to the theater, and she was ready to go in plenty of time. While she'd been dressing, however, she'd heard a lot of commotion outside and noticed the air seemed to smell like smoke. She looked out the window and didn't see anything that gave her pause, so she figured it had to be someone on the street. She was not yet used to the noise and bustle of this house, so close to the road.

At about five minutes before their appointed hour, there was a knock at the door. Expecting Walter, Suzette answered it herself and was more than surprised to see Doc Louis and Marguerite Beaufort instead.

Marguerite—who was dressed impeccably—addressed her in French, explaining, "Walter sent us to take you to the theater in our carriage. He sends his apologies, but he is running late due to a fire his company had to put out. It was not a terribly large one, thankfully. But he said he will meet you at the theater and will get there more quickly by himself on horseback. Are you ready to go?"

Blinking in surprise, Suzette thanked them, and they all took off. "Is Walter alright? He did not get hurt, did he? And Isaac? What about him?" She shuddered to think of the dangers of being a firefighter. Up until now, she had imagined the men living in luxury at Aylesbury Company. The reality of putting out a raging blaze had seemed so removed from possibility. Suddenly she had a deeper respect for both Walter and Isaac.

Doc Louis smiled at her, saying, "Your men are fine, Suzette."

"My men? Whatever do you mean? I barely know either of them and make no claim." She frowned.

"Yes, well… we'll see about that," he answered softly. "Are you ready for some marvelous music? This is going to be a real treat. Several of our talented locals will be playing tonight."

Suzette's mind was in a blur all the way to the theater. *Why would Doc Louis assume there is anything between me and either Walter or Isaac, much less* both *of them?* She had meant to ask about the evening's program, but his comment struck her dumb. Once they arrived and a playbill was offered, she didn't bother to look at it. She didn't want to seem condescending, but what could these locals know about the kind of music she'd heard in Europe? She was more interested in conversing with Marguerite.

They took their seats and chatted a while before Walter came rushing down the aisle, huffing like he'd been running. It was easy for him to take his seat next to Suzette as they were seated in the front row. Jasper and Royal occupied two seats at the far side of Doc Louis, and Suzette wondered why Adeline was not with them. She hoped one of the children wasn't ill. As soon as Walter sat down, he apologized. "I'm so sorry to be late. I needed to clean up before seeing you, and I had to let Isaac have the first crack at the bathtub. He was in a bigger rush to get here even than I was. Please forgive my tardiness. We'll all share the carriage going home, at least, and we can lead my borrowed horse back to his owner at Aylesbury Company." Then he laughed sheepishly. "I hope I didn't trade smoke smell with horse smell. I don't often ride, but I would have been too slow on foot."

Walter seemed nervous to Suzette as he babbled on and on. It wasn't like him to act so jumpy. She smiled reassuringly and said, "I am just glad to see you. Everything is fine." She could not help but notice how handsome Walter looked as she admired his profile, but privately she wondered where Isaac was sitting and why he hadn't joined them in the front row with his friends. She buried a sense of disappointment that came bubbling up when Walter mentioned Isaac was there in the concert hall. With whom was he sitting? She restrained herself from craning her neck and studying the faces in the audience—even though that was exactly what she wanted to do.

As soon as she squelched that thought, the stage curtain opened, and there sat a lovely concert grand Bösendorfer right in the middle of the stage, backed by a small stringed orchestra. Some of the musicians looked rather young, she noticed. She stifled a cringe; would she be sitting through a children's recital? She sighed inwardly, thinking back to the incredible music she had heard in France. She doubted she would hear its equal for years to come.

Then, much to Suzette's complete astonishment, out walked Adeline, once again dressed to perfection, looking stunning, and accompanied by... *Isaac?* Isaac was dressed in exquisite formal attire, and he carried a violin and bow. Adeline curtsied and took her seat at the piano, and Isaac bowed to thunderous applause. *Apparently, they are quite popular,* Suzette thought, surprised and curious.

Walter turned to Suzette while Isaac tuned his violin to the piano and whispered, "This is one of their favorites, and I understand that the orchestra has come together extremely well. Some of them are Isaac's students. Such a pleasure!" When the music began, the orchestra—which sounded surprisingly good—had a rather long opening, during which Suzette felt herself grow nervous for Isaac. She immediately recognized the beautiful Concerto for Piano, Violin, and Strings in D minor that Felix Mendelssohn had composed at the incredibly young age of fourteen. This was a challenging piece to play, and she worried that he would struggle.

Suzette need not have worried. As he played his opening

section, the notes swept through the hall with a clarity that made her jaw drop.

Adeline then entered and enhanced Isaac's tone with a lovely marriage of piano and violin delight. She continued to play with strength and surety, and Isaac's music was so perfect it brought tears to Suzette's eyes. Together, they were playful, rousing, and deeply emotional, and their timing was impeccable, with a thrilling give and take between the two instruments. The music took Suzette's breath away. She could not understand how such a large man could play so delicately and accurately, and she grew warm inside, watching him sweat as the music grew in intensity. This was no backwater town show—this was a true concert. She was embarrassed for doubting the quality of what she would encounter here. She was learning that San Francisco was far from the wilderness she had expected.

After all three movements of the concerto, the crowd jumped to their feet, shouting, stomping, and clapping with abandon. Isaac and Adeline glowed with satisfaction and tried to look modest as the audience carried on. Eventually, the musicians were allowed to take a rest.

During the intermission, Walter entertained Suzette with an interesting and sometimes humorous account of what it was like when he and Isaac were gold miners a few years back. It was hard for her to imagine proper Walter sweaty and muddy, panning for gold in all sorts of nasty weather, but he assured her he had. He also told her about a stall shower he and Isaac had invented and built so miners could wash away the worst of the grime that clung to them. "The water was icy cold," Walter chuckled, "but it was better than feeling constantly dirty."

Suzette shook her head as Walter explained that their neighboring miners had paid well to use their soap and shower contraption. Apparently, their invention was a success for many reasons.

Throughout their conversation during the intermission, Suzette was delighted by the fact that Walter had taken her hand and seemed to stroke it absently as he spoke. His hand was warm and firm, and this new feeling made her need to concentrate extra hard on his words.

The orchestra was absent after the intermission. When Adeline and Isaac lit into Niccolò Paganini's Caprice nr. 24 for violin and piano, Suzette felt her heart soar. She even wondered if Isaac played it just for her, but then told herself she was being silly.

The crowd cheered over and over for them, and the two virtuosi seemed to glow with happiness as they both thanked the audience and waved themselves off stage—not before Isaac looked Suzette right in the eye and winked. After multiple curtain calls, they returned to the stage, played a quick caprice, and finally retired for the night. They were both pouring with perspiration in the candlelight, and Suzette realized she was nearly as wet as they were—from crying. She'd been moved beyond belief.

After dabbing her eyes and wiping her face with her handkerchief, she asked Walter, "How did they manage such an ambitious program?"

He beamed at her proudly. "Oh, this was nothing. The

selections were more impressive, but they are accustomed to playing for hours on end. They used to entertain at The Discovery all night long. Most of that was for dancing, and they improvised a lot. It was great fun. Now they take their music more seriously since they teach at their academy at Hart House and are called upon frequently to give concerts."

"How does Isaac have the time to do all of that and still work for you?"

Walter's head jerked back a tiny bit, and he answered with a blink, "Isaac is the busiest man I know and has the energy of six men. He has several talented woodworkers who answer to him, but he doesn't work for me. Whatever gave you that idea?"

Suzette blushed and stammered, "Ah…" Isaac's work clothes and gruff style had caused her to assume—but she didn't want to say that Isaac had seemed like a common laborer in her eyes. Especially since her image of him had transformed so completely this evening.

Until now, she had seen him as a confident, talented man, though perhaps a little rough around the edges… Tonight he looked like a god. The man exuded power and artistry. In fact, Suzette would go so far as to say that he might be a genius on the violin.

She was also sure he was the most handsome man she'd ever seen—and that was saying something, considering her attraction to Walter. But then looking at Walter's intelligent, thoughtful expression, she amended her thoughts. They were equally handsome—just attractive in different ways.

"Isaac is a full partner at Roja Wais. Didn't you ever wonder about the name?"

"I did not actually think about it. Does it mean something in English that I do not know?"

Walter chuckled. "It's our names. Royal, Jasper, Walter, Isaac. Ro-ja Wa-is."

"I see." *I have been such a snob and a complete fool.*

"If Isaac weren't such a loyal and generous man, he'd probably be the wealthiest of all of us. But he is determined to keep his furniture business as part of our company rather than making money for himself beyond what he does for Roja Wais. He's said over and over that if it weren't for us, he'd never be here. Anyway, Isaac probably didn't even notice that you misunderstood. Shall we go and congratulate them backstage?"

Suzette wasn't so certain that Isaac would be as forgiving for her gaffe in assuming he was somehow less important than the men she now realized were his full partners. *At least,* she told herself, *I did not say anything to him directly insulting him... I hope.* "Yes, I would love to go congratulate Adeline and Isaac," she agreed. And off they went, following Jasper and Royal to the dressing rooms in the back of the theater.

Adeline's door was open, and she stood amidst several bouquets of flowers, laughing and drinking champagne with Isaac. Walter rushed in and hugged Adeline and then Isaac, extolling them with praise, "You were outstanding! Both of you! Exquisite, and your orchestra was marvelous." He clapped Isaac on the back again as if he couldn't help himself.

Meanwhile, Suzette kissed Adeline on both cheeks and

carried on with her own praise; then she stood before Isaac, pausing for a split second before leaning toward him to kiss both of his cheeks as well. Isaac, however, seemed to have a different idea because, after the first air kiss, he turned his face and captured Suzette's lips with his own. It was brief, but a current of surprise zinged through her all the way to her toes. Walter stood by, grinning at them, and then Isaac winked at Suzette once again. *He has some nerve.* Then, surprising herself, she thought, …*I like it!*

"Will you let me work on your Stradivarius now?" he asked with a cocked eyebrow.

"If you can build violins the way you play them, then by all means, yes. Did you make your instrument?"

"I did."

"Then it is settled. Please accept my enormous congratulations for an outstanding performance tonight and my humble apologies for ever doubting you."

Isaac gave her a wry look and chuckled softly. He did not, however, remove his arm from around her waist where it had suddenly taken up residence.

Suzette looked at Walter, whose eyes were riveted on Isaac's arm around her, and to her amazement, he looked pleased. There was no hint of jealousy or possessiveness in his gaze—just happiness. Then he did something that astounded her. Walter moved in and placed his arm around her and his other arm encircled Isaac. Walter kissed them both on the cheek, looking like the proudest, happiest man in the world. Suzette blinked a couple of times at them until the moment was shattered by Royal.

"Everyone, please come back to Hart House tonight where we can all celebrate and have enough space to let these two performers sit down and relax. We'll break out the best champagne and have a congratulatory supper!"

"That sounds grand!" Walter exclaimed. He looked at Isaac and then Suzette. Isaac grinned, and Suzette looked happy, if not slightly confused. "We'll be there."

"If you'll just excuse me, I need to go to my own dressing room for a moment," Isaac explained. "Then we can be on our way." He began to peel off his jacket as he left Adeline's room. Walter remained with his arm around Suzette's waist, and she could not resist snuggling a bit closer to him.

Adeline and her men bustled out of the room as well, so Walter led Suzette out with them and turned toward Isaac's dressing room as the others headed outside to their carriage. Without knocking, Walter pushed the door open, and he and Suzette were greeted by the sight of Isaac standing in the middle of the room in nothing but his trousers, holding a clean, dry shirt in one hand.

If Suzette had thought Isaac was magnificent in his tuxedo, seeing him out of his tuxedo was a revelation. The man reminded her of a statue of Atlas she'd once seen. She tried to swallow the gasp that erupted from her as her eyes went wide.

"Oh, my apologies for barging in," Walter said with a laugh. "I forgot we weren't at home. I guess I'm just anxious for the festivities tonight, and I didn't think."

"Nothing to worry about," Isaac assured him. But did he

give a few extra little muscle flexes while he donned the shirt?

He is certainly taking his time doing up the buttons, Suzette thought. *It is a pity he has to do them up at all.* Then she noticed that Walter seemed to be enjoying Isaac's display of muscular brilliance as much as she was.

Soon the show was over, and Isaac said, "Let's go."

Walter seemed to come to his senses and added, "I need to drop off Dooley's horse at the firehouse on the way to Hart House. It won't take more than a minute. Doc Louis and Madame Beaufort are probably waiting for us in the carriage."

By the time they made it to Hart House, the party was in full swing. Several more friends had joined them, and the kitchen staff was busily setting out a buffet. Champagne filled everyone's glass, and the guests all looked as cheerful as can be. Adeline was not present at first, but soon she came gliding down the stairs in a less formal gown, looking refreshed.

"Suzette! I'm so happy these dear men persuaded you to join us." She looked between Isaac and Walter with an expression that was nearly as fond as how she regarded her own two husbands.

"Thank you for inviting me, and again I must tell you how entranced I was with the concert tonight." She nodded her thanks to a servant who held out a tray of champagne glasses.

Walter spoke up, "May I make a toast?" He didn't wait for a response because he was used to speaking his mind in front of these people and knew they all loved him for it. "Cheers to two of the finest musicians in the country and definitely *the* finest in California. Thank you for entertaining us with your magnificence once again." Then he turned to Suzette and said, "And cheers to new friends whom I trust will soon become as dear as the old ones… or at least, that is what I hope. Thank you for gracing our city with your beauty and elegance."

Suzette found herself blushing, and she shyly looked at Isaac, who'd narrowed his eyes a bit at Walter. His jaw seemed to be ticking a little as well. If she didn't know better, she'd say he looked a tiny bit jealous. He'd been so accepting of having Walter take her to the concert, but now it seemed there was some other emotion afoot. His look faded away as he regarded her with a gallant expression and asked, "May I bring you something from the buffet?"

"Oh, let's all go, Isaac. Let the lady choose for herself," Walter said before she had a chance to speak up. He put his hand behind her back, only to find Isaac's hand was already there. So he left his on top of Isaac's and gently propelled them forward to the buffet table.

Suzette felt a little boxed in by the two men, but for some reason, she loved the feeling. *What is coming over me? Is it because I am in Hart House, or is there something in the San Francisco air that makes women think of more than one man at a time? And what is going on with these two? I wonder if, judging from his comment, Walter expects me to make a choice. How can I? Do I want to? I do not know if I could honestly lead either of them on, given my strange circumstance. They both seem interested, or is that my ego talking to me?* Her head spun with question after question.

Soon they had plates laden with delicious-looking treats, and they looked around for a place to sit. There was a conversation area designed for three in the main parlor, so they sat there. Isaac looked especially happy to be off his feet finally.

"Are you exhausted, Isaac?" she questioned him. "You have had a very busy day and night, from what I understand."

"I'm fine," he assured her with a smile, dismissing the topic. "I have a question for you, Suzette, and I hope it isn't impertinent, but I can't help but wonder..."

She furrowed her brow a little, but her curiosity got the better of her. "What is it?"

"How does it happen that a lady as lovely as yourself is not married?" He peered at her thoughtfully at the same time Walter's attention snapped to her face. Apparently, they both wanted to know.

Suzette felt her insides shrivel up. She thought—or rather hoped— she could avoid this topic forever.

Seeing her face lose all color, Isaac instantly retracted his question. "Forgive my forwardness. I don't mean to make you uncomfortable." *Why did I think it was my place to interrogate her in such a personal manner? I hope she will forgive me.*

She shook herself a tiny bit and answered, "Not at all. It is a fair question and one with a rather complicated answer, I am afraid."

"We're all ears," Walter said with what he hoped was an encouraging smile.

Suzette's appetite instantly evaporated, so she set her plate aside and folded her hands demurely in her lap. She looked down at them and answered softly, "I might already be married."

Both men blinked at her in confusion, and Isaac blurted out, "It ought to be clear one way or the other. How could you not know?"

"I went through a rather succinct ceremony to marry someone my father selected for me. Only Father was tricked. The man was not what he appeared to be. My father is an extremely obstinate man who never listens to anyone. He believed it was going to be an advantageous match, and that was that. No matter what the evidence showed later, he could not admit he was wrong."

"Please explain," Isaac implored her. He took her hand gently, although she seemed too in her own mind to even notice.

"For several weeks, this man—Monsieur Dernier—came courting me at my parents' chateau. During that time, they had to let some of the staff go because things of value began to go missing. No one ever saw them disappear, but they did with some regularity. Dernier always had impeccable manners—in public anyway—and arrived with recommendations from well-established members of society. So, he was never under suspicion. Now I suspect that it was he who stole those items right under our noses."

"So, he might be a thief, but why do you not know whether or not you're married to this… Derrière?' Walter asked.

Suzette stifled a giggle. "Dernier," she corrected him.

"Sounds more like a giant derrière to me," Walter argued as Isaac snorted.

Composing herself, Suzette continued, "As I said, I went through the marriage ceremony, so I believe I married *someone*. However, immediately after the ceremony, he disappeared. We searched and searched for him, and my father quietly hired men to look for him. The investigators did find the Dernier family, but they claimed no affiliation with anyone who matched his description." She hung her head in embarrassment. "He did not even stay around long enough to… consummate the marriage." Isaac's grip on her hand tightened, and Walter gave a sharp intake of breath. She looked up and continued, "My father was furious. He'd been led to believe the union would increase the family's fortune and land holdings." Her voice took on a bitter edge. "My father treated me like a business transaction. Perhaps that is why he allowed me to leave—I was no longer an instrument of financial windfall."

"Is that why you came to San Francisco?" Isaac asked. He stroked her knuckles with his thumb.

Suzette nodded. "There were already plans in place for Pascal to sail here, so at the last minute, I talked my father into letting me come as well. It did not take a lot of convincing. I assume because he believed it would be impossible to marry me off a second time. Someone needed to either produce my husband… or a dead body. I did not want to be confronted with either of those possibilities."

Walter grasped her other hand. "Suzette, I'm so sorry. Were you fond of this man?"

"No! I despised him. He was always overly polite when my father was around, but the few times we were alone—except for the servants in attendance—he behaved in a vile manner toward me and spoke German so no one else could understand. He was a pig. I tried to dissuade my father from making me go through with the marriage, but he told me it was my duty to the family to marry well and continue the family legacy. I tried to explain to my father that the man was cruel, but he told me I was just a typical bride who was nervous about getting married, and I ought to relax."

"Well, I don't understand," Isaac interjected. "If this man was so interested in your family and marrying into it, why would he simply disappear?"

"If you ask my father, it was I who hired someone to get rid of him. That was another reason he agreed to let me come to San Francisco immediately. He did not want anyone to build a case against me. This way, he could lie to people and say that my husband and I left the country together." She hung her head again. "It is such a mess."

Looking thoughtful, Walter asked, "What does Pascal think of this?"

"Pfft," she scoffed. "Pascal thinks only about his gaming and the quantity of his drink. He is the most indolent human being there is. He is my brother, and I know I ought to feel more fondness for him, but I have a very different association with him than I do with our elder brother Gustave. Pascal hates Gustave because he will inherit everything, but Gustave was mostly kind to me. I miss him. He is married to a lovely woman, and they have a beautiful family. I am glad he is happy."

"How do you and Pascal happen to speak such fine English?" Walter asked. "Not to change the subject, but I've wondered."

Suzette smiled her thanks and answered, "That is kind of you to say. We had tutors growing up. We had to learn to read and be conversant in French, English, Italian, and German, according to our parents. I liked English the best, probably because that tutor was the most interesting." She cleared her throat. "To get back to Pascal and Gustave… I spent most of the voyage here contemplating the possible involvement either of my brothers might have had in the disappearance of my so-called husband. They both knew I was bitter about the union. I believe, however, that Pascal would have been too disinterested to have orchestrated anything. Gustave, on the other hand, might have done something to protect me. His influence is even greater than my father's because he treats people with dignity and professionalism, so people are willing to help him when he asks. He may possibly have become aware of the man's duplicity and scared him off with threats. He may even have had him killed, for all I know. I would never ask and implicate him in any way. If he did something, it was a service to society. Forgive me if that sounds cruel or harsh, but Dernier, or whatever his name is, was a very bad person. A couple of times, he tormented me by telling me explicit accounts of things he planned to do to me after we were legally married, and he made it clear that I was his *property*." She nearly choked on that word. "They were not in the realm of normal marital activities. He planned to inflict pain and use torture devices." She lowered her eyes. "He always laughed at the effect his words had on me."

The men both gasped and squeezed her hands. It was then she became fully aware that they both had hold of her. She was again confused by her positive reaction to this, but she felt safe and comforted by them.

"That's monstrous!" Walter exclaimed, making a sour face. "He obviously loved intimidating you."

"Women are to be cherished and treated with the utmost respect," agreed Isaac. "And their opinions are as valid as any man's."

Smiling finally, Suzette said, "I cannot believe I have unburdened my deepest secrets to both of you, but I feel as if I can depend on your discretion in not spreading this story to all of San Francisco. For some reason, the two of you have earned my trust and my friendship more quickly than I would ever have expected."

"Both of us?" Isaac asked.

"Yes, indeed."

"Well, that's grand," Walter exclaimed with a wide grin. His eyes seemed to sparkle as he looked at Isaac and winked.

"In that case, would you like to continue to keep company with us? Together? At the same time?" His eyes looked across the room then and locked onto Adeline, who at that moment was ardently kissing Royal, who had his arm around Jasper. It should be an odd sight, but in this house, it seemed as natural as anything. They were all apparently having a conversation with Doc Louis and Marguerite at the same time as they were expressing their affection for one another.

Following Walter's gaze, Suzette felt her insides do a funny lurch, and she grew warm. She knew her cheeks had to be flaming. She also felt the stirrings of a longing that almost verged on jealousy for her new friend and the bountiful love she so obviously shared with her two husbands. *What would it be like?* She could barely imagine loving one person like that, but two at once? *Je serais folle de joie!*

It would be impossible for her to marry either of them, but what would be the harm in having two men to keep her company?

"I believe that I should like that very much," she blurted out with a ferocious blush.

"Well, isn't that grand?" Walter said with a satisfied chuckle.

Isaac looked surprised but content. He then handed Suzette her plate again and cajoled her, "Please, enjoy the meal." *What exactly does Walter have in mind?* He felt his insides go a little warm as he considered what this might mean for them. His eyes turned contemplatively toward Adeline across the room. *Maybe Walter and I need to have a chat with Royal and Jasper.*

For the rest of the party, late into the night, the three of them made the rounds, chatting with the other guests who all wanted to congratulate Isaac over and over. For some reason, each compliment gave Suzette a sense of pride. The feeling grew and grew inside her, as if she were somehow connected to Isaac's accomplishments.

She was glad he didn't seem to hold her previous frostiness toward him against her. She was also surprised and flattered that both men continued to touch her throughout the night, holding her hand or putting an arm around her waist as they made polite conversation. She noticed a few knowing looks—especially from Marguerite and Doc Louis, who at one point in the evening gave her a wink and a grin that made her choke back on a giggle. In truth, she was so happy it hardly mattered to her what those around her saw or thought.

Walter, in his own golden-tongued manner, sang the praises of Isaac over and over as the compliments continued. He was like a proud papa, she thought—though he looked at Isaac with a deep affection that seemed anything but fatherly. She guessed it would all make sense to her eventually, but for now, she would just enjoy it. No one looked askance at a woman on the arm of two men in this house; that was certain.

For all of his protestations that he was fine, Isaac began to look weary, so Walter suggested, "Let's walk Suzette home and then head back to Aylesbury Company to get some rest."

The walk back to her house was not long—just a few minutes up the hill. When they reached her door and escorted her inside, she turned to Walter and said, "Thank you so much for inviting me to join you tonight. This was probably the most enjoyable night of my life." She turned to Isaac and continued, "And thank you for your incredible music. I was transported into a new place. The Mendelssohn was magnificent, but the Paganini captured my heart. I cannot express in words how it moved me."

"Then express it a different way," Isaac whispered. He lowered his face and sealed her lips with his in a deep, soul-grabbing kiss. The man kissed like he played the violin. It was artistry—soft, yet firm—commanding and giving. As he did so, Suzette felt Walter wrap his arms around her from behind. Suddenly his lips were on her neck, leaving a trail of heated kisses that made her quiver inside. Gasping, she returned Isaac's kiss with equal ardor and grabbed his shoulders. He was so strong and hard, and Walter was so gentle and sweet, she could not believe this was happening.

But then it got even more surprising when Isaac pulled away and ended their kiss. He turned slightly and began kissing Walter the same way! She gasped again and blinked at them, noticing the surprise in Walter's eyes. Despite her shock, Suzette quickly became consumed with how beautiful they looked as they kissed each other. Then Isaac shifted once more, choosing this time to kiss Suzette's neck, leaving Walter free to kiss her lips. Walter immediately took over that task, plastering her with a deep, probing kiss she felt all the way to her toes.

Finally, Walter pulled back and said, "It's time to get our young man here home and in bed before he keels over. Thank you, Suzette, for accompanying me to the concert and for unburdening your secret onto us. I'm sure I can speak for both of us and say that your story is safe. You'd be surprised what lies beneath the surface of many San Franciscan lives. This is a city where people go to begin afresh, so you came to the right place. We'll say good night to you now and look forward to many enjoyable days… and nights," he winked at her, "together in the future."

"I'll see you in the morning and trade violins with you," Isaac added. And they were gone.

Suzette stood watching them through the window with her fingers to her lips as they walked away into the darkness. She'd never even dreamed that such feelings could race through her body.

She loved every bit of it.

ON THE WAY HOME, WALTER COULDN'T HELP ASKING, "WHAT possessed you to kiss me like that in front of Suzette?"

Isaac gave a soft laugh that sounded like it came from deep within him. "You've been wanting to do that for years and were afraid to ask. I finally decided to take the bull by the horns and see if you'd actually like it or just thought about it all the time."

"I don't think about it *all* the time," Walter protested.

Snorting, Isaac said, "You tell yourself that if it makes you happy. It's all fine; I discovered I liked it too." He swung his arm around Walter's shoulders and gave him a quick squeeze as they trudged down the hill to Aylesbury Fire Company. "I sure do hope there are no fires tonight. I'm exhausted."

While he might not have consciously thought about kissing Isaac all the time, as he'd protested, this gave Walter a lot to think about for the rest of the night. *Such possibilities!*

Nine

There were no more fires that night except for the inferno that ripped through Suzette. She was so aflame with want and confusion she could barely sleep. The magnificence of the concert was a pale backdrop for the vivid feelings the men had awakened in her. She was so confused. *What is happening?* She needed to speak to someone who might understand.

All too quickly, the sun came up, and she had to face the new day. *Isaac will be here soon, and I want to greet him looking and acting my best,* she told herself. So she dressed carefully and went downstairs to have some breakfast.

She was just finishing up when Fabienne led Isaac into the breakfast room. He carried a sturdy-looking violin case and gave her a beaming smile. *At least one of us seems to have slept well,* she told herself. *"Bonjour,* Isaac. Coffee?"

"Thank you, but I can't stay long. I need to meet with

someone soon, so I just popped in to exchange the fiddles. I'll try to get yours repaired as soon as possible. A week or so, depending on the extent of the damage I find when I crack it open."

Suzette gasped. "You open the violin? Does that not ruin it?"

He smiled. "It's standard procedure when doing a repair like that. Don't worry. I'll be gentle." Then he gave her a saucy wink.

"I think I might very much want to watch that. Would I be in your way?"

"Don't you trust me?"

Suzette gave him a flat look and answered, "Yes, I trust you, but you may as well be conducting surgery on one of my limbs. I am more than attached to that instrument, and I find I am curious to know what goes on inside. I promise not to ask too many questions and ruin your concentration. And I do not plan to stay all week." She laughed quietly. "I would just like to see how you get things started, and then I will leave you to it."

Isaac answered as they entered the music parlor where she had her violin stored, "It's a fine day, so why don't you stroll down to Aylesbury Company and join us for luncheon at twelve-thirty? If there is no fire, I can show you around, and then you can see the workshop I have nearby at Roja Wais. I'll be able to get started on the Strad this afternoon."

"I thought you were horribly busy. Am I keeping you from your other projects?"

"Yes."

Suzette blinked at his quick and frank response. "Then why are you setting aside other work to do this?"

With a twinkle in his eye, Isaac answered, "Several reasons. First, I have men who can do the furniture building I have contracted for right now. The designs are all complete. Second, they cannot work on the violin. Furthermore, I don't want you to be without your precious fiddle for too long—even though I am providing you with a lovely piece to play in the meantime. And I am quite honestly trying my best to make a good impression on you. Is that enough? I could probably go on." He smiled broadly. "Let's not forget also that I love violins and can't wait to get my hands on a truly great one."

"Oh! In that case, I will be happy to join you for luncheon, and I look forward to seeing your workspace. Thank you." She thought for a moment and added, "Will Walter be there as well?" Her face went a little pink, and it made Isaac laugh inwardly a little to see that.

"Unless he is called out to meet with someone about a plan for a building site, he ought to be there. If he isn't, will you still come?"

"Oh, yes, well, of course. I did not mean to suggest that he has to be there for me to be in your company. I simply wondered, is all." In truth, she was all jumbled up inside and didn't know what to think about either of them. Having Walter there as well definitely sweetened the pie, however.

Suzette could not resist opening the case he held and gasped when she saw what it held. "Isaac! This is a fine violin."

He laughed. "Try it out first. I find it can feel a little temperamental until you get used to it."

"Is this the instrument you played in concert?"

"I used it for the Paganini piece. This is one of my favorites. I wanted a different feel for the Mendelssohn, however, and used another instrument."

"Thank you for entrusting it to me."

He laughed harder. "You're the one who's trusting. This is worth a fraction of a Stradivarius. You'll find it has a lovely rich tone, but it was crafted recently, and while it sounds good, it will never compete with the legends of the Stradivarii. Does yours have a name, for instance?"

"I am afraid that if it did, it was lost somewhere in transferring from owner to owner. We shall have to come up with a new name for it."

"We can call it the San Francisco Stradivarius," he said with a wink. "There can't be another one with that name."

"Hmm… perhaps that makes it sound too modern," she said.

"Then maybe we ought to call it the Golden Lady. That has a certain mystique about it, the maple it's made from has a fine golden sheen, and the name suits the fiddle's owner."

"Are you trying to flatter me again, Isaac?"

"Only if it's working." He lifted the violin out of the case and handed it to her. Then he carefully transferred the Strad to his case. He watched her study the new instrument and added, "Go ahead and try it out."

"Oh, um…"

"Don't be shy about it, Suzette. I'm used to all levels of

ability. And I did hear you play a bit the other day when I identified the crack. I already know you play well, and I tuned this one before I left, just for you." He reached over and plucked the strings to show her they sounded right.

Suzette straightened her shoulders and reached for her bow. She placed the violin beneath her chin and paused a moment, seeming to be trying to remember something. She took a deep breath and put bow to strings. A warm, pure sound emanated immediately and turned out to be a hauntingly beautiful caprice by the Frenchman Pierre Rode.

Isaac grinned at her. "Breathtaking." He took in the sight of her shapely arms as she drew her bow up and down. Her nimble fingers danced across the strings as she drew out the sweet sounds. He noticed how she became one with the music and closed her eyes as she embraced the sound with her entire body. This was clearly someone who lived and loved to play. Finally, the last note died away, and she seemed to reenter their more worldly realm. She blinked as if noticing he was still there.

"You truly become lost in your music, don't you?" he asked. "That's a gift."

"There is nothing like it."

Cocking his head slightly to the side, he gave her an assessing look. "Oh, there are one or two things like it, actually." Edging closer to her, he raised his hand and stroked softly down her arm with one finger. His touch left a trail of heat. "Loving another person is similar. It brings you emotional as well as physical pleasure… or so I'm told."

"Have you ever been in love, Isaac?" She couldn't believe she asked him that.

"We'll see," he answered with an enigmatic look. He picked up the Stradivarius and strode to the door. "See you at twelve-thirty. I'm sorry I can't escort you there myself, but I'll just make it on time as it is." He nodded and left.

She stood gaping at the closed door. *What a puzzling man he can be.*

Suzette continued to amuse herself with Isaac's fiddle until a few hours later when there was a firm knock at the front door. Fabienne noticed that Suzette was engrossed and probably didn't hear it, so she answered the door and led the handsome, smiling man into the music room.

Startled, Suzette looked up from her music stand and gasped. "Walter! It is lovely to see you this morning. What are you doing here?"

Walter laughed and answered, "Isaac mentioned in passing that you would be joining us for the midday meal at the fire company today, so I thought I would come and escort you there. Are you about ready to go? The chef is prompt with his meal service."

"Oh! Is it past noon already? I am afraid I immersed myself in playing so much I lost track of the time. Just give me a moment, and I'll be with you." She set the violin down carefully and scurried away, leaving Walter gazing fondly after her.

In a few minutes, she was back, looking a bit more put together. Walter offered her his arm, and off they went. She found it was a short walk down Rincon Hill. "I have not yet paid much attention to the neighborhood, I fear," Suzette confessed. Eyeing the fine brick building that housed the fire company, she exclaimed, "This is a beautiful example of architecture, Walter. Am I to understand it was all your design? You are every bit as talented as Isaac, though in a different way." He escorted her inside, and she gasped at their luxurious surroundings. Wood paneling and heavy, masculine furniture gave it the look of a fine gentlemen's club. There was a sitting area with a marble fireplace, and in front of that sat two Dalmatians who relaxed at a man's feet.

"Meet our trusty helpers, Ember and Cinder," Walter said by way of introduction as the dogs rose, stretched, and approached Suzette to greet her. "They're friendly." She held out her hand and then stroked their heads.

"They are beautiful dogs," she said wistfully. "I miss our dogs that we had to leave in France. I am sure my brother Gustave is taking good care of them, however."

The dogs went back to lie down, and Walter took her arm again, saying, "Let me show you my favorite part of the building." He led her out of the sitting room and into a spacious library with shelves on all four walls that were filled with what had to be thousands of books. The center of the room had a sturdy table and chairs, and here and there around the room were more comfortable seating areas where one could relax and read for hours if they felt like it. About half of them were filled already with men who all looked up and unashamedly ogled her. One or two had a knowing grin for Walter, and one man stood and approached them.

Suzette didn't miss that the man was young and attractive, but as soon as he stuck out his hand and opened his mouth to speak, Isaac appeared as if from nowhere and wrapped his arm protectively—and more tightly than was probably necessary—around her waist. "Afternoon..."

"Alfonzo."

"Afternoon, Alfonzo. This is Suzette de Massey. She's here to visit Walter and me, and we're heading in to eat now." He spun her around before she had a chance to say a word, and off they marched to the dining room. Here, too, she could see Isaac's style represented in the furnishings and Walter's style in the overall look of the room. It was exquisite.

Once again, Suzette found herself flanked by the two men for a meal, and she was so conscious of their masculine presence she could scarcely pay attention to the lovely luncheon she was served. Throughout the meal, several men stared openly at her, assessing her and apparently liking what they saw. A few winked and tried to get her attention. Walter, as usual, had a collection of anecdotes to relay and kept up a stream of colorful stories, but Isaac barely seemed to listen. He was more interested in glaring at his ogling comrades. One by one, the men got his message loud and clear that Suzette was not there on display for their amusement, and they gradually went back to talking to one another.

Finally, after a delicious sponge pudding was served,

Walter jumped up and excused himself. "I'm terribly sorry to cut this short, but I have an appointment with a man who wants to build a playhouse. Apparently, he's a would-be playwright and needs space for his work to be performed. Interesting young fellow named Rosenbaum who's been making quite a name for himself around the city. Suzette, I'm sure you're in good hands with Isaac. If you're still at his workshop when I return, I'll see you both there."

Then he astonished her by bending over and kissing her full on the lips, before sauntering away with a spring in his step. A couple of whistles and catcalls punctuated his departure. Walter gave them a jaunty wave over his shoulder.

Suzette tried hard to keep herself from blushing, but she failed. She looked at Isaac, who seemed amused by her agitation, and asked, "Are you ready to go watch the operation now? I promise it won't be too painful."

She blinked a couple of times before registering that he was asking about the violin repair. "Oh, yes. Please give my compliments to your chef for such a delicious luncheon. I should very much like to see your workshop now." *I have never been kissed like that in public. If that is a local custom, it will take some getting used to. Not that I am complaining.*

Isaac rose and offered her his hand. His engulfed hers, making her feel doubly warm after Walter's unexpected kiss. She tried to ignore the questioning looks from around the room that sized her up. Instead, she concentrated on looking at Isaac. "Where is the violin now, Isaac?"

"I have it carefully locked up in my workshop. I don't want to take any chances with it," he answered softly. There was no reason to advertise its presence to anyone, even if these men were his friends.

It was a fine day, and Suzette enjoyed strolling along with her hand in the crook of Isaac's arm. Several people greeted him in a friendly manner, and Isaac smiled and nodded but seemed to prefer to keep walking rather than stopping to chat.

His workshop was a flurry of activity where several men toiled over various pieces of furniture in different degrees of completion. Isaac paused to answer some questions and then led Suzette into his private office in the back. Unlike the main work area, this part was spotless and free of sawdust, and the walls had musical instruments—some finished, some in the process of being built—decorating the space. Isaac closed the door, shutting out a great part of the noise. She hadn't realized how loud the pounding, sawing, and sanding was until it was muffled by the heavy door. "Have a seat if you'd like," he said, indicating a comfortable-looking chair across from his worktable. Then he took a key from his pocket and unlocked a large, sturdy cabinet in the corner of the room.

"Oh! You truly meant you had it in a safe place. Thank you, Isaac." She felt a tiny bit of relief pass through her, seeing him gently place her instrument down on a padded surface. He seemed already to be taking exquisite care of her precious Strad.

As Isaac studied the violin, Suzette perused her surroundings. A framed parchment caught her eye behind his work area. She smiled as she read the words inscribed on it:

"I lived in the wood until I was slain by the relentless axe. In life, I was silent, but in death, my melody is exquisite."
-Motto carved on a violin by luthier Gasper Duiffoprugcar
1514-1572

How fitting for a talented woodworker and violin maker, she thought to herself.

Isaac sat silently assessing the violin for several minutes, and Suzette found herself growing increasingly worried. Finally, after turning it over and over and looking at it from all angles, he sat back and regarded her with a serious expression.

"Is it in terrible condition, Isaac?"

"Oh, not at all. However, I notice a few things that I would recommend. There is the crack that I'll need to patch in the back. That won't be too difficult, but were you aware that the D-string peg is also cracked?"

"Yes, I have seen the crack, but my instructor advised me that it might be wrong to change too many of the Strad's original parts. It did not seem to be causing any harm."

Nodding thoughtfully, Isaac answered, "It's quite acceptable to replace broken parts, and a new peg will not decrease the violin's value, I assure you. But also, the bridge doesn't fit correctly. The whole fiddle could also use a serious cleaning, inside and out. I'll need to make a new peg and stain it to match the others. And I'll also make a new bridge for you.

This one doesn't appear to be very old. Did you have it replaced in the last couple of years?"

"I did, yes."

"Whoever did it made a mess of the job, I'm afraid. See how the holes in the design are rather closed up? These design elements need to be larger to give the instrument a cleaner, brighter sound."

"But the luthier in France designed that one to make the instrument's sound more mellow. It was certainly an improvement over what was there when I originally received the violin."

"If you don't like the new one, I'll save this one and put it back. It's not a difficult job, but the bridge is an extremely important element in creating music. Too much wood here, and it imparts a dull sound." He reached behind him and took one of the violins he had hanging on the wall off of its support and showed it to her. "See how this one looks so light and airy? It's a much better design. I guess some people would call a dull sound mellow, but doesn't that defeat the purpose of violin music? The clearer tone, the better in my thinking."

Suzette's shoulders slumped, and she mumbled to herself in French. Looking up, she seemed resolute and said, "I trust your judgment, and frankly I was never overly pleased with the so-called mellow sound, so please do whatever you think is necessary. I no longer need to listen to people my father hired to give me poor advice. Maybe I will discover that I play better than I thought after all." She laughed and was happy to see Isaac more relaxed after she gave him the go-ahead. "Please proceed."

For the next hour, she watched Isaac work silently, removing the strings, the bridge, the pegs, and finally, he ever-so-carefully took a knife and slid it around the edge in various places, eventually popping the violin apart. Suzette gasped and stood to get a better view. The inside was filled with a layer of dust and grime.

"This is where I'll begin," he said, taking a firm brush and dislodging years and years of built-up dirt. She watched spellbound as he almost lovingly stroked along the grain of the wood with the bristles. When he seemed satisfied with that step, he took a softer brush and swept away the tiny bits of debris. Isaac's hands were large and calloused from woodworking, but he used extreme care and finesse. She couldn't help but wonder how those hands would feel stroking her body with the same degree of care. Snapping out of that thought, she came back to the task at hand, clearing her throat. Isaac looked up, almost appearing surprised she was still there.

He stood and stretched his back, giving Suzette a pleasant look at his muscles in the process. "I need to find a patch for that crack, and I'll want to match the grain of the wood as closely as possible. Then I need to fashion a new bridge." He gave her a rueful smile. "I'm sorry I haven't been the best of company. I tend to become fairly engrossed in my work."

"Not at all, Isaac. I love watching you work, and I am gratified to see my precious instrument in such capable hands. I was not expecting conversation to keep me amused."

"Well, that's a good thing. If you need conversation, Walter is your man. I'm more of a physical person."

"I am the fortunate one then. Perhaps I can reap the benefits of both of you."

"That's what I'm hoping." He wiped his hands on a clean cloth and came around the workbench toward her. Softly, he asked, "Does the idea of two men worshipping you excite you, Suzette?" She gave a sharp intake of breath as his hands grasped hers and pulled her up, bringing her close to his body. Heat and power radiated off of him like a furnace, and he was hard everywhere. Isaac lowered his face to her neck and nuzzled her gently. He seemed to be breathing her in. "The idea doesn't frighten you, does it?" He began to nibble at her earlobe.

Suzette tried to keep her voice steady as she answered, "It does frighten me a bit because I have very little idea of what to expect, but the touch of fear excites me more than you can imagine." He pulled back a little and looked deeply into her eyes. She could see both happiness and lust in his expression. "Kiss me, Isaac."

"I am happy to give you whatever you want." He leaned in and stroked his lips across hers. He was gentle this time as though he had nothing to prove and all the time in the world to enjoy their contact. Gradually, he increased the pressure until their mouths seemed fused, and he invaded hers with his demanding tongue. His hands slid up her back, pressing her into him, and his hips jutted forward involuntarily, letting her know just how excited he was to be this close to her.

Her soft little moans were stirring him up like mad, but he

knew he couldn't do anything other than this with his workers just outside the door. Anyone could come walking in and find them in a compromised situation if he took things too far. And no sooner had he had that thought when the door opened, and Walter came strutting in looking happy.

"Well! Nice to see you're still here, Suzette," he chuckled. "I see that our Isaac has been taking good care of you." He closed the door swiftly and locked it. It took him only three strides to close the distance between them.

Isaac was in no rush to end their kiss, and he let it fall away as slowly and gently as a spring rain. Stepping back slightly, he grinned at Walter. "She was watching me work on the Strad, and it was time for a break." He winked. "Join us, Walter. Suzette is amenable."

"Will you kiss each other again?" she asked almost breathlessly.

Walter's eyebrows shot up, and he laughed softly. "Of course. Isaac? Is it fine with you?"

"Come here." Isaac grabbed Walter's arm and pulled him into their embrace. This time he let Walter initiate the kiss, and he was not sorry. Walter's mouth crashed onto his with obvious excitement. The feel of Walter's whiskers against his face felt foreign, but not any less exciting than Suzette's smooth skin. Both men felt Suzette's hands go into their hair and stroke them as they ravaged each other's mouths.

"Have you been in love with each other for a long time?" she asked. That caused them to break apart and stare at her.

"In love?" Isaac asked at the very same time as Walter emphatically stated, "Yes."

Isaac's eyebrows shot up as he gaped at Walter.

"Surely you knew," Walter said softly. "You made that comment…"

"Lust, curiosity, perhaps. But love?"

Suzette's eyes went back and forth between the men. She wasn't certain what to think.

Walter cleared his throat and stepped back half a pace. "Isaac, I have loved you probably since the first day I met you when you threw yourself into my wagon while holding onto your precious tools and violin case, running away from that ridiculous man with the shotgun."

Suzette gasped. "Wha…?"

"We'll explain later, dearest," soothed Isaac. "Funny story, actually."

"In that moment, my life changed," Walter affirmed. "All for the better."

"And yet you never said anything to me?" Isaac's brows furrowed as he considered this.

"You never gave me any indication that the feelings were reciprocated, and I certainly did not wish to make you uncomfortable or want to leave me. Your friendship was too important to lose."

"Walter, we've been together every day for years. We've seen plenty of men, including two of our closest friends, demonstrate their affection for one another publicly. Were you so afraid that I would turn against you? I think my feelings are a little hurt. You are the single most important person in my life. The best friend any man would be lucky enough to have. I even kissed you, and still you acted coy about it. I'm confused."

"Isaac, you are an incredible man. I am in awe of you. I cherish every moment in your company. If all you want from me is friendship, then I will remain a happy man. If you choose to love me back, I won't know how to contain my joy. And if we can add our lovely Suzette to the mix, life will be beyond incredible. It's almost too much to hope for."

"I already agreed to be with both of you gentlemen. I am the licky one here," Suzette said with a shy smile.

Both men stared at her until Walter asked, "You must mean 'lucky,' right?"

"I rather prefer her word," Isaac chortled.

"Oh, dear. Did I misspeak?" she asked.

"It's all a matter of perception," Walter replied and then nuzzled her neck. "Lick, luck. It's all good in the name of love." He looked at Isaac. "Do you think you could ever love me back the way I love you?"

"Walter, how can you even ask me that question? I do love you. I just never considered whether I was actually *in love* with you. But now that you ask, if I were to lose your affection, I would be devastated." He lifted his hand and gently stroked Walter's cheek. "I may not have the kind of experience it takes to love another man, but I'm sure we can figure it out together." He looked at Suzette. "How do you feel about physical love between two men? Does it bother you? Excite you?"

Suzette gave them a shy smile and answered, "A few years ago, I was walking in our gardens and came across two men on my father's staff. They did not see or hear me as they were deeply preoccupied. I am somewhat embarrassed to say that I watched them as they made love to each other. I hid behind a hedge and peeked at them through the leaves, but what I saw was beautiful to me. They had such obvious affection for one another, and they were fine-looking men. I grew terribly warm watching them, and I have never forgotten it. I must further confess the sight of their lovemaking comes back to me in moments of loneliness…" Her eyes dropped as she added, "often at night."

Isaac made a strangled noise as Walter's breath grew ragged.

"So, no," Suzette continued, "The sight of two men together does not bother me—it definitely excites me. Do you think I am strange because of that?"

Walter laughed and answered, "No stranger than Adeline. She adores Jasper and Royal, and I'm sure they don't hold back around her. This is a city where all kind of love happens."

She let out a small huff of breath. "You might say actually that I am more aware of what happens between two men than I am between a man and a woman, after what I saw."

"We will have to remedy that as soon as possible then," Isaac purred into her ear. "I think, in some ways, we'll all have to figure this out together unless we get some advice from our friends. You can always speak to Adeline and Madame Beaufort if you have questions."

Suzette stepped back a little and regarded her men. "What exactly are we proposing here? Are you men looking for fun and sexual gratification? Do either of you want a wife? You know I cannot be one without knowing whether or not I am married. Do you want children? I am sorry to sound so businesslike, but I am curious as to what to expect."

Isaac and Walter looked at each other with guarded expressions, and then Isaac softened. "I love children," he said.

Walter smiled at Isaac. "You would make a wonderful father." He turned to Suzette. "You don't know us well enough yet to say whether you would want to marry either of us even if it were legal. But I, for one, think we all have an incredible connection that we need to pursue. You won't find two other men who could treat you as well as we can promise to do. Let us love you… and love each other in the process, Suzette. I think we all owe it to ourselves to try."

Suzette stood smiling thoughtfully at them and asked, "Can you both come to my house this evening? We can have supper and then… well… see what happens."

"Yes!" Walter answered enthusiastically as Isaac said, "We'll be there. Thank you."

Ten

After a quick flurry of kisses all around, Suzette took her leave. She had much to do before the men arrived. "Please come at eight o'clock," she directed them as she scurried out the door.

Arriving home, she peered around and established that Fabienne had everything in sparkling order, so she summoned the two women with a bell.

"I will have company tonight, so I need the evening meal to be special and to be sufficient to feed two hungry men," she directed Delphine. "Do you ladies need to go shopping?"

After discussing a possible menu with Delphine, Suzette took off on her own toward Hart House, hoping she would find Adeline at home and not terribly busy. As luck would have it, Adeline herself opened the door and gave Suzette an enormous smile. "Welcome! Please come in, Suzette. I was actually just thinking about you, and here you stand. May I offer you a cool drink?"

"Thank you, that would actually be wonderful. I am quite out of breath. I need to get used to these hills in San Francisco. I am sorry to barge in unannounced, but I need to ask some questions, and you seem to be the best candidate to answer them."

"Let's go sit in my small sitting room then. It's quiet and private in there on most days." She rang a bell and requested lemonades be brought to them by one of her servants. Looking at Suzette with a knowing smile, she said softly, "I'm not at all surprised to see you." She led Suzette into a cheerful room with soft furnishings and a beautiful writing desk. They took their seats on a settee and waited for their refreshments before Suzette began her interrogation.

Finally, she cleared her throat and promptly blushed scarlet. "I do not know where to begin."

"I'll make it easy on you then. You are not making a mistake if you're worried about Isaac and Walter." Suzette looked startled and then relaxed, figuring that Adeline knew exactly what was going on. Adeline continued, "They are two of the finest men you will ever meet, and they are completely smitten with you. I'm sure you will be the envy of the town when people see you on their arms in public. No one will look aghast. I seem to have paved the way admirably." She laughed.

Nodding, Suzette smiled. "I see that. Isaac and Walter are admirable men, and I find I am equally smitten—to use your word. I could not decide between them if I had to with a knife to my throat."

"Then what are your concerns? Clearly, you have some."

"I do not… ah… know how… know what… you know?"

Laughing good-naturedly, Adeline answered, "I see." She took a small sip of her drink and set it down. "I had the counsel of Marguerite Beaufort to help me along, and my husbands, let's just say, have great imaginations." She looked Suzette in the eye and asked, "Are you a virgin?"

"I am. And that is somewhat odd because I may possibly have a husband somewhere, or I am a widow. I know not." She proceeded to give Adeline the abbreviated version of where her maybe-husband might or might not be. "You see, I ought to know more than I do, but shortly after we recited our vows, he vanished into thin air. He disappeared before anything at all happened between us, and my own mother never told me anything. She was, I am afraid, sorely abused mentally by my father and rarely spoke up about a thing. Not that she would have known how to approach having two lovers at once, even if she was accustomed to speaking her own mind." Suzette took a sip. "Please, Adeline, can you tell me anything? I do not want to get personal about your life, but I am grasping in the dark here. I know that kissing Walter and Isaac is like magic, and watching them kiss each other makes me get the shivers. Apart from that… well, I do not wish to disappoint them."

Adeline grinned at this news. "I can imagine. They're both fine-looking men, and they have shared a deep affection for one another for several years. But I doubt anything you could do would disappoint either of them. They have not been with a woman together, as far as I'm aware. Separately, they surely must have sampled a few, but nothing serious. I think they were waiting for someone like you to come along."

Just then, little Marigold came bursting into the room laughing and ran to Adeline, hollering, "Mama!" and threw her arms in the air, clearly wanting a hug. Adeline laughed too and smothered her little girl with kisses and hugs before the nanny appeared, looking embarrassed.

"She got away from me, ma'am. I'm sorry. I hope she's not interrupting anything important."

Hoisting Marigold into her lap, Adeline answered, "There is nothing to apologize for. You know that in this house the children are welcome to express their affection for their parents at any time." She looked at Marigold. "Are you hungry, dear one?"

"Yes, Mama! Hungry!"

"Then I say let Nanny Jane take you to get something to eat in the kitchen, and I'll come and find you in a little while. I'll let you play the piano if you're a good girl.'

Marigold's eyes went huge. "Pano! I play!" Then she looked at her nanny. "Hungry too."

Adeline set her daughter down and caught Suzette's expression as Marigold was led out chattering about sweets to her nanny.

"You want children, don't you?"

"More than anything. I was afraid after my fiasco of a marriage it would never happen, but I am equally glad that I never had to bear any with that hideous excuse of a man."

She looked down at her hands. "I discussed it briefly with the men, and they seem amenable to children. I suppose it would be inevitable anyway if we continue in what I assume they want to happen." She made a face. "I do not mean to make it sound at all as if they are pressuring me. They have made their desires known and are leaving the rest up to me to decide. Watching you and your husbands made me realize what seems impossible is possible, and I want it. I want it all."

"I think you need to relax a bit about the intricacies of what happens in the bedroom, Suzette. However, if you want some excellent advice on that score, you ought to make an appointment with Marguerite for a dress design and some fittings. The woman is a font of knowledge and can express herself unabashedly about the topic of sex. Her opinions are most enlightening." She smiled sweetly then and continued, "I would feel awkward revealing anything personal or suggesting something for you to try with two of my dearest friends. I will say that, like you, I could not decide between my two suitors, and they made it easy for me to accept them both. I have never been sorry. I think the potential for you, Walter, and Isaac is the same. Just relax and don't try to do anything too soon, especially if it makes you uncomfortable. They're good men, and they will understand how to make you feel good."

Suzette gave a nearly imperceptible shiver and smiled. "They do already."

"Oh, you have no idea, Suzette, what is in store for you. I wish you the very best of luck. And do go see Marguerite for a new gown and some advice. She used to live in a suite at The Discovery with Doc Louis, but they finally built a house here on Rincon Hill where she maintains her dress design business. Doc Louis has his medical office more in the middle of town now. In fact, would you like to send a messenger to her now and request an appointment? I can summon a boy for you who will return her reply to you."

"Yes, thank you." And that is what they did. A boy brought word back to Suzette a couple of hours later that Marguerite had an opening for an appointment the next day and was looking forward to seeing her. Suzette had a sneaking suspicion that Marguerite had an idea that this was for more than picking out material for a new frock.

Eleven

"We should take her flowers, shouldn't we?" Walter worried and fidgeted as he tied his tie for the third time. He had never been nervous around a woman before, but this seemed completely different from anything he'd experienced in the past.

"Yes, Walter. Flowers are important. I've already taken care of it. Didn't you notice them? They're right over there," Isaac indicated with a nod to the pretty bouquet on the side table.

"Oh, good. Thank you, Isaac. I don't know what's gotten into me. Why am I such a sack of jitters?"

Isaac gently took Walter's hands in his and said, "Stop fussing. Your tie is perfect, and you're perfect. If you're worried Suzette will ultimately reject us, you'll always have me. You know that, don't you?" He leaned his forehead against Walter's and heard Walter's sudden intake of breath.

"Think of this as a new adventure in our friendship. We've been through hell and back, and this might just be the ultimate pot of gold we were always seeking. I'm sorry I wasn't aware of the depth of your feelings sooner and was too obtuse about my own, but it's never too late." He stepped closer to Walter so their bodies touched. He could feel Walter hardening as he pressed against him and found that he responded in kind. He lowered his lips to Walter's and kissed him. Walter's hands went around Isaac immediately and stroked up and down his hard, muscled body.

"We have on too many damned clothes," Walter whispered, eliciting a rumbling laugh from Isaac.

"I'm sorry, but now isn't the time. Come on, let's go, or we'll be late. I sure hope there are no fires tonight to spoil our plans." Isaac squeezed Walter's shoulder and realized just how much more often he'd been touching Walter since Walter's confession of love. He liked it.

A FEW MINUTES LATER, THE TWO MEN WERE SHOWN INTO Suzette's parlor by her maid. Their hostess was nowhere to be seen, but they could hear angry voices arguing in a different part of the house. They couldn't understand the words, but the frustration in Suzette's voice was evident. Casting her eyes down, Fabienne backed out of the room and closed the doors, thus cutting them off from further noise.

"I wonder what's going on. Do you think we ought to go see if Suzette needs us?" Walter mused.

"Unless we hear screaming or something breaking, we'd probably be better off letting her work it out. It must be that ratbag brother of hers she's having words with."

As soon as Isaac finished his statement, Suzette swept into the room. Her color was high, and she seemed slightly out of breath as she plastered on a smile. Pascal, also red-faced, peered over her shoulder at them, squinted menacingly, and then turned on his heel. He jerked open the front door and slammed it behind him.

"I take it Pascal won't be dining with us tonight?" Isaac asked with a soothing smile.

"In fact," Suzette explained, "I asked him to join us for dinner. He wanted to rush off to do whatever it is he does each night. He was not happy with me when I told him he was being rude and should have been a gracious host in his own home. He is also at something of a crossroads in his life and needs to sort it out. He does not seem equipped to do it, however, and I am tired of persuading him. I thought perhaps he could speak to the two of you and imagine some possibilities, but he preferred once again to ignore me."

"As delighted as we are to have you to ourselves, I am sorry you had words with him," Walter said, thinking that Pascal's expression looked like he was upset over more than being late to wherever he was heading. *Does he mind leaving his sister unchaperoned? If so, he has every reason to.* Then Walter held out the bouquet and added, "These are for you, Suzette. Thank you for having us. I mean, inviting us." He looked at the flowers and suddenly felt like a fraud, so he blurted, "Isaac picked these out. He just let me carry them."

Suzette stifled a giggle as Isaac rolled his eyes heavenward and said, "Our suave and sophisticated Walter is overcome with nerves. We need to be gentle with him tonight." Then he winked at them.

Walter took a deep breath and announced, "It's not every day that one's wildest dreams begin to unfold in a most positive manner all at once. I find that I am beside myself in the presence of both of you, and I scarcely know what to do with myself. There, I've said it."

"Try this," Isaac whispered. He took Suzette by the hand and brought her forward leaning into Walter, he gave a nod to Suzette, who also smiled, and they both began kissing Walter's neck. Suzette nibbled at his ear as Walter inhaled sharply and grasped them both with his hands.

"Yes, just so. That's grand," Walter closed his eyes and sighed. "Oh my, yes."

They all reluctantly stopped when they heard a gasp at the door. Delphine stood there, gawking at them and trying to pull herself together to announce, "Pardon me, but dinner is ready."

With as much nonchalance as she could muster, Suzette thanked her and pulled away from the men. "You both know the way to the dining room. Thank you for the lovely flowers. Delphine, can you please have Fabienne find a vase for them and put them upstairs in my room? They smell so lovely; I want to enjoy them all night."

DINNER WAS DELIGHTFUL. DELPHINE HAD MADE A DELICIOUS Bouillabaisse according to the way she'd been taught in her seaside village in France. She also served them sourdough bread and fresh vegetables from neighboring growers.

"Pascal ought to be ashamed of himself for leaving such a meal. This is wonderful, and Delphine has used our local ingredients to her benefit. I'm sorry he felt compelled to leave the house," Walter said.

"Delphine assures me that there is plenty for him if he wants it when he returns. My brother is a spoiled child sometimes. Do not concern yourself with his annoying behavior, dear Walter." She sipped her wine and looked fondly at the faces of the men she already thought of as hers.

After eating, they retired again to the parlor with glasses of brandy. It was still too warm for a fire, so the room was softly lit by kerosene lamps now that the sun had gone down. Suzette sat in the middle of her settee, and the men flanked her on either side. It was a somewhat tight fit that no one seemed to be bothered by in the least.

"You look exquisite tonight," Isaac told Suzette. "And I bet you're as sweet as the lovely dessert we just enjoyed." He leaned in and sealed his lips over hers, growling happily when he detected the flavor of brandy and essential Suzette in equal measure. "I was right. Delicious. Let Walter have a taste." He took the liberty of placing his hand on her thigh and nodding toward Walter. As she turned to Walter, Isaac put his other arm around her shoulder and reached all the way to Walter with his hand. He stroked Walter's cheek with a gentle caress, causing Walter to rub Isaac's hand with his face like a cat.

With Isaac's touch on his cheek and Suzette's lips on his, Walter felt his arousal spring to life. *This has to be the best feeling in the world. Why was I so worried about telling Isaac how much I love him? I've been a fool missing out on his affection for all these years. Or maybe the time wasn't right, and we truly needed Suzette.* He reached across Suzette and placed his hand on Isaac's thigh, causing Isaac to grin and chuckle. Walter stroked up and down Isaac's muscled leg. *What a contrast, and how delicious to have this man who is all hard and truly sublime and this woman who is all fiery desire and beauty personified.*

Walter and Suzette kissed. Their breathing sped up, and Suzette thought her heart might just burst with happiness… or perhaps lust. Not knowing where to put her hands, she settled on stroking both their thighs, and this seemed to please the men, who scooted even closer to her. She was finally brought back to earth a bit when Isaac breathed into her ear, "It's up to you how far we take this tonight, Suzette. Walter and I want you more than anything, but we promise we won't rush you before you're ready for us. If you need more time to get to know us, you only have to let us know."

Suzette stopped kissing Walter then and smiled, saying, "I have never in my life been given a choice. I have been dictated to by my father, and I expected my married life to be more of the same. I cannot begin to tell you how much it means to me that you are such gentlemen about considering my desires as if I am equal."

Walter looked mildly horrified. "Suzette, you are absolutely equal to any man. We would never force you or neglect your feelings. This is 1855, not the dark ages! You are your own person. Women in San Francisco have rights and make up their own minds."

"This is just one more reason I am delighted to be here now. I had no idea how free I could be." She considered for a moment and then added, "I paid a call on Adeline today. She is a brilliant example of a woman who makes her own way."

Both men smiled at this news, and Isaac said, "She is a strong woman, and she will be a wonderful friend to you."

"She certainly had complimentary things to say about the two of you."

Chuckling, Walter said, "I'd hope so!"

"She also had me make an appointment with Marguerite Beaufort for a dress fitting and some, shall we say, more specific advice about what to do with two men at once. Adeline was reluctant to say anything specific to me regarding two close friends of hers."

Walter nodded and said, "Sage advice on all counts. I believe Madame Beaufort is accustomed to such things." He got a faraway look in his eye for a moment. "I'll let you in on a secret. A few years ago, she invited me to join her *with* Doc Louis in a… well… a sexual escapade."

Isaac laughed, "You never told me that!"

"Yes, well, I was a little shocked and frankly not particularly interested. She's a lovely woman, but I was not the least bit ready to engage with Doc Louis in anything other than polite conversation. He's an interesting man, and to show me that he bore no ill feelings about the rejection, he shared with me that ground-breaking study he'd worked on in France with a noted physician named Pierre Briquet. Together the physicians developed a treatment for female hysteria."

Suzette gave a tiny gasp and said, "It was in all of the French news. He worked on that?"

Walter nodded. "The report is fascinating reading, I must say, and fortunately he had it translated into English. After reading it, I shared the information with Isaac as Doc Louis swears it's not so much a medical treatment but a necessity for lovemaking."

Suzette looked confused. "How can a medical procedure help with lovemaking? I remember distinctly that my father had my mother go see the doctor about her female hysteria. She always swore the doctor was wonderful at treating her."

Walter laughed. "I am sure she felt that way. The point is, it's not just about hysteria. It's cloaked in that medical jargon, but it's truly about sublime female pleasure. Doc Louis swears it's vital."

Suzette looked confused, so Walter went on to explain, "The technique pleases and relaxes women tremendously, so I have no doubt innumerable women enjoyed their trips to the physician for treatment. Anyway, we're getting way off base here." He looked at Isaac. "We'll revisit this topic when the time is right for Suzette's pleasure to be guaranteed. For now, I want to confirm to you that I have not ever lain with a man."

"So, your interest is just in me, then?" Isaac asked.

"Yes. I've never harbored any secret desires for another man before you. There. Now you know it all."

"I'm honored, Walter."

"And I am the licky one," Suzette said with a flirty smile and a soft giggle.

"We need to explore that, don't we?" Walter asked.

"Would you gentlemen like to accompany me upstairs?" She stood and held out her hands. Her cheeks were rosy, and she looked at them imploringly with bright eyes.

At the very same moment as they grasped her outstretched hands, their brandy glasses began to jiggle across the table, and there was an odd rumbling sensation that they felt more than heard. Suzette's eyes became huge with surprise. "What is that? I feel almost dizzy!"

Isaac smiled comfortingly. "It's just a small earthquake. We have them fairly often, actually. I hope this one hasn't knocked over any lamps or candles because if so, we may be called to put out a fire or two. We might hear the firehouse bell ringing in a few minutes. Let's just hope all is quiet tonight."

"You mean the earth actually shakes like this regularly in this city?" Suzette asked, still wide-eyed.

"Yes, it happens," answered Walter. "Some are stronger than others, and the streets in San Francisco are so poorly made, we feel them moving around the buildings. But don't trouble yourself, Suzette. Your house was built to last. It won't fall down around you. We can personally attest to that." He looked at the door and indicated passing through it with a tip of his head. "Now, shall we?"

Squaring her shoulders, Suzette answered, "Yes. We shall, gentlemen." She led the way up the stairs to her bedroom with an air of confidence that was mostly for show. Inside, she was a trembling mass of nerves.

Twelve

On the threshold of her bedroom, she turned and looked at the men. "I want you to know this is what I want. I am most fond of and attracted to you both. I am not sure of my role in anything that happens past this door, however, so I am counting on you to tend to me carefully."

Isaac stepped in and wrapped her tenderly in his arms. "Thank you for your trust, Suzette." He kissed her as Walter came up to her from behind and caressed her gently. "We are also equally fond of you. I hope Walter and I will please you." They made their way into the room, and Isaac quietly closed and locked the door behind them. He turned back to Suzette and asked, "Has anyone ever touched you at all with love?"

"No," she whispered. "Never. I have only experienced your kisses."

"Walter, can you help her out of her gown from behind

while I work on things in front?" He looked down and chuckled. "Why do women's fashions have to be so complicated?"

"I shall speak to Marguerite about that tomorrow," she said with a smile. "Would you prefer that I summon Fabienne to help me out of my clothes?"

"Not on your life," Walter stated firmly. Then he kissed a trail down her neck, leaving a pattern of heat where his lips had been. "At least you're not wearing one of those confounded hoop skirts I see some of the newcomers wearing around town. They may be fashionable, but they get in the way and look dangerous." They all laughed at that, but their laughter died away as they concentrated on their tasks.

After undoing what had to be dozens of buttons and ties and dropping articles of clothing onto the floor, Suzette—clothed only in her light undergarments—commented, "The two of you need to catch up to my lack of attire."

As Isaac began divesting himself of his jacket and boots, she grasped a handful of Walter's shirt and untucked it from his pants. Finally, the men stood before her, shirtless in their trousers. She smiled at the glorious picture they made. Though slenderer, Walter's muscles were as beautifully defined as Isaac's, and Suzette gave in to the desire to run her hands over all of that warm, silky flesh and feel the ridges of their athletic bodies. Constant labor and firefighting had kept them fit.

"You are both exquisite, and aside from Isaac's arm, I have never touched the bare flesh of a man's body before tonight." With a worshipful look on her face, she stroked her fingers through the soft hairs on Isaac's chest and followed the path toward his navel. As her fingers trailed down his body, feeling the ridges and indentations, Isaac sucked in a breath. Suzette then took Walter's hand, and together they stroked Isaac and kissed his chest. "Show me what you long to do, Walter," she commanded as she stepped out of his way a bit.

Walter first took Suzette's face in his hands and kissed her deeply, then he bent down and buried his face in Isaac's midriff. Isaac moaned softly as Walter undid his pants and nuzzled his face into the newly exposed area that was covered only by his thin undergarment. Isaac's trousers hit the floor with a soft thud as he let go of them, and his stomach muscles tensed as Walter's face caressed him while his hands reached around and grasped Isaac's firm behind. Dropping to his knees, Walter inhaled the manly scent of Isaac's body. He reached for Suzette and pulled her closer so that she too could nuzzle her face into Isaac. Pulling back slightly, he whispered to her, "Isn't our man exquisite?"

Suzette hummed a sound of pleasure as she relished the feel of Isaac. She also put her hand behind his body and stroked up and down the back of his strong thigh. He felt to her like silken power all wrapped up in a warm package that thrummed with desire.

Isaac looked down at the unfamiliar sight of two heads leaning into his body at a very personal level of his anatomy and restrained himself from chuckling. He smiled at them, though they didn't see it. Gently, he stroked their hair and felt his own heartbeat pounding in his ears as if he'd sprinted a mile. He took several deep breaths and saw the front of his underwear begin to tent as he swelled with pleasure.

"See this, Suzette? Isaac likes what we're doing. This means he's excited." He raised his face to look up at Isaac and winked at him. "Touch him, Suzette. Our man will love that." He placed her hand over Isaac's stiffening cock and stroked it with her hand. Isaac hissed as Walter's hand slipped off of Suzette's and side-by-side his two partners' hands stroked him. Isaac fought to keep his eyes open. He was almost overcome with pleasure, but he didn't want to miss a thing by not looking. He had certainly felt the touch of a woman's hand on his body before, but never alongside a man's—and never with such profound affection. This was bliss.

Isaac could only take so much. The unexpected delight grew within him to such a degree that he knew he'd have to stop them before he exploded. Stepping back a bit, he asked in a choked voice, "Walter, shouldn't we take care of Suzette's pleasure now? I'm becoming quite overcome."

Suzette looked questioningly up at Isaac and replied, "I am experiencing great pleasure right now."

Snaking his arm around her, Walter said, "This is only the barest beginning, dearest. Isaac is right. We're being a little selfish." He helped her to her feet and led her to her bed. Considering it for a moment, he asked Isaac with a chuckle, "Do you think we ought to do something about this little French bed? We need to make her a larger one if we're all going to fit comfortably."

"I'll get on that as soon as I finish her violin," Isaac answered with a laugh. "For now, we'll just have to be snug. There are certainly worse things." He looked at Suzette. "Is everything right with you? Are you still comfortable with us?"

"I have never been more comfortable in my life. You are bringing out a feeling inside me that I have only imagined in the past. When I saw those men in the garden, my insides felt warm and wobbly, but now it is more like a furnace is raging inside of me. I need… something, and I cannot name it. More kisses, more hands, more… more."

Both men smiled at that. Walter sat on the bed and pulled her to him. Then Isaac lifted her off her feet like she weighed nothing and placed her in the middle of the bed. He climbed in beside her and reached for her face. He kissed her long and hard with no hesitation. His hand stroked down her face to the throat and then to her chest, and finally he cupped her breast, thumbing her nipple.

Suzette gasped at the feel of being stroked by Isaac's large hand, and then the bed dipped, and another hand appeared on her other breast. Walter lay beside her and stroked her hair away so he could kiss her neck. He caressed her breast, smiling to himself as he felt the stiff little peak. He couldn't resist giving it a swift pinch, which caused her to jump and whimper, *"Encore une foi!"*

"What?" Walter asked.

"She wants you to do it again," Isaac explained. "That much French, I know." He chuckled. "How about this, Suzette?" He bent down and sucked her nipple into his mouth through the thin fabric of her chemise. She gave a tiny cry that multiplied when Walter did the same thing to her other breast.

She let out a string of French words so quickly and in such a fever, the men could only guess at their meaning. Whatever it was, she sounded sultry and base but highly entertained. They chuckled at her fervor.

Isaac placed a hand on her belly as Walter stroked the inside of her thigh. Their tongues continued their barrage on Suzette's nipples, causing her to squirm and groan. Taking this as a sign to continue, Isaac untied the laces on the front of her chemise. The men sat back so that he could pull the fabric away from her breasts.

"Exquisite!" breathed Walter as Isaac dove back in and took her bare breast into his eager mouth. His tongue played a game with it, and Suzette's eyes went huge, and she squeezed her legs together. Her chest heaved with the heavy breaths she took in and blew out. This was something so beautiful and new, she wanted to savor every last second of it.

As Isaac continued to flick her nipple with his tongue and nibble gently on her with his teeth, Walter began kissing her exposed belly. His hand continued to stroke up and down her thigh as he tried to gently persuade her to open her legs, but she was just as set on keeping them locked together and writhing. He had a pretty good sense of how excited she was and knew how to satisfy the craving she probably still could not name.

Walter sat up finally and looked Suzette in the eye. "May we touch you now?" he asked in a soft but eager voice.

Suzette's eyes dilated as she answered, "Please. Yes."

Her bloomers were open in the middle as was the style, so

access was a simple procedure. Walter took Isaac's free hand and placed it on Suzette's other leg. "Relax your muscles, dear one. We will give you the greatest pleasure if you are ready for it."

"Do it, please!" She grasped the breast that Isaac had been playing with. She pulled and tweaked her own nipple, causing strange bolts of sensation to run through her body. She missed the feel of Isaac's lips and felt determined to keep the excitement going.

Both men's hands caressed up and down her inner thighs, and as Suzette forced herself to relax, her knees dropped open a bit. "There you go, dearest," Walter encouraged her. He scooted even closer to her so that his steely cock touched her.

Suzette was fully aware of both men on either side as they rutted their cocks almost involuntarily against her legs. The feeling was deliciously naughty. But then… "Oh!" she gasped. Two fingers were sliding over and around her most private, intimate parts, and the sensation nearly made her eyes roll back. Walter whispered something to Isaac about a "clitoris," and Isaac made a rumbling sound of agreement and nodded. Then Walter's finger began to stroke her in a circular motion that made her blood boil. She could barely contain herself; this unforeseen pleasure was so intense. And it got even better when Isaac's finger began to probe more deeply into her soft tissue. She felt her dampness grow, until the probing finger actually slid inside her body. Suzette gave a cry of surprise, and both men stopped what they were doing immediately.

Isaac's voice was full of concern when he asked, "Is this too much for you? Should we stop? We don't want to force you or make you uncomfortable."

"I am not certain what is happening, but if you stop it now, I shall surely die," she exclaimed. And she moaned as she felt the continuation of the circular stroking. The finger inside her slowly pulled back and pushed in again, and the feeling made her chest heave. She had never experienced such sensations.

"She's unbelievably tight," Isaac whispered. "Here, feel this." He slipped his hand away for a moment, and Walter replaced it with his. Suzette moaned in protest, however, as the circular stroking had stopped. Isaac took up the cause, making her purr in contentment once again.

Walter groaned with pleasure, feeling her warmth as she squeezed his finger.

Then something truly unbelievable happened. Isaac removed his finger and scooted into position, closing his *mouth* over her little pleasure nub! His firm tongue lapped at her, causing her to cry out again in ecstasy. She involuntarily clamped her legs together, squeezing Walter's hand. Both men chuckled at her reaction and felt their cocks grow harder and harder. This was delightful torture.

Isaac stopped for a second and asked, "Do you think she's ready for two?" He watched as Suzette's chest rose and fell with gasps.

"Yes," Walter agreed. "I think she's getting close." Then, addressing Suzette, he explained, "I'm going to use two fingers inside you now. My hands are large, and there will be some pain for a moment. Don't let it frighten you. It's normal, and it will go away quickly. Just try to stay relaxed and keep taking deep breaths." He nodded to Isaac, who placed his lips on her again and sucked her clit into his mouth. This caused her to nearly levitate off the bed. His tongue danced on her as though making music.

Everything about what was happening was warm and wet and incredibly decadent. Suzette gradually became aware of a strange, tingly feeling that seemed to emanate from deep within her soul. She could not even identify the source of the sensation other than to realize it was new and important. The feeling built, and just as she thought something within her might break, she felt a sharp, searing pain between her legs. Oddly, however, this pain enhanced her pleasure, and she became suffused with light behind her eyelids. As her body convulsed in a strange and delightful manner, Suzette emitted a guttural sound so foreign to her that she scarcely knew who she was anymore. But the pleasure... oh, incredible pleasure! Spasms ripped through her over and over, gradually diminishing in intensity. It was as if she had no control over her body's reaction, and she absolutely adored the sensation. It was freeing and felt like... love. A tear rolled down her temple and into her hair.

As her sensations died away, Isaac and Walter gradually decreased their ministrations on her body. Finally, they pulled away long enough to reposition themselves as they lay on either side of her. Isaac wrapped his arm across her, snuggling closer to her, and Walter stroked her face as he kissed her ear. Feeling wetness there, he leaned back and scrutinized her.

"Did I hurt you badly? If I did, I'm incredibly sorry. It was unavoidable at some point, and this seemed like the decent time to get it over with." He made a face at himself. "Oh, that doesn't sound very nice." He started to flop onto his back.

Suzette reached for him and said with a deep laugh, "If that is pain, I will take it any day. It was the most incredible feeling in the world. You both have given me something special I shall never forget, Walter."

"You don't have to worry about forgetting it, Suzette," Isaac assured her with a chuckle. We'll be happy to do this every day for the rest of our lives, with the exception of breaching your maidenhead for the first time. Now that it's done, it won't hurt like that next time, we promise. And this is just the beginning. There is much, much more you can look forward to." He nuzzled her neck and kissed her gently.

"What about the two of you? Did you experience anything close to what I felt? When I saw the men in the garden, it seemed to me that they were transported most rapturously before they pulled apart."

Smiling, Walter explained carefully. "We felt your pleasure, and that pleases both of us immeasurably, but for us to experience a similar climax, we actually need more… uh… contact than what we've had."

"I see," she said thoughtfully and then asked, "May I see? Can you do what they did?"

Walter looked eagerly at Isaac and waited for his reply. He would not force the issue. To his sheer delight, Isaac announced, "We can arrange something like that." Looking at Suzette, he told her, "Sit up a bit and get comfortable. We're new at this sort of thing, so I have no idea how long it might take. He raised up onto his knees and reached for Walter's hand. Walter smiled enigmatically and raised up to his knees as well. "Take the rest of your clothes off, Walter," he ordered.

"Yes, sir!" Walter scrambled out of his drawers and the socks he'd forgotten to remove. He stared as if spellbound as Isaac also slipped out of his cotton drawers, leaving him gloriously naked. Walter had often seen Isaac naked throughout the years of their friendship, but suddenly he could look at him the way he wanted to. He could regard him with love in his eyes and with a sense of possession. Isaac was his man.

"You are as stunning as Suzette," Walter said as he eyed Isaac's body. A shiver ran through him as he thought of fulfilling the desires he'd held locked inside for so long. He knew it would have to go slowly, though.

Isaac cocked his head a little to the side as he admitted, "I'm not completely sure of what to do. I mean, we've both seen men in the mine camps have sex with each other, but it just seemed like animals rutting most of the time. I guess that's why I never truly considered it for myself. With you, though, it's different, isn't it?"

"Come closer, Isaac."

They were both back to kneeling on the bed facing each other, their stiff members jutting out proudly toward one another. Isaac scooted closer and reached his hand to grasp Walter's shoulder.

"You are both so beautiful," Suzette whispered reverently. "Please touch each other."

Walter gave her a sweet smile and said, "Lady's choice." He leaned in and kissed Isaac's strong neck. Isaac's eyes closed, and he sighed. His hand stroked up and down Walter's arm, but his other hand went to his own cock and grasped it. Walter also grasped himself, and they stroked themselves. Their bodies were close enough that the tips of their cocks touched each other's bodies—a completely new sensation for both men.

Walter stopped and took hold of Isaac's wrist, gently pulling him off. Walter's large hand then went around both cocks, and he pressed them together as he pumped them as one. Isaac let out a protracted moan, feeling this new sensation of another man handling him as well as the feel of a penis rubbing his own. It was… strange. When Walter whispered, "I love you so much, Isaac. Always have," and kissed Isaac's lips, Isaac gave in to the pleasure of the moment. "Help me out with your hand as well." Isaac nearly engulfed Walter's hand by circling his fingers around him, and then he squeezed.

Walter threw his head back and cried, "Isaac, yes!" as both men began to stroke into their combined fists.

Suzette was spellbound as she watched their tight ass muscles contract with each thrust. They may have never done this before, but it looked to her like a beautifully choreographed dance of masculine lust. She couldn't help plucking at her naked breasts and squeezing her legs together as she watched them. Her insides felt all squirmy once again as profound pleasure bubbled up inside her.

The men increased their pressure and speed as well as the intensity of their embrace until Isaac muttered through their kisses, "I'm about to come," and Walter seemed to nod and say something that sounded like, "I am too."

First Walter, and mere seconds later, Isaac shuddered and let out long moaning sounds that erupted from the depths of their bodies. Suzette could relate. She knew instantly they were experiencing the same transcendent joy she'd felt earlier. She quietly clapped her hands with happiness and grinned at them, saying, "That was nothing like what I saw in the gardens, but it was wonderful." The men's chests heaved, and they leaned into each other. Their hands were covered in a creamy liquid, and they seemed very satisfied with themselves.

"Suzette, we're not quite ready for what you probably saw in France. Give us time. We're all new to this," Walter explained. "This was perfect for us for now. Do you have a basin where we can clean up a bit?"

After taking care of some cleanup, Isaac asked, "Do you want your privacy, or would you prefer us to stay the night?"

Blushing profusely, she answered, "Oh, ah… if you would stay, that would be marvelous."

"Only on one condition," Walter said with a leer. Suzette looked at him questioningly, and he went on, "Don't put on any clothes to sleep. I want to feel your naked body all night long."

"Walter always has the best ideas," Isaac agreed.

Thirteen

The sun was just beginning to light the sky when Suzette became aware of the glorious feeling of being sandwiched between two hard, naked bodies. One was toying with her curls and the other kissing her bare shoulder.

Off in the distance, however, a bell began to toll insistently. Isaac and Walter immediately hopped out of bed grumbling and began to grab articles of clothing. Isaac looked frustrated for a moment and then said, "These are your pants, Walter. Give me those." He had been trying to put on a pair that were definitely too small for him.

Walter tossed Isaac the right trousers and looked apologetically at Suzette. "We are terribly sorry, dearest, but that's the fire bell. Someone's morning cook fire must have gone awry, so we need to leave immediately."

Isaac was yanking on his boots as he said, "Last night with you was beautiful, Suzette. Thank you. We'll be in touch with you later." He dashed out the door while Walter leaned over to give her a quick kiss.

"I'm so sorry that duty calls. Go back to sleep if you can. You might need your energy later." He winked and left her speechless as he sped out behind Isaac.

The bed was so warm and cozy and smelled faintly of her men. She breathed in the scent and drifted back to sleep with a smile on her face.

An hour later, she sprang from the bed, donned a dressing gown, and went in search of some breakfast. She was ravenous and did not feel like delaying eating for one more minute. She had just enough time to eat quickly, bathe, dress, and get to her appointment with Marguerite Beaufort.

"Good morning, Suzette. Ah, something has put roses into your cheeks today, I see," Marguerite said by way of greeting. As her shrewd assessment took in Suzette's appearance, Suzette felt instantly that she'd been found out. Her cheeks flamed at the thought. Marguerite laughed good-naturedly and exclaimed, "Ah, just as I thought. You must tell me all about it, my dear friend. Come in so I can measure you and show you some fine fabrics and new designs, and then we can have some refreshments and discuss your exciting life."

For the next hour or so, the two women discussed current fashion in Marguerite's design studio—what they liked and what they found displeasing. A servant came in with cool drinks for them, and several seamstresses were noisily laboring in a room right next door. It was apparent that business was booming for dress design in San Francisco, and it was also apparent that the workers chattered like magpies.

Finally, Suzette broached a topic she wondered about, and it made Marguerite laugh. "You want to be able to divest yourself of your clothing easily? What prudent woman does not wish this from time to time? But remember, there is a certain something about making your lover wait. You can be a seductress as you disrobe, can you not? Maybe one should not be in too big of a hurry, no?"

"Ah. Perhaps not." Suzette nodded.

"Although, we would not want big clumsy hands being so rushed that they ruin your precious garments. These gowns will be of the finest silks, linens, and velvets." She then winked at Suzette and continued, "I always take male hands into consideration in my designs. You will not, for instance, ever find a row of tiny buttons that your man will be tempted to rip. Early in my career, I decided I would design gowns that did not require wasting my seamstresses' time with endless repairs. You will see what I mean when you come for your fitting." She set aside her sketchbook and asked, "Now, I hear that you are the one who has finally captured the hearts of the two finest bachelors in San Francisco." Suzette tried to curb her embarrassment. "And I must confess a small amount of jealousy over Walter James. He spurned our advances in such a gentlemanly manner, you would have thought it was my idea rather than his."

"Yes, I understand he was quite taken with you but was unsure about an offer of intimacy that included Doc Louis. That is in no way a negative comment on either of you," Suzette rushed to add. "I believe it had more to do with his feelings for Isaac."

"Yes, my dear Louis and I have observed the men for a few years and realized Walter was besotted with that clueless partner of his. Isaac Stark has been making the poor man mad with frustration. Do you mean to tell me that good things actually do come to those who wait?"

Laughing, Suzette answered, "They do indeed. Walter has professed his love for Isaac, and Isaac—although somewhat surprised at himself—for Walter, and the two of them have become quite affectionate as a result. I think Walter ought to have spoken up sooner and more plainly, and he may not have had to wait so long."

"Then again, perhaps they simply needed a third all along. You are a very lucky woman with those two men." She sipped her drink. "Now, what questions do you have for me? I am an open book. My beloved departed husband and I often played with extra partners in our marital bed. Sometimes it would be another woman for his enjoyment, and other times we would take a man to bed. That arrangement suited us both greatly."

Once Marguerite ascertained Suzette's complete lack of knowledge, she became a font of information. She was not shy about explaining sexual acts, specific configurations, and positions, and she highlighted several of her favorites with colorful descriptions and hand gestures. At one point, she grabbed for her sketchbook and drew a picture when she could see that Suzette wasn't grasping the fine detail of the act. After they studied the picture, Marguerite tore it out of the book, held it over a lamp until it caught fire, and tossed it into her empty fireplace, where they watched it turn to ash.

"We do not want to scandalize anyone," she laughed. "You will love being penetrated by both men at the same time," she promised. "It can be done in several different ways and in many different positions," she said matter-of-factly. "It is as close as the three of you will be able to get, and the sensations everyone can feel are incredible. But the men also need their chance to be in the middle, so do not be selfish about it."

Suzette suppressed a shiver at the thought.

Marguerite had a luncheon brought in and dismissed the help so they could continue to talk privately. Suzette left after three hours of having her head filled with ideas she never considered in her life. She felt almost dizzy with possibilities. She forgot to even worry about the fire her men had run out to handle. She felt brave and energetic after her meeting with Marguerite and could not wait for the first fitting so she could ask more questions. Just talking and thinking about the possibilities with her men made her insides get that familiar jumbly feeling, and she didn't know what to do with herself.

When she arrived back at her house, she found Pascal frowning over a letter. The stationery looked familiar. Pascal looked up at her and made a disgusted face.

"Is that a letter from Papa?"

"What do you think? Of course, he's wasting no time in hounding me. We just arrived, and I am already supposed to have launched myself into a successful career. The man is delusional."

Suzette made certain her voice was gentle when she answered, "Pascal, we have been here for over a month, and I am sure he is just trying to encourage you."

"He wrote this before we left France. He had to have, or it would not be here this soon. And it makes no mention of you, so it had to have been written before you decided to come with me. Papa is just trying to bully me into doing his wishes."

"Do you know what you would be interested in doing?" She knew she was treading in dangerous territory. Pascal could go off any minute if she pushed too hard, and he was already upset.

"Suzette, do you really expect me to make important arrangements this quickly?"

"Have you asked around when you go out at night? Surely there are some men you might talk to at The Discovery. Some reputable men. What do you do all night?" She had a pretty good idea that it was just drinking and gaming, but she could hope he had at least made some friends.

"Pfft! The men I meet are not interested in *talking*."

"Then I think you should speak to Walter and Isaac. They employ many men in their company and…"

"You think I should be a common laborer?" Pascal threw down the letter and stomped out the front door muttering, "I do have certain plans, you know. I am just not ready to implement them. And my own sister has no idea of my worth."

As the door slammed, Suzette thought to herself, *He has that right. I have no idea if Pascal is worth anything.* She decided to put him out of her mind for now.

Fabienne came into the room and handed Suzette a note, saying, "A boy dropped this off for you a little while ago."

Thanking Fabienne, Suzette unfolded the letter and read:

> *Dearest Suzette,*
>
> *Walter and I have secured three tickets to a play for tonight, and we hope you can join us. We would also like to take you to a new restaurant near the theater for supper before the entertainment. Unless we hear back from you that you cannot make it, we will come and get you at seven o'clock.*
>
> *Yours most affectionately,*
> *Isaac*

Fourteen

Dinner was mediocre at best, but the company was divine. All through the meal, the three of them told stories and laughed until their sides hurt.

"We should have eaten at Aylesbury House," Walter sighed finally. "But at least this was a change of scenery. I hope you weren't terribly disappointed, Suzette."

Waving her hand dismissively, she countered, "I am just happy to be with the two most wonderful men in this city. The overdone food is not a concern. What is the play about that we are going to see?"

"All I know," said Isaac, "is that it's a farce. This is a local production and a new playwright, so… we'll see. Best to keep an open mind."

As it turned out, Suzette was a bit mystified by San Francisco humor, and much of it was lost on her. Laughter is contagious, however, so she smiled and chuckled along with the rest of the audience. It didn't matter to her. She was happier than she'd been in years. Both men held her hands and occasionally gave her a little buss on the cheek as they checked to see if she was having a good time.

The night was warm, so after the play let out, they decided to take a stroll around the business district. The men attempted to point out some of the sights to Suzette. She instantly became aware, however, of the lack of women on the street. Men ogled her and a few tried to draw her into conversation, but Isaac and Walter glared at each one and hustled her away. These men weren't quite as polite as the gentlemen at Aylesbury Fire Company, or else they were fool-hardy and did not know about Isaac's strength and his suppressed temper. Some women may have enjoyed the attention, but it quickly became obvious that Suzette was not one of those women.

One incredibly pushy character tried to stroke Suzette's blonde curls as he cried, "You remind me of my Mary!" The man shook his head and looked close to tears. "I never shoulda left her to go prospecting for that damned gold."

Suzette cringed as Isaac and Walter pulled her away from his grabby hands. Once away from the man, her expression morphed onto a coquettish smile, and she said, "I am anxious for more of you men. Shall we go home?"

"You don't need to ask me twice," Walter answered with a laugh.

Isaac's eyebrows twitched and he grinned happily. "Let's go. Your place, Suzette?"

As soon as they entered her door, the men began removing their ties and shucking their jackets. "It's such a warm night," Isaac complained.

"You do not need an excuse to take off your clothes, dear Isaac," Suzette chuckled. "Shall we go upstairs? Or would you both prefer a brandy first?"

"I only need the two of you," Walter said as he stroked her cheek.

"I'm not thirsty," Isaac replied. "Walter's right."

Once in her bedroom, Suzette turned to them with a coy smile and said, "I had a long chat with Marguerite Beaufort today about what to do with two men. She made it all sound so thrilling, if not a bit naughty." She looked down for a moment as shyness took over but then shook it off. "I want the things she told me about. She explained how each of us might take turns being in the middle, as that is most advantageous for a lover."

Walter and Isaac just stared at her for a moment, and Isaac finally spoke up. "I hadn't actually considered that. Walter? How does that sound to you?"

Walter's expression morphed from incredulous to avid in seconds. He seemed to vibrate with need as he answered, "Oh, I am quite certain I would love that." He looked at Isaac. "Would you mind?"

Laughing softly, Isaac answered, "Not in the least. It

sounds interesting, if I understand the implication." He watched as Walter closed his eyes for a moment as if he needed to calm down. Isaac put his hand up to Walter's face and stroked his cheek with a loving gesture.

"Shall we try it then?" Suzette asked. "She also gave me some ideas of how to make things go… comfortably." She opened a cabinet beside the bed and produced a small box and a bottle of oil. "She said this would do it."

Walter eyed the bottle and grinned. "Yes, I can see how that would grease things along." He opened the stopper and sniffed. "Ah, olive oil. Perfect. I've read about it." He eyed the box and asked, "What is in that?"

Suzette took a breath and looked thoughtful. "It is to prevent pregnancy. She says it does not always work, and it is not particularly comfortable for everyone. It's a kind of a barrier. But…"

"Dearest Suzette," Walter said. "It is completely up to you, but if you should get pregnant from our actions, I, for one, would be thrilled. Isaac?"

"I would be ecstatic. We've been waiting for someone like you for years. However, as Walter said, it's your decision to make." While this exchange was going on, Isaac was systematically removing all of his clothing. Eyeing them, he asked, "Anyone need any help with your clothes?" Apparently, the subject of babies was done as far as he was concerned.

Suzette put the box back into the cabinet.

Chuckling, Walter observed, "Our man is apparently anxious for the *stimulating* part of tonight's entertainment." He eyed Isaac's obvious excitement and shivered. "Thank heaven for Marguerite and olive oil." He, too, began to shuck the rest of his clothing.

As soon as Walter stood naked before them, the two men helped Suzette out of her gown. They tried to be careful with the fabric as they knew it would be a shame to rip anything. Eventually, she was as bare as they were, and the three of them stood staring appreciatively at one another as a frisson of nerves attacked each of them.

Walter broke the silence by whispering, "This is like a dream come true with both of you. I am surely a blessed man." He kissed Suzette as Isaac began a careful exploration of her body with his hands. They all hummed with pleasure. As he continued kissing Suzette, Walter reached out and stroked Isaac's cock, which stood at attention. His other hand stroked Suzette's bottom.

After a moment, Walter led Suzette to the edge of the bed, where he sat her down. He and Isaac knelt down to kiss her thighs and spread her legs wide. "Look at how beautiful she is, Isaac. She is so pink and juicy, I want to taste everything." He kissed his way up the inside of her thigh and engulfed her clit into his mouth. Suzette let out a cry and tried to stay still, but it was nearly impossible not to squirm. Isaac sucked on her breast at the same time and then slid his finger into her beneath Walter's chin. She nearly levitated from the onslaught of sensations bombarding her. Walter added his finger alongside Isaac's, causing her to let out a long moan.

"Feel how tight and wet she is for you, Walter," Isaac crooned. "She wants your cock deep inside her."

"Yes!" Suzette trembled. "I want it."

Walter got up and reached for the olive oil. He started to drizzle some onto himself, but Isaac stilled his hand. "Let me do it."

"Yes, please." Walter could barely breathe as he watched Isaac pour a bit of oil into his hand and then massage it all over Walter's erection. Walter's chest heaved with emotion as he gasped with pleasure. "Oh yes. That's truly wonderful." Isaac's hands were large and calloused—so different from a woman's or even his own.

Isaac then bent down to lick every pink bit of Suzette his tongue could invade, causing her to squirm and pant. Finally, he raised up and guided Walter into her. "Here you go. Walter is going to make love to you now, dearest. Feel how he's filling you up?" He thumbed her clit as Walter pressed in.

Walter's moan was long and heartfelt, and Suzette grabbed his arms, gasping. Isaac grinned and watched spellbound as Walter sank into her. He bent down and licked Suzette's clit, and in doing so, also licked Walter. Within a few moments, Suzette was seized by an orgasm that blasted through her like an earthquake. Chuckling with happiness, Isaac stepped back and grabbed the bottle of oil. He stepped behind Walter and poured oil into his hand.

As soon as Walter felt Isaac's greased finger begin to probe him, he shuddered. Never in his life had he experienced anything like this. Suzette was warm and tight around his cock, and the man he adored was exploring his backside. *How many times have I dreamed of this?* he wondered. This was better than any fantasy he'd had. Walter widened his stance a bit to accompany Isaac's ministrations. "That feels incredible," he whispered.

Walter barely knew what to concentrate on—Suzette in front or Isaac behind. It was all just too good. And then a finger slipped inside him, and he cried out.

"Are you in pain? Is that too much?" Isaac asked.

"No. Keep going!"

Isaac drizzled more oil and began to push and pull with his finger until it seemed that Walter was loosening up. Eyeing the size of his own cock, he said, "I'm going to use another finger now." Carefully he slid another in, and Walter's reaction was much the same as with the first finger.

"You have no idea how grand this is. It's an incredible sensation. Keep going, Isaac!"

Suzette kept her eyes on Walter, fascinated by his reactions, and felt her spasms going on and on. She had no idea sex could be so amazing and wondered if women who only had one lover missed out on all of this fun. She smiled smugly to herself, thinking that she was truly a lucky woman. Her reverie was broken when she heard Isaac ask, "Are you ready for me, Walter?" Another shudder went through her, thinking about what Isaac was about to do.

In a choked voice, Walter commanded, "Do it, Isaac. Fill me like I'm filling our beautiful Suzette." Then he gave a huge intake of breath, and his eyes went huge. Isaac was probing him with his cock, and he could scarcely believe it. Deeper and deeper, Isaac pushed into Walter's body. Nothing ever had or ever would come close to this sensation, he knew for sure.

And then it got even better.

Isaac somehow touched a place deep in Walter's body that caused an electric current of pleasure so profound he thought he might faint away from the excitement. His eyes rolled up, and his head fell back into Isaac. Isaac kissed the side of Walter's head and was overtaken by the sudden need to pull away and pound back into his best friend's body, asking, "Why haven't I been doing this for years?" Over and over, he thrust into Walter, and Walter thrust in and out of Suzette—causing all three of them to experience pleasure beyond their wildest imagination.

Grasping Walter's hip with one hand to steady himself, Isaac reached around with his other hand and continued to manipulate Suzette's clit. She couldn't tell if another orgasm had begun or the first one was still happening as spasms of delight coursed through her body. She watched spellbound as the men both began to sweat. Their muscles flexed in the most glorious ways, and their expressions were positively transported into some new realm of pleasure.

Walter seemed to come to his senses a bit and asked in a shaky voice, "Do you want me to spill inside you or pull out, Suzette? You'll need to let me know quickly."

Looking at his handsome face that was so overcome with affection, she answered, "Do not pull away. I want to feel your love inside me."

That was all it took. Walter's shoulders heaved, and he let out a long, rumbling sigh of sheer delight as he emptied himself into her soft little body. Isaac's hand, which had been playing with her clit, grasped the base of Walter's cock and squeezed. He let out a second moan and shuddered. Then Isaac began to thrust harder and faster into Walter from behind. His tempo sped up until it became erratic and fevered, and he threw back his head, letting out a cry so primal, it was nearly frightening. Possibly to silence himself, his mouth clamped down on Walter's neck, where he left a light bruise and an imprint of his teeth. Walter had been marked.

"Mon Dieu. Incroyable!" Suzette breathed. Apparently, she was beyond being able to think in English.

They got the idea.

AFTER CLEANING UP AND CRAWLING INTO BED TOGETHER, ISAAC muttered, "The bigger bed should be ready in a few days. I'll have it brought over as soon as possible."

"Mmm, there is no rush," Suzette purred. "I love the feel of both of you curled up against me. May I be in the middle next time we make love, please?"

Walter chuckled and answered, "You won't believe how incredible it is, dearest."

Isaac grumbled, "My feet are hanging off the end of the bed. I'm glad it's not cold weather." Then he leaned over and soundly kissed both of his lovers. He was snoring in less than a minute.

"He's had a very long day," Walter explained in a whisper. "Good night, my sweet Suzette."

But she was also fast asleep.

IT MAY HAVE BEEN AN HOUR OR TWO LATER—NO ONE KNEW FOR sure—when there was an insistent pounding on Suzette's bedroom door that woke all three of them. They could hear Pascal slurring something in French. Suzette started to extricate herself, but Isaac, who was closest to the door anyway, said, "Stay here with Walter. I'll take care of him." He grabbed his trousers from the floor and quickly drew them up to cover himself. He didn't bother to button them, however, and in the moonlight both Suzette and Walter admired the way they hung loose on him. His back muscles were on perfect display as he stalked to the door with the grace of a panther.

Suzette immediately forgot about her brother and the nasty insults he was hurling through the door.

Isaac unlocked the door and flung it open with a look on his face that would frighten the devil himself. Pascal's mouth snapped shut and he stepped back for an instant. Then he puffed himself back up into a self-righteous snit and began to berate his sister once again. "I wanted to know why I found a man's tie on the stairs and wondered if the servants had male company tonight, but I see that it's my harlot sister. Did you know that she has a husband somewhere? That is, unless she had the man killed!"

"Go to bed, Pascal. You smell like a brewery, and you need to keep out of Suzette's affairs," Isaac growled at him.

Pascal tried to push his way past Isaac but discovered it was like moving a mountain. He craned his neck around anyway and his jaw dropped when he realized that Walter was in bed with her. The expression on his face went from judgmental to disgusted in a heartbeat. Shouting in French, he bellowed, "Suzette! Are you depraved? Wait until our father hears about this!"

"Mind your own business, Pascal," she warned him in English. "Our father is on the other side of the world, and I can make up my own mind without his or *your* interference."

With that, Isaac grabbed Pascal by the collar and dragged him down the hall to the other end of the house. "This your room?" he asked. When Pascal nodded, Isaac shoved him inside so hard, Pascal stumbled across the room and collided with his bed. "Sleep it off, man. And respect your sister. You won't want to answer to me if you continue to make nasty remarks about her or hurt her feelings in any way."

As he turned to slam the door, Isaac could hear the unmistakable sound of Pascal retching.

Climbing back into bed with his lovers, Isaac whispered, "Get some sleep, dear ones."

For the next several weeks, San Franciscans seemed to be on their best behavior, fire-wise. There were only a few small incidents that required the men of Aylesbury Fire Company to drop everything and hurry off to douse a flame. Even so, Ember and Cinder took their jobs seriously and heralded the passage of the firemen through the city as though the whole place was about to burn to a crisp.

It may have been the warm weather that prompted less need for hearth fires, but folks still needed to cook and illuminate their homes and offices, so there were a few mishaps. Still, it lulled the populace into a false sense of security about their safety and the need for vigilance. Everyone was required by a local ordinance to keep emergency water on hand in the event of an errant flame, but a few neglectful people used up their water for the wrong purpose and forgot to replenish it. This was courting disaster.

The men of Roja Wais continued to be extraordinarily busy, but Isaac fulfilled his promises to Suzette by returning her Stradivarius in better shape than she'd ever seen it. Also, he had an almost comically large bed delivered to her house.

And the three of them certainly made good use of the newer, more spacious sleeping arrangements. Gradually, more and more of their belongings drifted over to Suzette's house as the men were feeling more at home with her than at the fire company. Finally, it was Walter who spoke up about this over dinner one night. "Suzette, are we crowding you in your home? I hope you don't feel as if we are taking advantage of your hospitality."

"Ah, no. Not at all. In fact, I was wondering if you would both like to officially move in with me. I love having you here, and I cannot imagine it any other way." She looked shy for a moment and confessed, "I also find that I have fallen deeply in love with the two of you." She looked at both of them in turn, smiling sweetly. Their returning looks were heated, so this prompted a trip to the bedroom to celebrate. Amidst their lovemaking, first Isaac and then Walter proclaimed their deep love for her. Each of them felt happier than they ever had in their lives.

And so, they made their official exit from the fire company, although they remained Aylesbury firemen and still answered the call whenever they were summoned. They also made a deal with Suzette that they would pay Delphine and Fabienne's wages since they were now part of the household. Suzette protested on the grounds that she did not want to feel like they were taking care of her. They were adamant, however, that they had plenty of money and huge appetites, so it was their duty to do this. They also gave the two servants healthy pay raises due to the increased work they would be doing. Delphine was especially happy with this because she loved to cook for the appreciative men who showered her with compliments daily.

Isaac built and installed some beautiful bookcases for Walter in one of the parlors, and they hauled over his extensive collection of books. Suzette loved the way the room looked. Pascal saw it and snorted with derision. He wasn't fond of reading. He also was not at home most of the time, so his opinion didn't matter much to any of them.

Adeline, Royal, and Jasper were ecstatic for their friends and not a little smug about it. "I hope we've set a good example," Royal laughed one evening over Friday supper at Hart House. Suzette was now an accepted part of the family.

Pascal, although he did not spend a lot of time at home, let his opinions be known to his sister on a regular basis. "Those two men are taking advantage of you," he scolded time and time again, but never in front of Walter or Isaac. He was afraid to stand up to them, so he preferred to berate his sister privately.

"I want Walter and Isaac here, Pascal. It is on my authority that they stay. And they contribute regularly and generously to our expenses, which is much more than I can say about you. You seem to want to gamble and drink away our allowance faster than I can even imagine. Sooner or later, you need to do something productive. I am embarrassed for you!"

On those occasions, Pascal would nastily accuse her of

earning her keep on her back. A few times, he threatened to write to their father about her scandalous behavior. Suzette saw through that, however, knowing Pascal would never do anything that might decrease the allowance from their father. Nevertheless, Pascal would fume and storm out of the house, leaving Suzette shedding angry tears.

Isaac came home early one afternoon and found her in this state. Thinking something terrible must have happened, he enveloped her in his arms and asked, "Whatever is wrong, Suzette?"

She hid her face in her hands, mumbling, "My horrible brother. He makes rude accusations about my character while he is but a lazy good-for-nothing."

Isaac ground his teeth, thinking about what Pascal probably said. "Do you want Walter and me to speak to him?" He would prefer to pulverize the little gimcrack, but he knew that couldn't happen.

Sighing, Suzette answered, "It would probably do no good. He is too much like our father. Once his mind is made up, he closes like a vault."

"Suzette, would you be happier if you married one of us? I would be honored and thrilled if you would be my wife. I also would never cut Walter out if you and I were married because I know you love each other as dearly as I love the both of you."

Hanging her head, she answered, "Thank you, Isaac. As much as that thought pleases me, you know I cannot wed anyone until I know whether or not I am married or a widow. It would not be right. I have written to my elder brother

Gustave to see if anyone has been able to locate Monsieur Dernier yet. I have heard nothing back. Perhaps if the man is found, we can discuss this. I pray that will be sooner rather than later."

Isaac decided to speak to Walter anyway. Her brother was trouble, and Isaac certainly didn't want Pascal's opinions to ruin Suzette's life. But, for now, he had something to discuss with her. Wiping away her tears with his fingertips, he asked, "Suzette, I have already spoken to Adeline about this, and we wondered if you might be interested in joining us in the music academy. We have a waiting list for children and adults who want to take lessons, and the two of us don't have enough time to accommodate everyone. Now that I've heard you play many times, I think you'd be a real asset… that is, if you're at all interested. What do you think?"

Her eyes went round, and she produced a smile as she considered the possibilities. This arrangement would provide her with her own income, completely separate from her father and brother, and she could spend time meeting people who loved music. She couldn't actually think of any reason why she shouldn't do it. "Yes!" she beamed. "Thank you for putting your trust in me, Isaac. I would love to teach."

Laughing merrily, Isaac said, "Just remember that the young ones are often there at the wishes of their parents. They aren't all as dedicated as you and I probably were as children, but they are still enjoyable to work with. Addie and I try to keep the lessons fun, and eventually the cream floats to the top. We have some very talented students, but even the least talented ones learn to appreciate music."

And so, Suzette became known to many as Madame Suzette. She still was not certain of her actual legal last name anyway, so, even though she preferred de Massey, this appellation suited her. The children took to her immediately as she built up a warm, comfortable rapport with them. She was not going to become rich this way, but the parents paid well, and Suzette loved building her own private account that Pascal had no access to. The independence she felt with this arrangement was something she'd dreamed of for years.

Mostly, she tried to put her questionable marital state out of her mind. Gustave had no insight to impart to her through his letters, and France was a long way away, so she felt fairly comfortable in how she conducted her affairs.

Sometimes, however, the world is smaller than we think, and it's harder to escape one's past than it seems.

Sixteen

On a Saturday morning in the autumn, the three lovers were languishing in bed. They were tired from a late-night Friday supper at Hart House, where Adeline, Isaac, and Suzette were pressed upon to play after the meal was over. They sounded magnificent as a trio, and for Suzette, this was a real treat. She had not had many opportunities to collaborate with other musicians when she lived in France. So they happily performed well past midnight and eventually stumbled home, almost giddy with exhaustion. Walter felt so much pride for his lovers he could barely contain his enthusiasm, but the other two were just bone-tired and pleased with themselves. They all fell into bed and were asleep within minutes of returning home.

In the light of the morning, however, with their energy restored, they awoke with Suzette fondling both men to attention. Humming with pleasure, the men kissed her, kissed each other, and began making sweet love to their woman, stroking her with hands and mouths to a languid release. Isaac then pulled Suzette on top of him and settled her down onto his cock. He winked at Walter, who immediately reached for the ever-present bottle of oil. As Walter unstoppered the bottle and began to oil himself, Isaac placed his hands on Suzette's hips and raised her up and down rhythmically on his erection. He growled in appreciation, and Suzette closed her eyes in bliss, still feeling the pleasure of her orgasm pulsating through her.

Walter positioned himself behind Suzette and carefully prepared her for entry. She purred and moaned as he manipulated her backside. They had done this many times by now, and she never grew tired of being in the middle of her two beloved men. When his hard member breached her, she gasped and shuddered with pleasure. "Yes," she whispered looking over her shoulder. "That's it. Fill me with your love, Walter, like Isaac is doing."

Walter reached around her and stroked her, feeling Isaac's cock with his fingers at the same time as he felt the texture of it rub against him inside Suzette's body. This was sheer heaven, as far as he was concerned.

Their languid loving gradually became more and more frenetic as their collective excitement grew. Walter went from long, smooth strokes in and out to almost ferocious pounding.

Isaac's breathing sped up as he became transported by the warm heat of Suzette's viselike grip on him and the texture of Walter's cock rubbing against his over and over.

Suzette couldn't contain herself. She closed her eyes and breathed words that sounded as if they had to be filthy. They were in French, so the men had no idea, but it was obvious she had entered a new realm of decadent indulgence. The noises she made spoke of pleasure tinged with delicate pain and love so profound it nearly scalded them.

Isaac had a tell for when he was about to ejaculate. His breath hitched, and a moan escaped that vaguely reminded Suzette of a wolf's howl. She knew Walter would follow soon, chattering away about how good everything felt. The two men were generally in complete sync with each other with their feelings, if not their style. Her own orgasm had not actually ended completely but seemed to be building in intensity once again. She loved it when they all came together this way.

And no sooner had they all cried out in release when there was a loud knock at the front door.

Shrugging, Suzette said, "Ignore it. One of the girls will get it eventually, or the caller will go away. I do not want to move." She collapsed onto Isaac's broad chest and nuzzled him. Walter wrapped her in his arms, stroking her back with his face and breathing in the fragrance of her hair.

But Delphine and Fabienne did not answer the door because they had gone shopping. Suzette didn't realize just how late in the morning it was. The caller continued to pound on the door at regular intervals. Then they could hear the sound of a male voice hollering, but they could not make out the words. No one had the gumption to open a window so they could hear better.

Lying in a heap of intertwined arms and legs and feeling somewhat sticky, they weren't inclined to entertain any company at the moment. They were way too satisfied to move. But the pounding and the yelling continued.

Eventually, there was male hollering from within the house. Apparently, Pascal couldn't take the persistent visitor's knocking any longer. Angry footfalls thundered down the steps to the front door, and finally, there was silence for a moment. The three lovers snuggled closer and drifted off. This was short-lived, however, as the same footsteps pounded back up the stairs, and Pascal smacked her bedroom door several times. They could hear him sniggering nastily. His knocking grew in volume, and finally, he shouted, "Suzette, you whore! Get out of bed! Your husband is here to take you back to France, where you belong!"

Seventeen

"What?" Suzette cried. Isaac and Walter were completely in the dark about both Pascal's insult and his announcement, as he'd said it all in French. Still, they could tell by Suzette's demeanor that whatever he said had gone from bad to worse.

Walter disentangled himself from them, muttering, "Isaac, we need to learn French." As Suzette also rose from the heap of bodies on the bed, he asked, "What's going on?" Looking at her more closely, he could see tears in her eyes, a look of fury on her face, and she seemed to be vibrating with some emotion.

In English, Suzette hollered, "Get that man out of this house, Pascal. I have no desire to see or speak to him! And then you can apologize for your crude insult."

"No. Get out of bed and face your *husband*, you slut!

Now!" They could almost hear the sneering grin on his face as he berated her—this time in English, for their benefit.

Isaac sprang to his feet and yanked on a pair of trousers. Suzette was busily wrapping herself in a dressing gown, and Walter was pulling a shirt on. Isaac stomped to the door, unlocked it, and flung it open, nearly wrenching it off the hinges. Without even thinking, his arm dashed out and he grasped Pascal by the throat as he snarled, "Apologize for that slur right now, you good-for-nothing, lily-livered worm!" He didn't even notice that another man was making his way down the hallway.

All of the color drained out of Pascal's face as Isaac towered over him with a ferocious scowl. Isaac did not let go, however, until he heard the unmistakable sound of a gun being cocked. Swiveling his head toward the sound, he found himself looking down the barrel of a small silver pistol held by a stranger. He frowned and let go of Pascal at the same time that Suzette jumped in front of him and shielded him with her body.

"Get out of my house this instant," she shrieked, shaking with intense fury as Isaac's arms went around her protectively.

Then Walter stepped in front of Suzette, saying in a placating tone, "Put down that weapon, man! Nothing is worth killing anyone about."

The gun-toting newcomer gave Suzette a smarmy look and asked, "Are you all broken in for me now, my darling *wife*? And by two men! I am sorry I did not get to do the honors, but maybe this is better for what I want to do with you."

Suzette gasped in horror and embarrassment.

Walter chanced a look behind him and asked, "So, is this Derrière, Suzette? The man who claims to be your husband?"

Puffing himself up to his full height—which was actually shorter than Suzette—Dernier announced in a stuffy tone, "Not derrière! I am Baron Gilles Dernier, and I am here to claim my lawfully married wife. I was detained most tragically after the nuptials, but I am here now. We are supposed to be boarding a ship back to France in three days. My valise is downstairs, and I expect a servant to bring it up to the bedroom immediately. I've had a long, arduous trip and need some rest and the comfort of my wife."

Suzette scoffed, "Oh, so now you claim a title? When did that happen?"

With his nose in the air, Dernier glared at her. "As you know, the nobility in France has only recently had their titles restored by decree from Emperor Napoleon III. My family is one that received that honor." He brandished the gun around as if to make a point, causing Walter to wince.

"Title restoration happened years ago, and you are a liar!" She nearly spat the words at him. "I think you are nothing but a charlatan and a thief. What proof do you have that you are whom you say you are, and that I even married you?"

"Can we all sit down and have a polite conversation about this, please? Without a gun?" Walter beseeched. "And could you perhaps allow Suzette to get dressed?"

Dernier looked at his weapon as if he'd forgotten it was in his hand. "I should shoot you on general principle for being caught in a bedroom with my wife," he growled at Walter. "But I suppose I do not wish to miss and accidentally harm her. That would be a shame. I have been so looking forward to our wedding night pleasure at long last." He carefully lowered the gun and put it into his pocket, leering at Suzette the entire time.

Isaac whispered in Suzette's ear, "Maybe he'll shoot himself in the balls with that stupid little gun."

She tried to squelch a laugh, but it came snorting out of her nose anyway. "I will see you all downstairs after I am properly attired. Pascal, since you let him in, perhaps you can see to your guest's refreshment."

Pascal gaped at her. "Why?"

"Because you were the fool who opened the door to this man! Grow up, you imbecile!"

"You cannot talk to me like that!"

"I can, and I shall since you deserve it." Suzette gave a haughty sniff, spun on her bare foot, and stormed back into the bedroom with Isaac still managing to hold onto her. He glared at Pascal and Dernier and asked Walter, "Coming?" Walter followed them in and slammed the door, locking it firmly.

Instantly Isaac whispered, "How can we get Suzette out of the house without those two interfering?"

Walter looked thoughtful as Suzette stepped out of her dressing gown and began pulling on proper clothes. "I have an idea, but it's quite a risk."

Eighteen

A few minutes later, Walter, now fully dressed, found Pascal and Gilles Dernier muttering with their heads together in the main parlor. As he expected, Pascal had done nothing as far as offering any refreshment. Walter schooled his expression into one of sublime politeness as he asked, "May I bring you some coffee, Mr. Derrière? There should be some in the kitchen."

Dernier sniffed at Walter with an amused expression. "Doing women's work, are you? And it is Baron Dernier, you fool."

"I'm offering you more hospitality than you deserve, Mr. Grand Derrière. You aimed a gun at us. I will assume from your impolite response that you do not need refreshment." He turned around and wandered away with an air of nonchalance, heading toward the kitchen, muttering, "I'd like some coffee at least. And maybe one of Delphine's fine pastries…"

He rattled around in the kitchen for a while, making several loud noises, and returned with a steaming cup in one hand and a pastry in the other.

Pascal looked longingly at Walter's food. Walter just stared back at him, then took a bite and hummed, "Mmm. Delphine is a jewel. She makes such wonderful confections." He sipped his coffee and announced, "Suzette should be down shortly. It takes her a while to get dressed in the morning. I'm sure Isaac is doing what he can to help make her presentable. He's very thoughtful. And dexterous. The man is quite clever with his hands."

As Pascal glared at him, Dernier squinted his eyes at Walter and then frowned. "What is that horrible smell? Is that smoke?"

Walter wolfed down the rest of his breakfast and raised his nose in the air. "By Jove, you're right!" He leapt from his seat and ran back toward the kitchen. Suddenly he shouted, "Fire! Evacuate immediately!" He ran for the front door, yanked it open, and cried, "Fire!" as loud as he could, alerting the neighborhood. The cry went from house to house quickly, and soon they could hear the bell tolling from Aylesbury Fire Company. He bustled Pascal and Dernier out saying, "Take shelter as far away from the house as you can get! Quickly, men! Save yourselves. I'll see to Suzette!"

Pascal and Gilles stumbled over each other to be the first outside and took off down the street like scared rabbits.

Walter quickly went back into the kitchen and fanned the acrid black smoke so that it made its way to the open front door and gave the appearance of an inferno. At the same time, Isaac escorted Suzette—who carried a small bundle of possessions—down the stairs. He grabbed her violin case from the parlor and sprinted out the back door into the garden. Walter gave them a quick signal as to which direction the Frenchmen had gone.

Sneaking through some neighbors' gardens, Isaac and Suzette made their way up the street to the house across from Hart House. Isaac checked the main thoroughfare to make certain that Pascal and Gilles were nowhere to be seen. Not finding them, he whispered, "Come on. This way." Out in the street, they crossed it and sauntered up to the front door as if they had all the time in the world and were there to give some music lessons. Isaac used his key and ushered Suzette inside.

BACK AT THE DE MASSEY HOUSE, HOWEVER, PASCAL AND GILLES made a sudden about-face. Gilles shouted, "I need my valise! Everything important to me is in it! I cannot let everything burn! Someone, get it for me!"

And Pascal shouted, "I need to get the violin! It is the most valuable thing in the house. We cannot let that burn up!" He'd had his eye on that violin for years, thinking it was one possible way to come up with a large sum of money should he ever need it in a hurry.

The two of them arrived back at the front door at the same

time as the firemen, who immediately barred the Frenchmen from entering the premises. Richard, the firefighter with the Dalmatians, explained to them as if speaking to children, "We can't let you inside. We're trained professionals, and we'll take care of things. Now, kindly get out of the way."

"Do you think I look stupid?" Dernier shouted. "I am not running *into* a burning house. Just make sure someone who is in there grabs my luggage in the foyer and sends it out to me."

As he began to organize a bucket brigade up the front steps, Richard glared at Gilles as billows of black smoke poured out the open door. Through that miasma, Walter appeared, dragging a suitcase that he heaved at Gilles none too gently, causing the man to land with a hard thud on his derrière when he caught it. Walter thought to himself that the landing was rather fitting.

"Why is that case so heavy?" Walter asked. He got no reply from Gilles who glowered at him from the ground. Walter continued, "I recommend you go book yourself a room at The Discovery, Derrière. It will smell better there."

Richard recognized Walter immediately, of course, and asked, "How did you get here so quickly? Where's the fire, Walter? I don't see any flames."

Walter dragged Richard just inside the door and answered, "I took care of it. No need to call the men in. It's been contained. We only need to open the windows and air things out for a while now."

At that moment, Delphine and Fabienne returned from their marketing expedition laden with packages. Both of them looked thunderstruck at the commotion in front of their residence. "What is happening?" demanded Delphine. There were barking dogs, gawking neighbors, lots of smelly smoke, and a whole team of virile men carrying heavy buckets of water up to the front door, where Walter and a stranger seemed to be holding everyone at bay—at least momentarily.

Pascal ignored everyone and angrily pushed and shoved his way past Richard and Walter into the house. Turning to the parlor where Suzette practiced, he craned his head around and held his nose because of the smell. It didn't take long before he realized there was no violin in the room. Storming back out, he cried, "We've been robbed!" No one paid any particular attention to him, however, because he was hollering in French.

Delphine and Fabienne quickly understood from Walter's blasé attitude that nothing was terribly wrong, so they ignored Pascal and turned their attention to the firemen milling around. They smiled and made eyes at the men, who were all too happy to flirt back. Fabienne had a fondness for dogs, and she engaged Richard in a conversation about Ember and Cinder as she admired their beautiful coats. Richard seemed to swell with pride as he spoke of his dogs to this pretty young woman with a delightful accent.

After about twenty minutes of confused questions flying around and everyone talking over Pascal—who seemed to think if he shouted louder and louder, someone would finally listen to him—the crowd gradually began to disperse. There wasn't much to see after all, and the neighborhood seemed safe from becoming a raging inferno.

Finally, Pascal got through to Walter that he was certain the Stradivarius had been stolen. Walter feigned a horror-stricken expression at that news. "You must go report the theft to the authorities, man! Without delay! I'll stay here and air out the house. We can't leave it all open and unguarded, so someone needs to be here. I'm used to smoke, so it won't bother me as much as it would you, so why don't you make yourself useful and go find Sheriff Scannell? He's probably in his office."

Pascal was not at all used to taking orders, but he was also unaccustomed to having a purpose in life other than general indolence, so this errand seemed to invigorate him somehow. He puffed out his chest with self-importance and answered, "Yes, a fine idea. I shall do that right away." He took off in the general direction of downtown, leaving Walter to wonder what might become of him—but only for a few seconds. He didn't really care all that much.

Finally, it was just Richard and his dogs left chatting with Fabienne. Delphine had made her way into the house to deposit her heavy purchases. Walter asked Richard, "Would you like to come in? It's a little smoky, but we have fresh coffee and pastries." He noticed the smile on Fabienne's face when Richard accepted.

Gilles Dernier, who had at least picked himself up off of his ass, was still loitering in the street. He tried to follow them back into the house now that the threat of fire was gone, but Walter slammed and locked the door before the wily Frenchman made it up the steps and past the threshold. They all ignored his knocking and bellowing after that.

"I cannot understand how a man could travel around with a valise as heavy as his. It felt like it was full of lead weights," Walter mused. He then met Delphine in the kitchen and apologized to her. "I had to close the flue, which I will open again, and I'm dreadfully sorry for burning a couple of your aprons. I grabbed whatever I could in a hurry that I thought would make a lot of smoke. "I'll clean this up for you." He eyed the charred mess of rolled-up newspapers, a potato sack, and pieces of singed fabric in a large cauldron. In the center of this mess was a small horsehair-stuffed pillow that was still smoldering. It smelled hideous, but it had done the job.

Across town, Pascal was on his sheriff-finding mission, wandering around asking people where to find him. He could not pronounce "Sheriff Scannell" to anyone's satisfaction, though, so he wasn't having much luck. It was also at least an hour before it occurred to him to wonder what had become of his sister. Finally, by process of elimination and a little bit of luck, he located the sheriff's office on Broadway. The sheriff, as it turned out, was out by then for his lunch break. It was another hour before Pascal would have the opportunity to speak to him and report the supposed theft, so he spent the time while he waited working himself into a frenzy about the seriousness of the crime.

The sheriff was not much of a music lover, so hearing that a violin had disappeared did not do much to stir him to action, even when Pascal asserted with flamboyant gestures and a loud voice that this particular piece was worth thousands of dollars. The sheriff shrugged and said with as much sincerity as he could muster, "We'll look into it."

Pascal left, comfortably assured he'd handled things well by making a good case.

He was wrong. Scannell forgot about him the moment Pascal left. In truth, Scannell was deeply embroiled in a political scandal related to ballot box stuffing allegations. He was far too busy trying to take care of his own reputation to give a damn about a violin owned by a drunk French maniac.

On his way home, Pascal had to pass by several disreputable gaming houses, and finally, the temptation became too great. Thinking he deserved a treat, he wandered into one in the Sydney-Town area, despite the warning he'd received upon arrival from Jasper about safe places to gamble. This place was a far cry from the honest casino at The Discovery; it was run by ruthless thugs. Even though it was still early in the day, and he'd had nothing to eat yet, he ordered a whisky (they did not offer any food) and sat down to play some cards. This was a big mistake. His fine clothing and accent give him away to the clientele. Instantly Pascal became a target for the dodgy proprietors.

deline, Jasper, and Royal were appalled at the story they heard from Isaac and Suzette. Suzette had to back up and tell the story again about her forced marriage to the man and the subsequent search for him directly after the wedding ceremony.

"Even if you did say vows," Royal explained, "you could claim desertion, and the marriage would be annulled by any sensible judge. No one in their right mind disappears and then reappears months later to claim spousal privileges. And you're not even sure of his real name? This is nonsense."

"You think I should speak to a judge?" Suzette asked. "I never even considered annulment because I doubted I would see him again. I thought the most likely scenario was that he was dead—or at least that's what I had hoped." She hung her head for a moment and then looked up again. "I thought it possible that my elder brother Gustave might have been responsible indirectly for Dernier's demise. I do not believe he cared for the man any more than I did. It was only my father who saw him as a possible match for me, and that decision was based on greed."

Jasper burst out laughing and said, "I don't mean to make light of your situation, Suzette, but I'm sure that for the right price, the judge who married us would give you an annulment document. Does anyone remember his name?" He looked at Royal and Adeline expectantly. Things had changed dramatically in San Francisco in the past few years. But they just looked back at him with blank expressions. Then they all burst out laughing.

"We weren't at all interested in his name," Adeline explained. "We were so anxious to be married, he could have been anyone with an official-looking sign over his door. For all they were worth, the marriage documents burned to the ground with his building that very night too."

Isaac pointed out, "The important thing for now is to keep Suzette away from that awful man until we can deal with him somehow. Can you put her up here for a while, Addie?"

"Of course, we can! You and Walter are more than welcome to stay as well. We have plenty of room."

"I just hope my brother Pascal does not figure out where I have gone. He might be in league with Monsieur Dernier, for all I know."

Jasper looked thoughtful and said, "We'll post some of our watchmen on duty round-the-clock until this is all resolved. We don't want any trouble for you. And if Pascal is in cahoots with the man, I'll be quite annoyed with him. In fact, I'll get word to Séamus and Timothy to make certain Pascal is kept well-entertained at The Discovery. He's less likely to cause trouble if he's doing well at the tables. And the man does spend an inordinate amount of time there, from what I understand."

"Does he ever make trouble?" Suzette asked. "I noticed them talking quietly about him one time when we were all here for dinner. They did not seem overly fond of him."

Jasper gave her a rueful smile. "He started out trying to throw his weight around and accusing anyone who beat him of cheating, but when they offered to ban him from the premises, he calmed right down and became a much more compliant customer. He is well tolerated now."

"That is a relief," she sighed. Then, quite suddenly, Suzette's color changed from a healthy pink to a pasty light green, and she put her hand up to her head. She swooned a little, prompting Isaac to grab for her.

"Suzette, dearest, what's wrong?" Suzette didn't answer, but her chest heaved a little, and she clutched her stomach.

Adeline gave Suzette a shrewd look and asked, "Have you had anything to eat yet today?"

She shook her head, putting her hand to her mouth.

"Have you felt like this on other mornings lately?

Suzette thought for a moment and nodded, still with her hand to her mouth, she muttered, "This time it is worse."

Adeline nodded sagely and ordered Isaac, "Take Suzette into the dining room and make yourselves comfortable. I'll make sure you both get something to eat right away."

"Oh, I do not know if I can eat anything…"

"Trust me, Suzette. It will make you feel much better. It always has for me." And with a wink, she turned on her heels and strode off to the kitchen.

Jasper and Royal looked at each other and grinned and then turned their smiles on Isaac, who looked back at them blankly. "Don't look so worried, man!" Jasper chuckled.

Royal smiled broadly at Suzette and announced, "Congratulations!"

She blinked at him and then fainted.

Now in a panic, Isaac scooped her into his arms before she had a chance to fall. He held her to his chest with a horror-stricken look. "Why are you all grinning at her? What is wrong with you? What's wrong with Suzette?" he nearly shouted.

"Isaac, my dear friend, let's get the two of you upstairs to a bed, and we'll have a meal brought up to both of you," Jasper explained in a soothing tone. "My very strong guess is that Suzette is the picture of health, and she'll be just fine."

Isaac glared at Jasper. "She's clearly ill! Why aren't you worried?"

Royal laughed and said, "We've seen these signs so many times, Isaac, with Addie, and I remember the symptoms in my own mother as well. You're going to be a papa!"

"A...?"

Suzette roused a bit, blinked her eyes a few times, and then snuggled closer into Isaac's embrace. "I suppose it is true, my beloved," she whispered. "How could it not be?"

"Come on," Jasper directed. "Let's go pick out a room for you."

"I'll go see that the food is brought upstairs immediately," Royal added.

As soon as Suzette was comfortably situated in a pretty room upstairs, Adeline and two servants came in with trays of various foods. "I wasn't sure what would tempt you and what would repel you, so you'll have to decide by trying." She grinned at Isaac. "You can also help yourself to anything, Isaac. Suzette, I would start out with a bit of tea and some toast. If that makes you feel better, keep going."

Taking a deep breath, Suzette reached shakily for the cup of tea and sipped, and at the same time, Isaac held out a piece of buttered toast to her. She gratefully took it and began nibbling. In less than a minute, her color was rosier, and she smiled. "Oh, much better now. Thank you, Adeline."

"I knew it!" Adeline proclaimed with a satisfied grin. "This is terribly exciting, Suzette! Maybe we'll eventually have a cellist or violist who can play in an ensemble with us!" She laughed at her own joke. Then she seemed to realize that Isaac and Suzette were staring at each other and probably needed to be left alone for a while to talk. "We'll be downstairs if either of you needs anything." She took Jasper by the arm and walked gracefully from the room.

Alone, finally, Isaac was the first to speak. "You had me a little worried there for a moment, but it sounds as if everyone here knows what's going on, and they are convinced that we're having a baby." Tears suddenly appeared in his eyes as he continued. "This is the most wonderful thing I can even imagine. And I hope you understand that Walter and I do not care which of us is the child's father. We will both cherish the babe just as we cherish you." He leaned in and gave her a sweet kiss. Sitting back, he gave her a blinding smile and exclaimed, "I'll have to build a crib! Suzette, I am so happy, and I love you so much. Wait until Walter finds out."

"I am also happy, Isaac. It is a little scary, however. And I am sorry we are not properly married for the child's sake."

"If anyone gives this baby a difficult time, they'll have to answer to me. But now that we know Derrière is alive, maybe you can resolve things with him and eventually get married properly. You know my feelings on the subject. I'd be thrilled to be your legal husband. If you'd prefer Walter, I'm sure that could be arranged as well."

"I do not think I could ever choose between the two of you."

"I understand, even if it would be in name only." He looked thoughtful for a moment. "I wonder where Walter is. I thought he'd be done at the house by now and would have made his way over here. He knows where I brought you. I hope no one has given him any trouble about creating a fake fire and summoning the Aylesbury men." He watched for a moment as Suzette began to explore the tasty morsels Adeline had provided and appeared to be ravenous all of a sudden. He smiled to himself thinking how beautiful she would look as she blossomed with their baby growing inside her.

They continued to chat about babies and how little either of them knew about raising them as Suzette filled and emptied her small plate over and over. Finally, she gave a contented sigh that turned into a huge yawn and eyed the pillows on the bed she was sitting on. "Isaac, if you do not mind, I am suddenly exhausted. I am just going to close my eyes for a moment."

Thinking back to the numerous naps Adeline had taken throughout the day during the early months of her pregnancies, Isaac understood. "I'll just get comfortable with you here." He scooted behind her and wrapped her in his arms. Leaning over, he kissed her forehead, noting that she was already sound asleep. Shaking his head, he thought, *I'm glad I've been around at least one woman who was expecting, or I'd be worried sick.*

Twenty

Back at the de Massey residence, Gilles Dernier was causing such a loud fuss by hollering and banging incessantly on the door that some of the neighbors came out to challenge him.

"Either quit this rumpus immediately, or we'll be forced to get the police involved!" shouted one irate individual. "Decent people live here, and we don't want our lives disrupted by the likes of you."

"Get out of here, you mischief-maker," shouted another. "You're nothing but a nuisance! If they wanted to let you into the house, they'd have opened the door by now, and we're sick to death of you and your noise. Leave!"

Understanding at last that he was not going to get anywhere by creating a scene—and definitely disliking the idea of police arriving—the self-proclaimed baron hoisted his travel bag and trudged down to the street away from the house. He only made it as far as the end of the front path, however, when he had to resort to dragging his luggage. It was too heavy for him to carry more than a few feet. When Walter hurled it at him almost effortlessly, it had given him an understanding of the man's strength. If he planned to confront Walter, he'd have to win with finesse and cleverness; it was clear he'd never overpower the man. And that other man, Isaac, appeared even larger and probably a lot stronger still. This was going to be a challenge. *But how clever can these American simpletons be?* he asked himself with a smirk.

As he was making his awkward progression along the street, he was suddenly aware of some snarling, howling animals making quite a lot of noise behind him. He stiffened with fear as they seemed to be closing in. With his heavy baggage keeping him stationary, he felt like a sitting duck.

Richard, with Cinder and Ember accompanying him, spied the Frenchman struggling with his heavy burden and—just to be ornery—gave the dogs the signal to give their alarm cry. He tried to stifle a grin as the dogs bounced around noisily, nipping near Gilles's feet and trying to get him to move along out of their way. Richard knew they would never bite the man, but he'd understood from Walter and Fabienne's description of the events of the day so far that "Derrière" was nothing but trouble. Ambling up behind him, Richard asked politely, "Need some help?"

"Yes!" he cried, flinching. "Call off these curs immediately!"

"Ember! Cinder! Quiet." The dogs stopped barking at

once, settling down to sit, panting at Gilles with their tongues lolling out.

Instead of thanking him, Gilles glared at Richard and looked angry enough that he might want to kick a dog. Undaunted, Richard asked, "Know where you're headed? That's a pretty heavy load you have there to be dragging around all over San Francisco."

Sticking his nose in the air, Gilles assumed what he thought was his most officious air and answered, "Since my rude wife and her men will not allow me entry, I require some suitable lodging for the night." Then he considered the possibility that Richard might actually know something and asked, "Would you perchance have a recommendation?"

Stroking his chin in thought, Richard narrowed his eyes and answered, "If you want a great meal and a safe and comfortable place to sleep, I'd recommend the hotel up on the hill called The Discovery." He pointed in its general direction. "It'll cost you though; it's not cheap. There are a couple of other places around town that are almost as nice—the Barrington Arms and the Wilson House. Then there are some boardinghouses down at the wharf that are cheap. They look somewhat like ships because that's what they used to be. You won't get a very good place to sleep, but it also won't break the bank for you. Just be careful." Figuring that was enough helpful information, Richard patted his thigh to signal the dogs and took off.

"Wait!" shouted Gilles. When Richard turned back to look at him over his shoulder, Gilles went on, "You need to offer me some assistance with this." He indicated his bag by poking it with the toe of his boot. This man with the dogs was about the same stature as Walter, making Gilles think that these were a strange breed of large people in San Francisco. Therefore, he reasoned, they must be used to hauling things around for aristocrats such as he.

Pursing his lips, Richard seemed to consider Gilles's request for a moment and then answered, "Nope. You got yourself into this by overpacking, and I have to get back to the fire company for lunch. You're on your own." He took a step away and then stopped, turning once more and giving Gilles a steely look. "Also, I'd recommend you stop harassing my friends if you know what's good for you. We Aylesbury men stick together." With that, he resumed his long stride away. The dogs' tails wagged cheerfully as they followed him.

Eventually by kicking, scooting, rolling and sometimes lifting his overly heavy luggage, the ersatz Baron Gilles Dernier made it to the base of Rincon Hill and considered his options. The first order of business was to employ someone to help him transport his bag as he'd done to get up to Suzette and Pascal's home. It was a pity that man with the cart had left as soon as he'd been paid. The area was teeming with men of all sizes, and it didn't take him long to locate someone who'd carry it to a decent guesthouse for him. Compared to the boardinghouses at the wharf, it was a slice of heaven, though he did not doubt there were fine hotels somewhere around. At least it was centrally located, he rationalized, and he had a room with an actual door that closed. The floor was dirt, however, and he hoped it didn't flood. *It will do until I can move in with Suzette*, he reasoned with himself. *And I can keep my precious possessions safe.* With that thought, he went in search of some food and a place to do some serious plotting. *I need to get that delectable little harlot of a wife back. She would look so fetching in my shackles.* He sighed. *I cannot wait to put my mark on that perfect alabaster flesh of hers. I am fortunate that the fool she calls her brother told so many people where to find him if they ever made it to San Francisco. That older brother of hers ought to be shot for causing me so much trouble though. After finally losing his men, I had to hide out for weeks before I could escape France. That bastard put a price on my head! I did think, however, that Suzette would welcome the idea of returning home, and she and her father would be my ticket to freedom. Who wants to live in this frontier farce of a city? Inconceivable! I will just have to convince her with my charm.*

At first, Gilles was attracted to the de Massey's fortune and couldn't wait to move into the chateau and live like the aristocrat he'd always believed himself to be. He had created an elaborate story that he'd conjured up so long ago he'd begun to believe it himself. In truth, his mother had been a lowly maid at the Dernier estate for a while—until she was fired for stealing. He was her bastard with an unknown father, though he'd decided that the lord of the manor himself had to be his rightful parent.

Gilles did not even know his true father's last name, but his mother's surname was Anouilh. Someone once laughed in his face saying that this meant his full name translated into Little Goat Slow Worm, and he never wanted to think of either creature with any relation to himself. As soon as he heard of his mother's brief association with the Dernier family, he adopted that for himself. When his mother found out he was parading around, telling people he was a Dernier, she slapped him.

The truth was that his mother had been so drunk the night he was conceived, she had no idea which farm hand or sailor had impregnated her, and each time Gilles questioned her about his "real" father, Dernier, she'd slap him. When he got to be thirteen, she threw him out of their one-room hovel.

The only way he survived after that was by becoming a very adept thief. Small in stature, he hid well and listened. He learned to speak like the rich people and stole everything he could get his hands on. Gradually, he stole or swapped his purloined goods for finer clothing than he'd ever worn, and little by little, people began to look at him like a person rather than a speck of dust. Not able yet to purchase a residence, he spent most of his nights in brothels, and it was there he discovered he had some particular tastes that only a few could properly satisfy. His favorite madame was a German woman who taught him from a young age all sorts of nasty tricks as well as how to speak her language. He decided it was a useful skill. The vocabulary he learned was not particularly suited for polite company, but he learned to speak in detail about the wicked things he loved to do.

But then he'd been introduced to Suzette by her father. The elder man also had some rather distinct desires that he satisfied regularly in an establishment for gentlemen with certain needs. Monsieur de Massey befriended Gilles and believed all of his nonsense about being an important man with a vast fortune and was all too happy to offer up his daughter as a sacrificial lamb.

When Gilles saw Suzette with her shiny golden curls and her lithe little body, he craved conquering her perfection so badly he convinced himself that she would be excited to be shackled and tortured into sexual bliss by his whip. He tried to brag to her in German of the delights he could bestow upon her body with a careful slice of a razor here and there, the burning crimson mark of his palm across her buttocks that he would soothe by spraying her with his urine, and the stripes of his delicious silver-tipped flogger across her breasts. She'd been stoically silent and gave him no response in the way of reaction, so he'd taken that as acquiescence—or being overcome with the very idea. Eventually, however, she faked not understanding him so convincingly he began to doubt the family's assertion that she could speak German at all. Nevertheless, talking to her that way gave him a satisfying erection, so he persisted.

With the many fantasies he had floating through his mind, he could barely contain himself throughout the ceremony and decided that he needed to relieve his aching erection before he could so much as raise a glass in toast.

Right after the vows were finished, Gustave's men found him playing with himself noisily in the toilet. They kidnapped him with alarming speed and efficiency. Gilles was incensed at missing out on his wedding night and marking that porcelain skin of his new bride.

As wily as he was, eventually he'd escaped his kidnappers, but word got around about the price on his head. He sold most of what he had and bought passage to San Francisco. He'd only kept his most favorite "equipment" and a few changes of decent clothes.

After a long, disgusting journey all the way to California, seeing his lovely Suzette was like a dream, but to have her come out of a bedroom half-dressed and with not one but two apparent lovers was more than he could stomach. She was his, by Jove, and he was going to claim her.

Twenty-One

Once the kitchen was cleaned out—with Walter's help—and scrubbed to its former pristine condition, he apologized to Delphine about ten more times and promised both of the ladies that they would receive bonuses in their pay for the trouble he'd caused them. He explained more about Mr. "Derrière" and made them swear never to let him in the house. "If you see that man around here, I want you to get word to us immediately and do not even speak to him, understand?"

Fabienne was still floating around dreamily thinking about Richard and his lovely smile, deep voice, and sweet dogs, so she was in fine, if distracted, spirits. Delphine took him a bit more seriously as she dished up some stew for Walter's lunch.

As soon as he finished his meal, he grabbed a few things and took off for Hart House—not directly, however. He wandered up and down the hill and stopped in at the fire company for a while just in case Derrière was anywhere around and following him. Before he left the fire company, he changed his clothes and put on one of their signature Aylesbury top hats. "This ought to be good enough," he said to Richard as he removed his glasses and stuffed them into his coat pocket. Then he hurried out the door and back up the hill to his friends and lovers.

WHEN HE ARRIVED AT HART HOUSE, WALTER WAS SHOCKED BY Royal's announcement that Suzette was in bed. He was immediately worried that she had taken ill. "Isaac is with her," Royal continued.

This relieved Walter's fears only slightly. Of course Isaac was with her if she was ill. There was also the possibility that they could have gone to bed to spend time together, but the whole situation was unexpected, and it set Walter's nerves on edge.

"Third bedroom on the left." Royal grinned at him.

"It's rather bad manners, you know, to be poking fun at two people in bed together, even if it is the middle of the day." He jerked off his hat and jammed his glasses back on.

Royal laughed and waved at the staircase answering, "Just go on up and see what they have to say, Walter. No offense is intended."

Walter grumbled something beneath his breath and strode up the stairs.

Tapping lightly in the door, Walter opened it to a sight so sweet, it took his breath away. Fully clothed, Isaac was lying propped up by some pillows, and Suzette was cradled in his arms. Isaac has such a look of adoration on his face, it nearly brought Walter to his knees. Suzette's curls were tumbling across Isaac's broad chest, and she looked like a sparkling, serene Madonna in the afternoon light.

Isaac's eyes snapped to Walter and a smile as broad and bright as the sun took over his face. "Walter!" he whispered, "we have the best news!" Isaac kissed Suzette's forehead and said, "Wake up, sleepyhead. We need to talk to Walter."

Suzette's eyes fluttered open, and for a moment she seemed to be getting her bearings, and then she, too, grinned like a smug cat. She stretched and yawned and sat up to give Walter her attention. "Adeline says I am pregnant!" she announced. "She has been through it herself and knows the signs."

Walter stood stock still, letting the words sink in. They could see the instant he registered what she'd just said. His eyebrows flew up, and his smile lit the room. "Are you sure? Do you need to see a doctor? How long do you think you've been pregnant? This is wonderful! Isaac, aren't you excited? Oh, Suzette!" He strode closer and dropped to his knees in front of her. "I love you so much, and this is going to be the grandest thing *ever*." He grabbed her hands and kissed them. "I wonder if we'll have a boy or a girl. Isaac, we're going to be fathers!"

Suzette and Isaac laughed at his exuberance and surprise, and then Isaac answered finally, "I share your excitement, Walter. This is wonderful news. I'm already planning what the baby's crib will be, and Auntie Adeline is debating which instrument he or she will eventually learn to play." He burst out laughing again in joy and wrapped his arms around Suzette even tighter.

"Why were you sleeping in the middle of the day, Suzette? Are you feeling unwell?"

Suzette looked lovingly into Walter's eyes and answered, "No, not now—just terribly sleepy. I was feeling a bit faint, and my stomach felt upset, so Adeline fixed it with some food and tea, and the fact that I came around so dramatically made her certain I was with child. She admitted that she had already suspected it was possible before today. I am so glad the two of you brought such a good friend into my life. With you, Adeline, and Marguerite, I am very fortunate." She looked down for a moment and then said, "I hate to think of what my life would have been if I had stayed in France. My father would have manipulated me into something horrible, I am sure. Whatever benefited him the most. But here, I am free to love the two most wonderful men in the world and we are going to have a child—making us a real family."

A happy tear rolled down her cheek that Walter swept away with his thumb. Then he laid his head in her lap and murmured, "Hello little one. We don't know you yet, but we all love you more than anything in the world."

"Walter?"

"Yes?"

"Will you and Isaac make love to me now?"

Walter sat up and looked into her eyes. Isaac was already kissing the side of her face, and his hands had begun to caress her body. "If it pleases you, dearest, we can certainly do that. I'll just go and lock the door. I know our hosts would never be shocked by anything we do, but I still think it's best if we keep it private."

"Of course," she mumbled as her mouth met Isaac's.

After making sure the lock was secured, Walter began shucking his clothes. As soon as he got down to his drawers, he advanced on the lovers who were still kissing. Reaching for Suzette's frock, he deftly began to dismantle her clothing. She was making such happy little sounds with Isaac, it made him grin from ear to ear. *They are simply spectacular together*, he thought. Isaac disentangled himself from her kisses and stood to tear off his own clothing. Soon everything had landed in a heap on the rug. Walter never tired of the vision of Isaac's well-honed body, and he drank in the sight.

"You need to congratulate each other for our happy news too. Do not forget," Suzette chided them with a mischievous smile. She loved to watch her men together. Winking at her, Walter grabbed Isaac and planted a huge kiss on his lips. He also reached around and grabbed Isaac's strong buttocks with both hands. "What will it be, Suzette? You should do the honors and decide for us today."

She looked thoughtful for a brief moment and then answered, "I am feeling like I want both of you to pour your love onto me at the same time."

Isaac, looking pleased and then hopeful, turned and

opened the stand next to the bed. "Well, would you look at that? Our hosts and hostess have prepared the room for the likes of us." He drew out a stoppered bottle of olive oil similar to the one they had at home. "We're lucky because I didn't think to grab ours when we left so quickly." Then he looked thoughtful and added, "Or maybe they have this in all the bedrooms just in case they want a change of scenery." He snorted at his little joke, and they smiled at him as he shrugged. "Well, it's obviously not for cooking up here."

Slowly and lovingly, the men finished removing the rest of Suzette's clothing, and then Isaac used the oil to prepare Suzette's backside for his entry. As he carefully manipulated her and got her to relax her muscles, Walter kissed and massaged her breasts and thighs and gradually moved to licking and probing her from the front.

Suzette felt overcome with sensation. She was ultrasensitive, and her men were extra sweet to her. Isaac kept kissing her neck as he fondled her from behind, and she stroked Walter's silky hair as he sucked her on her most sensitive spot. His fingers slid in and out as she grew wetter and wetter for him, especially when he found that special spot that always gave her a jolt. Finally, she could feel both men's fingers inside her, nearly touching. Walter's tongue never stopped its assault on her until she shuddered with a glorious release. "Now, please," she sighed. "I am ready for you."

Grasping Suzette by her hips, Isaac positioned her over his erection and let her slide down onto him. It never failed to make her gasp at the initial intrusion of her backside, but the fullness she felt was almost all-consuming. Isaac groaned happily as she engulfed him.

Once they were situated with Isaac deep inside, Walter took himself in hand and stroked. He was so excited he was leaking all over his own hand and chuckled at the sight. He positioned himself at her slick opening and slid inside. They all three couldn't contain their moans as he wrapped one arm around her and focused his other hand at her clit again. "Can you climax once more for us, dearest?" he asked, stroking her as he began an in-and-out rhythm with his cock. He stroked her from the inside over and over, rubbing along Isaac's massive erection at the same time. He always felt so joined and so right when they all made love this way.

With that thought, he felt his orgasm roar through him with no warning. It happened so fast he hadn't even had time to make his typical remarks about the sensations he enjoyed. Speeding up the manipulation of her clit, he hoped he could at least bring Suzette around to come with him. And it nearly worked. She stiffened and groaned her release a split second after he emptied himself into her. Now it had to be Isaac's turn.

Softening, Walter slipped out of Suzette's body and knelt in front of his lovers. He bent down to lick her opening and fondle Isaac's balls at the same time. Suzette still writhed with aftershocks as he sucked her clit into his mouth again but pulled away when Isaac started to pump in and out of her from behind at a rapid pace.

Isaac's face became contorted and dotted with perspiration as his climax grew nearer and nearer. He kept up an almost punishing pace until he gave his signature lupine howl. Walter had to smile at it. He caught Suzette's eye, and the two of them grinned. They loved their Isaac so deeply. At least this time, Isaac had been a little quieter than he generally was at home.

Twenty Two

Pascal considered himself a crafty gambler, but he couldn't seem to do anything right today. The more he lost, the more he drank, until he was almost swooning off of his chair. What he didn't know was that he'd happened upon the most crooked establishment in all of San Francisco. The entire time he'd been playing, a person behind him revealed his cards with silent signals, and the dealer was extremely adept at dirty dealing from the bottom of the deck.

As he lost hand after hand, Pascal became angry and then belligerent to the point that the bartender offered, "I'll heave you out the door m'self if you don't shut yer trap and quit complainin'!" This had a brief effect on Pascal's bluster. He lost the next hand too, however, and stood to put up his fists.

"Something is not right here!" he shouted. Unfortunately, he forgot his English and cried this in French. All he saw were blank faces glaring at him.

The bartender had had enough of him and decided to make Pascal useful, so with a nasty gleam in his eye he suggested, "We 'ave a private room in the back for special customers. Maybe ye'd be happier playin' wi' them."

Too far in his cups to recognize the sinister look on the barkeep's face, Pascal answered, "Yes, of course. A private room is exactly what I would prefer. Show me the way." He grabbed what he had left on the table and stepped toward the bartender. He drew himself up to his full height, standing proud with his chest puffed out. Unfortunately, he ruined the look by releasing a loud belch.

The dealer smirked and intoned in an oily voice, "It's been a pleasure doin' business wi' ya. Enjoy yerse'f."

Pascal staggered, his balance corrupted by drink. Swallowing hard, he reached and gripped the bar in an attempt to steady himself.

The bartender said, "B'fore I send you to the back room, relax at the bar, and I'll give ya a drink on the house. Yer looking a lil' rough, and this'll perk you right up." He poured out a measure of dark liquor into a new glass and ordered, "Drink up."

"*Oui, merci,*" Pascal muttered before throwing back the drink with a shudder.

Taking a handout was never advisable in these surroundings. About fifteen seconds later, Pascal's eyes rolled back, and he slipped off his stool. He landed in the arms of the bartender's accomplice, who dragged him quickly through a door behind the bar.

Once out of sight, the barman removed Pascal's coat as

well as his fine leather boots and the large gold ring on his finger. Then he emptied Pascal's pants pockets and shoved him through a trapdoor in the floor. He laughed nastily as the Frenchman landed in an unconscious heap on a filthy mattress, then he called out to a boy in the alley behind the bar, "Let Phineas know we have a new sailor for 'im, and tell 'im he has about twenty minutes to come fetch this wombat."

He flipped the kid a penny, and the boy admired the newly-minted coin for a moment before scurrying off with a grin.

ABOUT THREE HOURS LATER, PASCAL AWOKE RETCHING WITH A headache that tolled like cathedral bells. He could barely open his eyes to see his strange surroundings and wondered why his feet were cold. His body felt bruised and stiff, and the air smelled like salt, puke, and sweat. Whatever surface he was on was hard and would not hold still for some reason. He passed out again.

Another hour elapsed before his fog lifted enough that he was able to sit up. The first thing he registered was that there were about ten other men around him who appeared to be likewise disabled. But then one of them, who looked a bit more alert than the others, cried out, "Damnation! We've been shanghaied!"

It appeared that Pascal had finally acquired a new profession—though one that neither he nor his father would have readily endorsed for him. He was now a newly-inducted crewman aboard a trading ship bound for Hong Kong. He would be spending the next few months seeing the world and working hard to learn some skills… And if he didn't, he'd be tossed overboard to feed the sharks.

Twenty~Three

The watchmen looking out for Suzette's safety reported after each shift. After three days of quiet, everyone was lulled into a false sense of security. However, Jasper had a startling bit of news that he shared with everyone over dinner.

"I spoke with Séamus today, Suzette. He told me he hasn't seen your brother once at the casino since the man you call Derrière showed up in town. This has me a bit worried."

Suzette blinked at him and gasped. "I think I should go home and see if he's there. He might be injured or unwell."

Taking her hand gently, Isaac spoke up. "I'll go after we finish eating. We don't want you falling into a trap of Derrière's making. He could be plotting something and using Pascal as bait."

"I'll go with you, Isaac," Walter announced. "I hope no one is making trouble for Delphine and Fabienne either. We probably shouldn't have left them there with that awful man at large."

Jasper then added, "I also asked Séamus if he'd seen a Frenchman by the name of Dernier ask for a room at The Discovery. I described him from what you said about him, and Séamus told me they don't have any French guests that he knows of at the moment. So, his whereabouts are anybody's guess."

An hour later, Walter and Isaac, with Bert—one of the watchmen they had along for extra muscle—opened the door at the de Massey house and heard a man's voice coming from the kitchen. It didn't sound like Pascal at all, so they looked at each other questioningly. Nearing the kitchen, they also heard quite a bit of female giggling.

"This doesn't sound too bad, but I wonder what's going on," mused Walter.

Rounding the corner, they found Fabienne sitting on the lap of... "Richard! What are you doing here?" Isaac exclaimed. Then he laughed and amended, "Never mind. I see what you're doing." Richard seemed to be stroking Fabienne's thigh with one hand while holding a drink in the other. Delphine sat across from them at the large worktable, also on the lap of another one of their Aylesbury brothers. He was newish to the firefighting company, and Isaac remembered that his name was Alfonzo.

The faces of the young women fell, and they jumped to their feet, adjusting their skirts. Fabienne started to apologize in French while Delphine managed to get out, "We are sorry. We did not expect you back this evening, and we have not had much to do for days now, and…" Her words petered out as she realized her employers were smiling.

"It's fine, Delphine. You are entitled to have some fun. But may I ask if Pascal has been around much lately?"

Her eyebrows shot up, and she answered, "No. We thought he was with you. He has not been here since the fire. Have you not seen him either?"

Shaking his head, Isaac gave Walter a serious look. "This doesn't sound good." Turning to Bert, he asked, "Can you use your resources to see if you can find anything out about a man who calls himself Baron Gilles Dernier? He's a skinny little cuss with black hair that hangs down past his chin. Looks kind of like a girl, if you ask me. He has a valise he's very fond of that he can barely lift. That's about all I can tell you about him. And see if you can locate Pascal de Massey? The last we saw of him, he was headed to the sheriff's office, but that was days ago. He's blond like his sister and a few inches taller. I think he has brown eyes, but I've never paid much attention. He would have been wearing nice clothes, and he always has a large gold ring on his finger. Suzette told me it was some kind of family crest or whatnot. He speaks English well, but not as fluently as his sister. And mostly, he loves to gamble and drinks too much."

"Yes sir, Mr. Stark. I'll get the men to work on that right away. We have eyes and ears all over the city, so I may have to pay a few of them…"

Walter nodded and said, "Just keep track of your expenses, and don't spare any. We'll make sure you're well compensated. I'm sure Suzette wants to know where her damned brother is, even if he isn't always the most pleasant person to be around."

"Agreed," said Isaac. "We'll let you get started, and we'll go tell Suzette what we know so far." Turning to Richard and Alfonzo, he added, "You two men might want to keep a close eye on these ladies as well. I don't trust Derrière one bit, and he may just come back here to cause trouble because he's angry and can't find Suzette. I'd feel a lot better if Delphine and Fabienne either stayed at Aylesbury with you, or you two move in here with them. You can still hear the alarm bell from here."

Fabienne blushed crimson and shook her head. "Oh, I…" she stammered.

Isaac waved his hand dismissively and said, "Whatever arrangements you make are up to you. You can even come back to Hart House with us if you prefer. We'll continue to pay your wages, but we're not bringing Suzette back here until things are cleared up with Derrière. He's a real trouble-maker. Now that Suzette is expecting a baby…" Fabienne and Delphine gasped, and Isaac grinned. "I know. It's wonderful news, isn't it? Anyway, we absolutely need to guarantee her safety."

Richard grasped Walter's hand and shook it vigorously.

Walter smiled broadly. "Thank you. We are ecstatic about the news." Then Walter very uncharacteristically wrapped his arm around Isaac's waist and kissed him on the cheek. He nodded at Richard and Alfonzo and continued, "That's the way it is with us."

"Well, then, congratulations. I can't exactly say I'm surprised, but I'm happy for you. And you're not the only men from Aylesbury who are together." Richard looked over at Alfonzo, but he was busily kissing Delphine's neck and whispering into her ear.

The final decision—accomplished with much blushing done by the ladies—was to lock up the de Massey house for now and let Fabienne and Delphine move into Hart House for a while. They weren't quite ready, it seemed, to move into a fire company that was filled with men, even if they enjoyed the company of Richard and Alfonzo. The men assured them that they still wanted to keep company with them, and the sisters looked pleased at that.

"Can we help the household staff at Hart House?" Fabienne asked. "We do not wish to be a burden."

"I'm sure that can be arranged," Walter answered. "There is always plenty going on there."

<h1>Twenty~Four</h1>

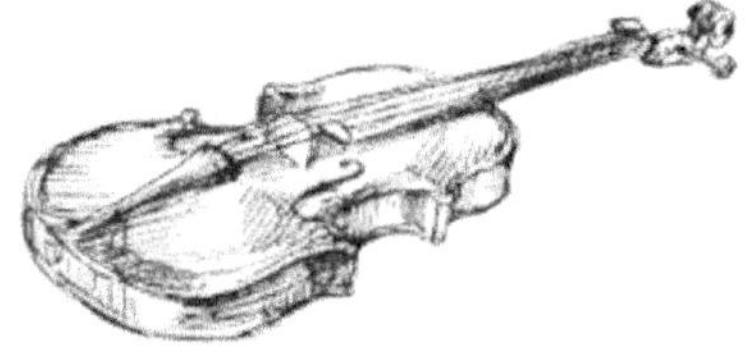

A week passed before they heard anything newsworthy about either Pascal or Gilles. The team of investigators hired by the men of Roja Wais finally turned up an individual who had an interesting story. They dragged him to the office, and Isaac went to fetch Suzette.

As soon as Suzette laid eyes on the man, she let out a startled gasp. "That is Pascal's ring! Where did you get it? Please tell me! Is my brother alive?"

"I didn't steal nothin', miss, if that's what yer thinkin', and I didn't hurt no one. I won it fair and square in a game," he said in a sincere, if worried voice. He wasn't sure what his fate would be and sure didn't want to be accused of murdering anybody.

"Did you win it from my brother Pascal?"

"I don't know no Pascal, but the man I won it from didn't have an accent like yers."

"Then who was he?" Walter asked.

"I dunno. Some rough character from Sydney-Town. I was surprised I beat him, and I was afraid he'd stick me with a knife b'fore I made it out safe. It was only cuz someone else come in and distracted 'im so's I could leave real quick. They was arguin' somethin' awful and I grabbed it an' ran outta there."

"Were you in Sydney-Town when you were gambling?" Walter asked.

"Uh, yeah."

"I take it you're new to San Francisco."

The man nodded.

"Don't you understand how dangerous that is?"

"I do now."

Isaac produced a small pouch of gold and thrust it toward the man. "Will you take this for the ring? It doesn't sound like you stole it, but it clearly ought to belong to Miss de Massey. It's a family heirloom." The man's eyes lit up at the gold, and he quickly made the exchange. "You are a lucky man that there was a distraction because I can say with authority that they never meant to let you out of there with anything of value."

Suzette looked sadly at the ring. "Thank you, Isaac." Then she looked at the man's face and asked, "So, you did not see *anyone* around there in nice clothes who appeared out of place or who spoke with a French accent?" She was grasping at straws, she knew, but this man was, so far, her only clue to her brother's whereabouts.

"No ma'am. Just some tough-looking sorts. I was ready to

get outta there when I won this. It's a bad place, and I sure won't be goin' back."

Walter asked, "Do you remember the name of the establishment? Or anything specific about it?"

"Yessir. Not the name, but the place smelled real bad. I mean like pig shit. Excuse me ma'am. Turned out there was a boar in the corner sleepin' in a pen. It looked half dead, to tell ya the truth."

All of the men of Roja Wais looked at each other and grimaced. "Not again," Isaac moaned.

"What?" Suzette asked with alarm.

Walter put his arm around Suzette and spoke softly. "It's more than likely that if your brother went in there, he only went out again unconscious. He was probably shanghaied."

"I do not know this word. What does that mean?"

"That place is notorious for capturing unsuspecting men by drugging or hitting them over the head and selling them off to work on trade vessels. That's what almost happened to us and how Royal got shot rescuing us." Suzette gasped at him. "It's a long story for another time. We all survived, as you can see, but it was a terrifying experience. Sydney-Town is bad in general, but that place is the worst of the worst."

Jasper was nearly shaking with irritation. "I warned that damned fool to stay away from that part of town! Sorry, Suzette. I don't mean to malign your brother, but..."

"But he is a stubborn person, and this sounds like just the kind of trouble he would get into." She looked at the man who'd handed her the ring. "Thank you for telling us your story and for providing me with this." She clutched the ring tightly. She looked at Isaac and then Walter and added, "I do not know how to feel about Pascal any more today than I ever have." She looked down and then shook her head. "Perhaps he will show up again. Perhaps not. I just hope he is still alive somewhere." She looked at Walter and Isaac and added quietly, "I think I would like to go back to Hart House now."

Jasper and Royal looked at each other and nodded silently. Royal spoke up, "Suzette, this doesn't mean we'll stop looking for Pascal."

"Thank you," she said softly. "I know he is difficult, and at times he can be almost horrible, but he is still my brother." She left on the arms of Walter and Isaac with her head bowed. They could hear her muttering to her men, "I wonder what to tell our father about this. It's too bad they took Pascal instead of Dernier."

ACROSS SAN FRANCISCO, IN A SEEDY PART OF TOWN, ANOTHER Frenchman was partaking in a different kind of entertainment than Pascal had sought. Gilles Dernier searched around until he found the area that had the most interesting brothels—just like old times. He found a madam who provided the more brutal kind of sexual release he craved and who welcomed his valise full of specialized equipment. He moved his belongings out of the guesthouse and into the brothel as soon as he found someone to drag it there for him.

His sea voyage had been long, and he was so far unable to reestablish his connection with Suzette, so he reasoned that it was fitting to take care of his needs for a while. The madam he located saw in him an opportunity to train some of her new girls in ways that a few men needed and paid good money for.

Their arrangement worked out so well for both of them, Gilles began to feel some real affection for the madam and, for a while, nearly forgot about his so-called bride. He should have known in his twisted little heart that their marriage wasn't legal. He was never a Dernier and had married under false pretenses. *But how is anyone supposed to know that? Would they believe a silly woman's assertions?* he asked himself. *Surely my word is worth much more, especially since I am a baron.* Now and then, visions of her money and her beauty would grab his imagination, and that craving would resurface, but for the most part, he was happy with the madam.

For a few weeks, all news about Gilles seemed to dry up. He stayed indoors with the madam and wallowed in the depravity of her establishment. They taught each other some tricks, and Gilles had a wonderful time instructing her girls. He also spent some time under the influence of her ready stash of opium, so when he wasn't wallowing in sadistic sexual encounters, he was nearly comatose. He thought, *This life in San Francisco is not half bad.*

Eventually, he announced to the madam that he would go in as half-owner of her business, thinking he could make a killing at it and could teach her how to run things the way he'd prefer. Naïvely, he thought she'd be thrilled with the proposition. He had not counted on the prevailing independent attitude amongst San Francisco women.

Her answer to that was to bundle him out the door with his case full of possessions. "I don't need some man to take over half of the business I've built up on my own. What are you thinking? That I am some helpless woman who needs a man? Hah! You are nothing but a greedy, meddling muckety-muck." He had outstayed his welcome and was past his usefulness to her. She slammed the door in his face.

At least, he comforted himself, this time his valise was more manageable. It nearly broke his heart when he realized that it was not because he'd built up more strength to carry his equipment—it was because his lovely shackles were missing. The madam had apparently purloined a few items that she enjoyed.

On the streets once again, Gilles weighed his options. He was running low on funds, so it was either time to go back to being a thief or find his beloved wife. Or both. He was already teetering on the edge of reality, and the disappointment of losing his hold on the madam and the lovely brothel seemed to shift his mind further over the cliff. He no longer consciously realized that he had made up his background out of thin air and truly began to believe he was a nobleman who was entitled to whatever he wanted. He adopted an officious air whenever he had to deal with anyone—when he wasn't sneaking around stealing everyone blind. He found himself an abandoned two-room building on the outskirts of Sydney-Town where he took up residence and began to fill the place with his "treasures," all of which he kept under sturdy lock and key. He vowed he would make it perfect for his wife, and she would love it there with him. *How could she not? I will treat her like the noblewoman she is—married to me.* The space began filling up with discarded detritus he picked up all over the city as well as some more valuable items that he stole. He could not discern the difference because his grip was so tenuous on good judgment. He was greedy… and mad.

Twenty~Five

Life at Hart House was chaotic and noisy. Two ladies, four gentlemen, a staff of nannies and household workers, kitchen help, and the children all made for a lot of activity. And then, when you added in the ever-present rotation of music students and the resident practicing musicians, it was never really quiet. Because their offices were nearby, and Isaac had lessons to give, all of the men came and went at various times of the day.

So far, at least, no one had caved into Marigold's persistent demands for a puppy, but it was just a matter of time. Adeline's usual response was, "When you're a little older, my love. Then you can take responsibility for a puppy." She had a sneaking suspicion, however, that Royal and Jasper were already looking for the right dog. And it didn't help that Richard and Alfonzo showed up now and then to visit Delphine and Fabienne, and they usually brought Ember and

Cinder. Marigold was beside herself each time the dogs arrived.

Suzette loved it at Hart House. She had grown up in a monstrous chateau with countless rooms and grounds that seemed to go on for miles, and she'd been lonely. Her tutors and her music had provided her only entertainment. Here, although by San Francisco standards Hart House was grand and quite large, it didn't even come close to comparing to her life in France. Whenever she turned around, someone was chattering away about interesting gossip or household affairs, and Friday night dinners with as many friends and family members who could show up became Suzette's favorite time of the week. Adeline never acted as though Suzette and her men were in the way in the least, and besides, she was used to having Isaac and Walter around. Adeline seemed to thrive in the chaos as much as Suzette did. Suzette also adored her music students, and she found playing with Adeline and Isaac immeasurably fulfilling. She could hardly imagine a happier existence.

Weeks went by without a word about Gilles Dernier. As time passed, Suzette worried less and less about her ne'er-do-well husband. The group hypothesized that he must have left town on his own, or somehow managed to get himself shanghaied along with Pascal. The watchmen were looking for him in places where they may have found Pascal; no one thought to look in the dens of iniquity—the worst of the brothels the city had to offer. So, they never located him.

Although they loved the chaos and life of Hart House, Suzette, Isaac, and Walter did miss their relative privacy.

They agreed that they all felt a tiny bit thwarted by having to be quiet at night. So, when absolutely nothing came to light about her so-called husband, they somewhat reluctantly decided it was time to move home again. They reasoned that Suzette would still spend much of her time at Hart House teaching, practicing, and performing, and at night she would have Walter and Isaac with her, so she would not be left alone.

As a precaution, Suzette decided to leave the Stradivarius in the Hart House music room under lock and key. She did not want to be walking back and forth with it every day.

And then something truly wonderful happened.

Isaac and Suzette were just sitting down to dinner when Walter came bustling into the house, nearly breathless with excitement.

"Where have you been all day, Walter?" Isaac asked. "We tried to wait for you, but I skipped lunch, and I was about ready to eat my shoe, I was so hungry. We decided to go ahead without you."

"I have a letter from France!" Walter exclaimed, grinning ear to ear. "Wait until you hear this!" He flapped two envelopes in front of him as he plunked down into one of the dining room chairs. Just then, Delphine came in and set a steaming bowl of soup down in front of him. "Thank you, Delphine; it smells delicious." He set the letter down, picked up his spoon, and shoveled in a mouthful. "Mmm! One of your best!"

"Walter! You cannot leave us in suspense like this!" Suzette huffed at him. Her eyes were laughing, so he could see that she was not truly upset with him—just a little frustrated.

"Oh, yes, of course." Walter was clearly as famished as Isaac and told his story between mouthfuls of soup. "Well, back when you first told Isaac and me of your dilemma regarding Derrière, I decided to do a bit of sleuthing. With Doc Louis' assistance, I wrote a letter to the patriarch of the Dernier family in France and asked him whether he had a son or even a nephew named Gilles. I explained a bit of Suzette's situation without naming her directly. And today I received a letter back from him that Doc Louis translated for me. The gist of the real Dernier's reply is that he has three daughters and no sons, and his nephews are named Robert, Hugo, Pierre, and Guillaume. They are all married and living in France. Then he made it clear that he has no illegitimate children who might wish to claim the name for their own. He goes on to say that their last name is not a common one, and he feels confident saying that anyone who claims it is an impostor." Walter paused and took a sip of wine, but kept his finger in the air, indicating that he had more to say. "So then," he continued, "I took Doc Louis' translation to a judge here in town and discussed it with him. He told me that there's no way Suzette is married to the man who claims to be someone he is not, and you can't be married to a person who does not exist. He stressed that he would be happy to give you an affidavit that absolves any fake marriage Derrière claims with you. He said, essentially, that you may consider your sham marriage to be annulled." He lifted the two envelopes as evidence. One appeared to have been passed through many hands, and the other was crisp and new.

Walter beamed as Suzette and Isaac stared at him, and then Suzette jumped up from her chair and threw herself into his arms, laughing and crying happy tears, nearly upsetting the soup.

Isaac looked pleased, though not a little skeptical, at Walter's announcement. "How much gold did you pay the judge, Walter?"

Waving him off, Walter answered breezily, "Immaterial. It's done. Suzette is free of that rascal for good. Isn't it grand?"

Suzette, who had been peppering his face with kisses, finally returned to her seat. "This is a happy day for me, Walter. I cannot thank you enough."

"Does this mean you want to marry one of us now?" Isaac asked hopefully.

Walter interrupted before Suzette had a chance to reply. "I also spoke to the judge about that, and he recalled having married a woman to two gentlemen a few years ago. So clearly it was the same judge who married Royal, Jasper, and Adeline. He said he had no problem with doing that again. He was—since I know you're going to ask, Isaac—eyeing my sack of gold rather pointedly when he made that statement, but what does it matter?" Walter then stood and dropped to one knee and asked, "Suzette? Isaac? What do you think? Shall we all get married?"

Isaac let out a hoot of laughter and exclaimed, "What a wonderful idea! Suzette? What do you think?"

Blinking back more tears, she said softly, "This is better than my wildest imagination. I would be so happy to marry both of you. When can we do it?"

Looking a tiny bit embarrassed, Walter admitted, "I made an appointment with the judge for us to meet with him and marry tomorrow afternoon."

"You were pretty sure of yourself then," Isaac laughed.

"Of course I was. I know you both love me as much as I love both of you. Any other outcome would be preposterous."

AND SO, THAT IS WHAT THEY DID. THE NEXT AFTERNOON, Walter, Isaac, and Suzette donned their finest clothes and met up with their best friends Jasper, Royal, and Adeline, and they had a heartfelt, if brief, ceremony in the judge's office. The judge had a bit more time to plan this marriage, so he was more eloquent about it than he had been with his first three-person wedding. Rather than simply saying, "You're married," he used their actual names and had them make vows to each other. He seemed terribly pleased with himself, especially when Walter handed him a good-sized sack of gold.

Adeline threw together a celebration for their friends back at Hart House that night, and everyone they knew showed up to celebrate another unconventional union. Many of the men from the Aylesbury Fire Company came, several customers of Roja Wais, as many people from The Discovery who could get away, and those people they knew through their music teaching and performances. On and on, neighbors, friends and relatives came and went all evening—celebrating with the happy newlyweds. Walter, Isaac, and Suzette were the talk of the town.

And word got around; unfortunately, not everyone who heard the news was happy for them.

Twenty-Six

Once the festivities dwindled down, the newlyweds made their way back to the de Massey house. They should have been tired by then, but they were so energized by their good fortune and love for one another, they were positively giddy.

There was a damp chill in the air that night, and they were pleased that Delphine handed them all warm drinks as soon as they arrived home. They were also happy to see that Fabienne had lit the fireplace in their bedroom. It cast a soft light and set a romantic mood.

"I just can't believe that everything fell into place for us all at once," Isaac mused as he sat on the edge of the bed. Kicking off his boots, he reached out a hand to both of them and drew them close. "Walter, you are amazing. I will be thankful for you for the rest of my days. You've saved me more than once, and now you've also saved our Suzette, and you made it possible for us all to be together this way. I love you so much. And Suzette," he chuckled, "You didn't know what to make of me when you met me. I thought you hated me, and still, I wanted you so ferociously. I recognized the passion that you tried so hard to keep locked down. And look at you now—married to not one but *two* men. As if just one could ever satisfy you." He nuzzled her neck as she sighed with a soft laugh. As he placed his hand on her abdomen, he continued, "And growing inside of you is our miracle and our future. My love is brimming over to such an extent I can't contain it." He thought for a second and added, "Maybe I will write a musical piece about it. My magnum opus. I wonder if I could…" His voice trailed off, and he kissed her.

Walter watched them kiss and added, "Isaac, you can do anything you set your mind to. You are the most talented individual I have ever known. You are brilliant and creative, and you have always been the truest friend to those you love." Walter tried to dash a tear out of the corner of his eye without his spouses noticing, but he failed. They smiled at him, knowing how sentimental he could be. "I loved you from the moment you jumped into my wagon back in Pennsylvania, and my love for you has only grown stronger and stronger with the passing of time." He put a hand to Isaac's face and stroked it lovingly. "And Suzette, when I came to your house and met you the first time, Isaac intimated that we had a very special new neighbor, so I knew something was up. But when I walked through the door, it was as if the sunshine outside dimmed in comparison because the true sparkling light came from you within these walls. You are talented and loving, passionate and loyal, strong and intelligent. I don't even need to mention how beautiful you are because, as nice as the packaging is, your true beauty emanates from within. I love your fearlessness and your adventurous spirit. I haven't had years to love you the way I have with Isaac, but the passion I feel for you could move mountains."

Suzette's mouth curved up in a satisfied smile. "Adeline was right when she told me you were two of the finest men in San Francisco. She has had a long time to get to know you, but I am the one who reaps the benefits of loving you both so dearly." She touched their faces gently. "Isaac, you are right. I did not know what to make of you. I confess that at first, I tried to fight my incredible attraction for you because I was afraid of it. It seemed you could burn me to ash with your fiery spirit. But when I saw you harness all of that passion inside of you and unleash it with your violin, I knew I understood your very soul in ways not many could. You seemed to somehow become uniquely mine with your music. But then I also saw your true affection with Walter and his for you, and I feared my heart would burst. I was already half in love with Walter, and the two of you together seemed to be an impossibility. Walter, you are all heart and brains—wrapped up in a kind, brilliant gentleman who makes me want to be a better person. I feel secure and warm when I am near you, and Isaac, I still feel as if you could burn me up as easily as look at me. When we make love, I sometimes pretend I am your instrument, and you are making music with my body." She took a long breath and smiled at them again. "So here we are now, thanks to you, Walter, all married and happy. Whatever shall we do about it, my loves?"

Nipping at her earlobe, Isaac whispered, "We could start by taking off our clothes, and then we can take it from there. Maybe we can make some beautiful music together."

"Yes, please," she answered.

And thus began the slow process of removing each other's layers one at a time. As soon as bare skin appeared, it was instantly covered with kisses and strokes. Finally, they all stood naked amidst a pile of their fine attire that was dropped haphazardly onto the floor. Walter bent down and picked up Suzette's gown and flipped it over a chair. "Don't want such a beautiful frock to be ruined," he said. Turning back to them, he saw that Isaac and Suzette were already lying down on the bed, and they were locked in a passionate kiss. He paused to admire their beauty in the firelight. "You are magnificent," he whispered. "I might be the happiest man on earth right now."

As Isaac and Suzette continued their kissing and stroking, Walter lowered himself to the bed and bent over them. He nudged their bodies apart enough that he could caress them. Isaac was already proudly erect, and Walter grasped him, sliding his hand up and down Isaac's shaft, eliciting a soft moan from him. Then he bent down and kissed Suzette's thighs and slid a hand upwards and into her damp warmth. "I need to make love to both of you at the same time," he declared in a soft, sincere tone. He then slipped two fingers into Suzette and swallowed Isaac's cock, causing them both to groan happily. Walter alternated sucking Isaac and then sucking Suzette's clit so adeptly, they were both writhing within a couple of minutes.

Walter could tell that his lovers were both riding the edge of bliss when he ceased his sucking. Leaning back with a chuckle as they protested his stopping, he reached for the bottle of oil in the bedside cabinet. Quickly, he drizzled some over his steely erection and administered some to Isaac as well. "Lie back, Isaac," Walter ordered, as Isaac sighed with pleasure.

"Now turn and face me, Suzette," Walter directed as he gently turned her around. He immediately feasted on her sensitive breasts that had swelled with her pregnancy. "So gorgeous," he whispered between kissing and sucking her nipples as she stroked his back. Again, he reached down with an oily hand and slipped in and out of her first with one, then two, and finally with three fingers. "You are so wet, you must love this, my dearest." She nodded again with what sounded like purring. "Now, Isaac," Walter ordered as he removed his fingers. "Slide that beautiful cock of yours into our wife. Don't you love that word? Our *wife* is wet and ready for us." As Isaac maneuvered himself into Suzette, Walter knelt down and licked Suzette's opening and Isaac at the same time. "You taste perfect together," he said with awe in his voice and then plunged his tongue inside her alongside Isaac. They both gasped at the foreign sensation. Walter then latched onto Suzette's clit and began a barrage of sucking and stroking her with his rigid tongue. Soon she gasped and stiffened in Isaac's arms as her climax barreled through her. Isaac continued to fondle her body from behind, periodically caressing and pinching her sensitive nipples. It was almost as if the room was too small to contain all of their combined love as their satisfied sounds filled the space.

"You are so beautiful in the throes of your orgasm, dearest. Are you ready for me now?" Walter asked. She nodded, and Isaac chuckled, so Walter carefully positioned himself and began to feed his cock into her alongside Isaac, the way he'd done with his tongue. Inch by careful inch, he pushed inside, reveling in the feel of her heated grip and Isaac's firm member sliding along his own, skin-to-skin. "This is it, my loves. The ultimate and closest way to be together. I love you both so deeply," he said with a hitch in his voice. Once he was fully seated inside Suzette, he threw his arms around the dearest people to him on earth. He kissed Suzette and then Isaac as he rocked in and out of her, rubbing against Isaac's cock.

"I would never have thought such a thing possible if Marguerite had not suggested it," Suzette moaned. "I can feel your love for each other *and* for me this way." She clenched her muscles, causing both men to hiss. This made her smile.

THE CLOSENESS AND INTIMACY OF SIMULTANEOUS PENETRATION aroused them all to such a degree it became difficult to maintain a slow rhythm. The warmth and pleasure of her orgasm still poured through Suzette, so she felt herself grasping and releasing her men over and over. The men coordinated their probing, relishing in the slide up and down of their textured shafts against one another. Suzette was gloriously wet, easing them in and out—and yet gripping them together at the same time. It was nothing shy of sheer bliss. Gradually they sped up their actions until they were rutting powerfully inside her and against each other. Over and over, they pounded, each of them lost in their own euphoria, and each of them in love together until Suzette cried out in ecstasy. Isaac was close behind with his howling release that never failed to make Walter smile. But this time it caught Walter off-guard with the profound reality that these people were indeed his forever. He cried out as paradise enveloped him. They all panted with heavy breaths and broad smiles as their synchronized heartbeats slowed back to normal.

Not too much later, Walter and Suzette were sound asleep. Walter's arm was draped over Suzette protectively. Isaac, however, was pestered—in a good way—by the idea that he might be able to compose something to honor their commitment to one another and the love he felt for his wife, husband, and baby. Snatches of a melody began to take place in his head as he stared unseeing at the ceiling. He and Adeline had certainly improvised many times when they performed for the dancers at The Discovery, but writing an actual composition was new for him.

The soft breaths of his lovers kept up a steady beat that propelled him forward in his thoughts. He visualized three hearts beating in union and then a tiny fourth joining them. Closer and closer he got to feeling that he truly had something, so he crept soundlessly from the bed, grabbed his shirt and trousers from the heap on the floor and started out of the room. He decided to grab his boots and jacket for fear that downstairs would be much cooler than this warm cocoon of heated bodies and a small smoldering fire.

He headed downstairs to the music room, where he located paper, pen, and ink. With the light of a candle and the moonlight through the window as his only illumination, he began to compose. Isaac had the odd sensation that he was merely transcribing a dictation he heard from heaven above. He could barely get his thoughts down quickly enough and was terribly sorry he didn't have either the Strad or one of his violins to try this out. "Tomorrow," he vowed to himself out loud and grinned happily at the score.

And then chaos reigned down upon him as the world seemed to shatter, and his composition became splattered with blood.

Twenty-Seven

Walter jolted upright in bed at the same time as Suzette. Blinking in the dark room, Walter craned his neck around, looking for an answer to why he'd been woken up so rudely and dramatically. Suzette felt behind her, wondering at the chill where before there had been a solid, warm presence, and she asked in a small, shaky voice, "Where is Isaac?"

"Stay here, Suzette, *please*. That was a gunshot!" Walter nearly shouted as the fog in his head cleared. He grabbed his trousers, yanked them on, and dashed out the door.

"Walter!" Suzette cried as the door slammed. She could hear his footsteps thundering down the hall. Then she could hear the sounds of Fabienne and Delphine's terrified voices drifting up the stairs. They were clearly out of their chambers in the back of the house and looking to understand the situation with Walter. Thinking that she might be of some service,

Suzette also rose—against Walter's wishes—and located a dressing gown. She somehow managed to get all tangled up in it before she could get it on enough to protect her modesty, however, so she ended up rather late to the scene unfolding downstairs.

As she reached the foyer, she found Fabienne scurrying into the music room with a broom and dustpan, and Delphine had a bucket of warm water and some clean linens. "Oh, do not go in there," she quickly ordered Suzette. "There is glass everywhere, and you will cut yourself too."

"Too? Who is cut?" Suzette demanded. "What happened?" But no one answered her, so she gingerly made her way to the door of the parlor, looking at the floor for any obvious shards. Not seeing anything, she looked up and nearly fainted at the sight that greeted her from inside the music room. Isaac was sitting at her writing desk with his head in his hands, dripping blood. Gasping, she only thought to get to him quickly and tend to him, but as soon as she bolted forward, strong arms grabbed her from behind.

"Stop, Suzette. You're barefoot," Walter ordered. "You'll injure yourself. We'll get Isaac to Doc Louis for stitches if he needs them, but right now, let Delphine handle the bleeding, and Fabienne will sweep up the glass. They thought to slip into their boots."

"What happened?" Suzette cried again. "Tell me! Why is Isaac down here in the middle of the night, and was that really a gunshot? Was Isaac hit by a bullet?"

"I can explain some of it," said a vaguely familiar-looking man who stood in the open front doorway. "Two of us were on watch tonight, concealed in the bushes. My partner Jake chased after the gunman, and I stayed here to continue guarding the house. We always work in pairs."

Suzette could feel her patience reaching its limit. *Gunman? This man needs to speed up his story!* She bit her tongue before she bit his head off, however.

"We saw Mr. Stark come downstairs about two hours ago. That was unusual, but he clearly had something on his mind that he needed to put to paper. His expression grew more and more pleased as he worked on whatever he was doing. Then we saw some motion in the bushes near the window where Mr. Stark was working. It was a strange man. He was dressed well enough, but he was a scrawny fellow with long dark hair. Jake poked me in the ribs as soon as we saw him. He fit the description of the man we were supposed to be protecting you from. We advanced as soon as we could, but…" The watchman shook his head. "It all happened so fast, it's a wonder Mr. Stark wasn't murdered." He briefly hung his head.

Suzette's hand flew to her mouth, and Walter's arm tightened around her. They were both shaking.

"We had nearly reached him when the moonlight caught on the metal of the man's pistol. He was aiming it at the window, pointing it directly at Mr. Stark. When I saw that, I leapt out of cover and dove for him. The gun still went off, but the shot went wild, and when I tackled the shooter, the gun went flying and crashed through the window. Glass went everywhere, and some of it landed on Mr. Stark's head and hands. He was probably protected somewhat by the jacket he has on, or he'd have been hurt worse, but I think he's still cut up pretty bad even so."

"Oh, Isaac," Suzette moaned. "We need to see if he got any glass in his eyes." A tear streaked down her face as that idea came to her. "I hope his hands are not too badly injured either."

"How did the shooter get away?" Walter asked.

The watchman sheepishly held up his hand, showing a bloody, mangled wound. "I was hanging onto him as hard as I could, even though he was thrashing around, but he bit me like a rabid wild beast! As soon as I flinched and yanked my hand away, the little bastard shook me off and ran. Jake took off after him, and I don't know what happened to either of them after that. I'm terribly sorry, folks. I feel like we've failed you miserably since we didn't apprehend the gunman before he did so much damage."

"But you saved our Isaac!" Suzette protested. "We will be grateful to you for that forever."

"Well, yes, ma'am. There's that. I just hope Jake shows up again with that stinkin' polecat in handcuffs."

"Yes, one can hope," answered Walter as they heard shuffling footsteps approaching. "Ah, here is Isaac now. Are you all in one piece? Can you see? Are you in terrible pain? Shall we take you straightaway to Doc Louis?"

Isaac stood in front of them, swaying a bit. One of Delphine's clean linens was wrapped around his head like a turban, but his face seemed mostly unscathed—if a little pale. He had some small scratches, but his turban was liberally oozing blood. "Yes,

Doc Louis... That glass almost scalped me, and it hurts like a... well, it hurts." He made a rueful face. "Thank you, Charlie, for no doubt saving my life. I... um... think I need to sit down." He plopped gracelessly down onto the floor in a heap.

Suzette crouched down and gently put her arm around him. "This is all my fault," she moaned. "I am so sorry, Isaac." Isaac seemed to be in too much shock and pain to register what she said.

In the distance, they heard the unmistakable sound of the Aylesbury Fire Company alarm bell suddenly beginning to clang.

"Oh no," sighed Walter. "They'll just have to do without us tonight. I hope it's not a serious fire."

Another man entered the front door, and Charlie brightened at first, but when he saw the man's woebegone expression, he deflated immediately. "Did you lose 'im, Jake?"

"Yeah, chasing that man is like trying to pick up butter with a hot fork. The last I saw of him, he set fire to the front of a dry goods store, and then he seemed to vanish into thin air. I reported the fire and beat it back here. He's a slippery bastard; I can tell you that."

"Probably trying to set a diversion or get Isaac and me to leave Suzette and go fight the fire," Walter mused. "Either way, the sheriff needs to hear about it." He looked at Suzette. "We need to get some clothes on and get our poor man here over to Doc Louis. We'll take you too, Charlie," he added looking at the watchman. "That wound of yours looks nasty. Or, better yet, let's send someone to fetch Doc Louis here, so we don't have to hitch up the horses and a wagon to get everyone over to him."

"I'll go get 'im," Jake said. "I know where he lives." It was too early in the morning for Doc Louis to be at his practice, although the sky was beginning to grow light. "I'll explain it to 'im."

About thirty minutes later, Doc Louis came bustling in with Marguerite. "I had to come and offer my support," she explained. "You must be frightened out of your wits," she said to Suzette as she embraced her. The two patients were sitting up in the kitchen where Delphine was still carefully washing Charlie's wound.

"This young lady makes a fine nurse," exclaimed Doc Louis, making Delphine blush. He looked at Charlie's badly mauled hand and made a *tsk*. "There is not a lot more I can do for this. I will give you some of my special ointment, and I have seen the best results when wounds are clean, so you will want to keep it that way. We hope no infection sets in with a bite like this. I would hate to see you lose that hand." Charlie shuddered at that suggestion, and Doc Louis looked at him kindly. "If you start getting red streaks or you run a fever, let me know. And make a tea of this for the pain." He handed him a packet of willow bark. "A bite is nasty business, but you are young and healthy, so I expect you will make a good recovery." He then turned to Isaac, who was being fawned over by Suzette.

"Not what most people experience on their wedding night, is it?" Doc Louis asked as he unwound the bloody turban. Suzette was becoming paler and paler, so he turned to Marguerite and said, "Let's get some toast into this lovely mother-to-be before she faints dead away. I will take care of your man, Suzette. He will be fine. Head wounds bleed a lot, so they are always dramatic. Well! Look at this. You still have a chunk of glass in your wound. I will clean that out and stitch up the top of your head, and you will not even have a visible scar from it. Your hair is going to look a bit odd for a while, however." He whipped out some tweezers and yanked out the shard before Isaac could even brace for it.

"Yaaghh!" Isaac hollered. "Ow." Then he looked contrite. "You probably think I'm acting like a baby," he grumbled.

"I am surprised the biggest cut is so far back on the top of your head. You were lucky the glass did not fly straight into your face. You just have this one cut over your eyebrow that I will also stitch up. That one will leave you a bit of a reminder."

"I was leaning over the desk writing," Isaac explained. "There was a loud report when the gun went off, and my immediate reaction was to put my arms in front of my face and crouch down, but it only took a split second for the glass to come flying into the room along with some object that I realize now was a large pistol. I've never seen anything like it. It was like a glass blizzard for a moment. I'm glad I didn't end up blind."

Just then, Walter returned to the house with Royal and Jasper. "How is he?" Walter demanded as he dashed in, wild-eyed and dressed haphazardly in trousers and a jacket with no shirt or cravat. He'd pulled on his boots at least, but his wild, unkempt hair made him look like a madman. He was normally so put together and proper, but this time he'd even forgotten his glasses. Rushing to Isaac, he asked, "Can you see properly? Are you in terrible pain?" He looked at Doc Louis, not waiting for Isaac's reply. "What can I do to take care of him?" He eyed the razor the physician took from his case and blanched. "What's that for?"

Doc Louis laid a friendly hand on Walter's shoulder. "I am merely going to shave a bit of Isaac's hair so I can sew this big flap here back to where it belongs. He's going to be just fine."

"Damnation, that bastard nearly scalped me," Isaac moaned. "This stings like an angry swarm of bees landed on me."

"Sorry to say, it will feel worse before it feels better. At least the cuts on your hands are mostly superficial, and none of the tendons were severed." Doc Louis proceeded to shave part of Isaac's head, then searched for more tiny shards of glass in the wound. He dropped several slivers into a dish set out by Delphine. Finally satisfied, he began to stitch. Isaac tried not to flinch too badly, but it was tough.

Walter sat down in front of Isaac and ordered him, "Take hold of my hands and squeeze them if it gets to be too bad—unless that hurts too much. I'm here for you. Take my strength." Then Walter got an idea to help distract Isaac. "Did I tell you about the story I read in the newspaper the other day…?" And he spent the entire time Doc Louis stitched Isaac's head telling ridiculous stories about local gossip. He may have made a few of them up, but the effort seemed to calm Isaac down somewhat. Walter's voice always had a calming effect.

While Isaac was being tortured with a needle and thread, Fabienne led a few more men into the kitchen. They were more of the watchmen who'd been employed by the men of Roja Wais over the years. It was getting crowded, so the men took their business to the dining room where Suzette and Marguerite were sitting. Delphine served them all coffee and fresh pastries.

"We need to come up with a better plan to keep everyone safe," Jasper pointed out, "We don't want any more folks getting hurt, and Isaac, Walter, and Suzette's safety is paramount. You two," he nodded to Charlie and Jake, "need to head to the sheriff's office straightaway to report everything you saw. We need to put a price on Derrière's head for attempted murder and arson. Maybe we can have some wanted posters put up in strategic areas in the city as well." He looked around and asked, "Are you well enough to make the trip over there, Charlie?"

"I'll be fine," he grumbled. "If the sheriff sees what that little snake did to me and hears what he tried to do to Mr. Stark, hopefully, he'll get the picture that Derrière is dangerous enough to pay attention." Then he added, "Maybe you could offer a reward for information on how to find him. Nothing loosens people up more than the promise of gold."

"Good idea," Royal said with a nod. He looked at the

watchmen who'd just arrived. "You men need to stand guard here at the house. Front and back. And when Suzette needs to come over to Hart House to give lessons to her students, she'll need an escort of two men at a time. But do not abandon Fabienne and Delphine here either. There's no telling what that madman might try."

Just then, they could hear Isaac cursing loudly from the kitchen, hollering that something burned like the devil. Doc Louis was applying iodine to his wounds. Walter's soothing voice continued non-stop throughout Isaac's ordeal. Suzette abruptly stood up, abandoning her toast, and rushed into the kitchen, announcing, "I must go to him."

Seeing the state of Isaac's wounds and stitches made Suzette get the shakes. "Oh, Isaac," she moaned. "Does it hurt horribly?" When all he did was grunt, she asked, "Can you tell us what you were doing out of bed in the middle of the night?"

His shoulders slumped. Doc Louis seemed to be done poking him over and over with a needle and scalding him with medicine. So, while Doc Louis wrapped bandages around his head and hands, Isaac answered, "I had what felt like a wonderful idea for a violin and piano piece. It was a trio for us to play with Adeline, and it seemed to be coming together beautifully. I was so excited to have you see it and play it with you. But then the glass window came flying at me, and the score is now a bloody mess. I don't know if I'll even be able to read it to copy it." He sighed. "I hadn't even begun the piano part yet."

"You'll get it back," Walter said in a bracing voice. "You

did it once, and you can do it again. Suzette and I have full faith in you."

"Why do you think Derrière was outside the house anyway? Surely, he didn't show up expecting to put a bullet through me in the middle of the night. No one is usually up at that hour. This was just a fluke."

Walter got a stricken look on his face and said, "We need to talk about this with the others. Can you make it to the dining room?" He put out an arm to help Isaac stand.

Doc Louis grabbed Isaac's other arm and said, "Take it slowly, young man." Together they led Isaac out to where their partners were getting ready to leave for the sheriff's office.

"Hold up, men," Walter commanded as he pulled out a chair for Isaac. "There is something else we need to consider." Everyone sat down again, and Walter looked around the room, his eyes resting on Jake. "You said he set fire to the dry goods storefront, correct?"

"Yessir, Mr. James. He tossed something through the front window."

"Doesn't it sound as if he was awfully well prepared to start a fire in that case?"

Suzette gasped as she grasped his meaning. "You think he was here to burn the house down and saw Isaac and decided to shoot him instead? That man is like the devil himself!"

Isaac said grimly, "It could be that he was hoping to flush you out and grab you during the commotion that always surrounds a fire. He probably thought Walter and I would be busy fighting the flames, and you'd be left unattended."

"As sorry as I am that Isaac was hurt, I am relieved that did not happen," she answered. Unshed tears sparkled in her eyes. "We all could have died." She unconsciously wrapped her arms protectively around her middle.

"Everyone is going to have to be extra careful from here on out," Royal stated. "That man is clearly insane."

Isaac seemed to sway in his seat and looked at Walter for help. "I need to go upstairs and lie down. I feel awful, and I've had no sleep at all."

Doc Louis gave Isaac something for the pain, and the result was that he slept away the better part of the day. Suzette came in a couple of times to bring him food and drink, and then she napped with him. Isaac found he was happiest and the most comfortable when he could wrap her in his arms. Without her there, he slept fitfully, and his head burned, so when she stirred as if preparing to leave, he strengthened his grip. Finally, when she'd slept as much as she could, she grabbed one of Walter's books and lay in bed with Isaac, reading while he slept.

Walter had business to attend to and left his two favorite people under the watchful care of a staff of guards while he and the other men conferred with the sheriff and made plans to keep everyone safe.

Lessons and work were canceled that day for Isaac and Suzette.

Gilles Dernier had his own plans to make. His first attempt at rescuing his wife from those lowly San Franciscans may have been a failure, but he knew his nobleman's intellect would eventually prevail. *Surely, they are no match for a baron such as I!* He was thoroughly convinced of his right to her and that she would welcome his attention. *I just need to secure passage back to France on the next ship, then snatch her away from those dolts. It ought to be easy. I have just had a bit of bad luck so far, and I was not prepared. Must not be too eager next time. I shall have all of my plans in place. Suzette will be so happy when I can show her how much I cherish her. She will enjoy my special talents. And her father will be so happy to see us back in France and together at last. We will move into the chateau, and life will be wonderful.*

His already tenuous grip on reality slipped more and more with the passage of time.

Twenty-Eight

All was quiet for a while. Isaac began to feel better when his head stopped throbbing, and Doc Louis was happy to see that his wounds showed no signs of festering. Likewise, the doctor's special ointment seemed to be working well on Charlie's hand, and he was healing without a dreaded infection setting in. Not everyone believed in Doc Louis' progressive ideas about keeping things clean at all times, but the proof was in his rate of success with his patients.

Suzette and Walter took good care of Isaac and did everything they could to make him happy. While his hands still stung from the number of cuts on them, his lovers cheerfully took it upon themselves to "do all the work" when they went to bed. They were extra affectionate with him and lavished his body with attention. He'd never felt so cherished in his life. His favorite was the night when Walter used his fancy oral skills on Isaac's cock and fingered his ass at the same time as Suzette sat on Isaac's face. Isaac momentarily lost his concentration when Walter stroked a certain spot inside of him that made him shiver and groan with pleasure. As Suzette gyrated on him in the most wanton way—exclaiming her profound pleasure in a frenzied mixture of French and English words, he felt transported to a new ring of heaven. Shooting down Walter's throat, Isaac came with a howl that was muffled by Suzette's damp, pulsating heat.

Walter gently pulled Suzette over beside Isaac so he could watch as Walter slammed into her from behind. Isaac ogled her jiggling breasts as Walter pounded into her over and over, and he longed to reach out to caress them. Since his bandages were still in place, he had them maneuver around so he could lean over and feast on her rosy nipples. This position was a bit awkward, but the heat of the moment eradicated any worry about that. Isaac watched spellbound as Walter ground his fingers against her clit and fed himself into Suzette again and again until she gave another long, quivering moan. Walter erupted with a shout of rapture.

"You two are just about the most beautiful sight I can even imagine," Isaac growled.

They enjoyed discovering new ways to be inventive until Isaac could comfortably use his hands once again, and each night brought them closer and closer together.

"I have never before felt so much love surrounding me," Suzette declared with happy tears in her eyes. "My life up to the time when I met you was like an empty box just waiting to be filled with surprises and miraculous gifts. You have both exceeded my dreams. I love you both so dearly."

When his stitches came out, Isaac was almost able to comb his hair over the worst of the mess.

"You are still beautiful to me—even with questionable hair," Walter assured him with a grin and a hug.

Isaac grunted. "I hope I don't scare any of the children, that's all." He was not particularly vain anyway.

"This new scar over your eyebrow makes you look dangerous," Suzette said with a wink. Then she kissed it and sobered. "I am so relieved that the glass missed your eye. And I am thankful that your wonderful, talented hands were not sliced up so badly you could not play the violin or do your magnificent woodwork."

As promised, when Suzette was without the escort of Walter and Isaac, she never ventured anywhere without a pair of armed guards, and often two more would follow surreptitiously so they could scan the surroundings for anything suspicious. Everything seemed fine—so far.

ISAAC GOT BACK TO WORK AND STARTED TEACHING HIS LESSONS again. Noticing, however, that he and Suzette seemed worried and distracted at times, Adeline came up with an idea.

"We have so many new students now after adding you as

a teacher, Suzette. Wouldn't it be fun to plan a recital? We could ask the National Theatre if we could use their stage for the afternoon one Saturday, and that way, all the families and friends would have good seating. It will be so much more exciting for them all to have it on a large stage rather than here at Hart House. What do you think?"

"I have never done anything like this, but it sounds wonderful to me," Suzette agreed.

"Perhaps to pay the theater back, we could offer to give our own concert—the three of us," Isaac offered. "That way, they could make some money. Are you ready for this, Suzette? It will be something to tell our child about in years to come—how he or she was on stage even before birth!" He chuckled at his own joke. "I don't want to overtax you, so we could pick pieces that are audience favorites but aren't all that challenging for us. We have a number of things to work on as it is."

Once they received a commitment from the National Theatre's manager, they had notices printed and began the process of polishing the students' performances for the stage. Then they picked out their own repertoire for their concert. They had six weeks to get ready. Isaac pointed out with a chuckle, "My hair ought to be somewhat back to normal by then."

The agreement with the National Theatre was that the student recital would be in the afternoon, and that same evening they would have the trio's concert. Thus began a flurry of plotting and planning.

All the while, they were being closely scrutinized.

They had no idea.

As a pickpocket in his younger years, Gilles Dernier had mastered fitting into crowds and going unnoticed. Now he called on that talent once again. Some days he would venture out in ratty old clothes with his hair under a shapeless hat and a patch over one eye, looking like a stooped beggar. On other days he would shave carefully and tie his hair back under a scarf that he knotted under his chin. Then he would put on a simple, shapeless dress and pad his body to look like a humble and somewhat chubby woman. He never made eye contact with a single person and could blend in virtually unseen, right under the noses of the people looking for him. In this manner, he learned Suzette's schedule as she traveled between home and Hart House with her men and her guards.

He began to formulate a plan in which he could hire men to ambush the guards, and he would sweep her away from them.

But then luck was on his side when he got hold of an announcement that there would be a free student recital and later a concert at the National Theatre. A new plan began to take shape. The timing couldn't be better. A ship was scheduled to leave for France the same day he planned to snatch her away from those awful Americans.

Gilles told himself over and over that he felt sorry for

Suzette having to put up with such cretins. He knew his noble birth placed him in much better stead for her happiness. He pitied her as she undoubtedly longed for him to return. If it weren't for those overbearing, protective men, he'd have spirited her away before this. They were just so much larger than he, it would take careful planning on his part to lure her away safely. He doubted they would do anything that could possibly harm Suzette, but he was not so certain they would be as careful with him.

One day as he observed his beloved wife's comings and goings, a touch of reality smacked him in the face. *Suzette's waistline is expanding! The foolish whore has gotten herself pregnant, and it is not my child!* Gilles' fury burned with the ferocity of a thousand suns. *She will need punishment for that transgression.* Staring at her profile from his vantage point where he sat slumped on a street corner, he squelched a shriek that threatened to bubble out of him and covered it up with a fake coughing fit. He was in his beggar outfit and suddenly sounded vaguely consumptive, so everyone around him gave him a wide berth.

Oh, how I am going to enjoy flogging you for your sins, my beautiful wife. I know you will act contrite but love it too, no matter how loudly you scream. He stood up from his begging position and scurried like a rat back to his abode, where he dressed in his preferred finery and set out to find a whore he could beat to a pulp. Unfortunately for him, his reputation preceded him, and when he got to the area where the brothels were, he was turned away over and over.

After multiple rejections, his frustration grew to an

inferno, and he lashed out, threatening to strangle one of the madams. Undeterred by his belligerence, the madam calmly nodded to a large man who stood just inside the door. The guard unceremoniously grabbed Gilles by the front of his fancy coat and shoved him. Gilles tumbled down the steps into the alley and lay in a heap. Slowly, one by one, he checked his limbs and decided he was bruised all over, but still in one piece. His pride took the worst hit, and this further inflamed his insanity.

Suzette and those terrible captors of hers have to pay!

Twenty~Nine

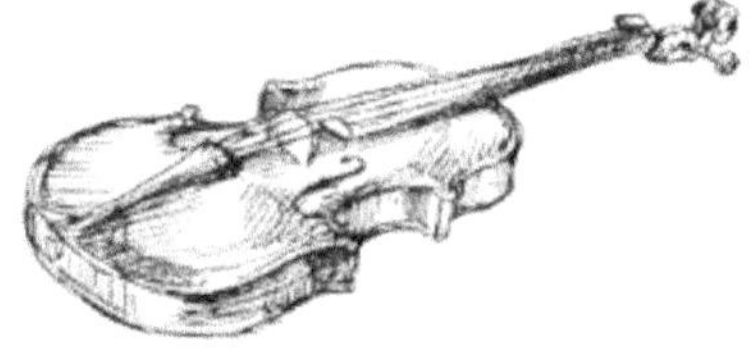

Suzette had never prepared anyone else for a performance, and she discovered that it was a rewarding experience. She worked with her students to decide what they would play, giving suggestions when needed, and listening to their wishes. Most of them already had a favorite, so making sure everyone was playing something different was her only major challenge. It all worked out finally with no hard feelings.

Then she and Isaac got another idea that they thought would be fun. After the students were done with their solo works, all of the violin, viola, and cello students would play a short piece together as an ensemble. Their students ranged in age from five to adult, so it would be something to behold. Some of the older ones were quite talented and had played with the orchestra when Isaac and Adeline gave their concert months prior to this, but for most of them, this would be a great new experience. Since Suzette was the newest teacher, she tended to have the least experienced students to work with; she loved them dearly.

They further decided that the musicians needed to rehearse together on the stage of the National Theatre. It gave the head of the watchmen fits to know that Suzette would be leaving the relative safety of her usual locations—her house and Hart House—to travel to the theater, but he had no say in their decision.

GILLES DERNIER WAS SCHEMING GLEEFULLY.

I know a thing or two about women, he told himself. *I just need to capitalize on that, and my plan will work beautifully.*

The date for the concert loomed closer and closer, and Gilles could feel himself growing more excited with each passing hour. He couldn't wait to get his hands on Suzette, and this thought created a tremendous need in him for release. At times he looked at what was left of his beloved equipment and rued the day that he lost his shackles, but he still had a sturdy rope and some beautiful items that could cause exquisite pain.

Shivers ran through him at the thought of using those tools on his errant wife. He fixated on what he would do to that pale skin of hers, and he would become aroused to nearly the point of pain. Over and over, he had to stroke himself to a frenzy, but his orgasms were becoming harder to achieve with simply his imagination for help. He even tried stroking his erection with the heavy hemp rope he owned, thinking it would give him greater friction. All it did was rub his skin raw. He found clothing to be terribly uncomfortable for a few days after that botched experiment.

He took to donning different disguises and capturing women and young boys in the alleys of Sydney-Town where he put them through a session of torture. He never raped anyone, much to their relief, but they'd been terrified, nonetheless. Holding a knife to their throats, he would tie them up and strip them bare while taunting them in French as he flogged or whipped them. His final act was always to ejaculate on the painful stripes he left on their skin. Not one of them understood a word he said, and they were left to wonder why they'd been abused by such a madman.

Sydney-Town was largely ignored by the police, so he was never brought to justice for any of this behavior. He released each of his victims with threats in English about what would happen if they told anyone about him and slithered back into obscurity—so sure he'd get away with doing it again. The familiar longing would send him out into the streets looking for his next target. Women started going out in pairs because the word was out that a madman stalked the alleyways. Errand boys had to earn their keep and tried to run swiftly enough not to be caught. Sometimes it worked for them. Some of them were not as lucky. The bad reputation for lawlessness in Sydney-Town became even worse, thanks to Gilles Dernier.

Thirty

Most of the preparations for the recital were done in private lessons, but as they drew closer to the performance date, the rehearsals in the National Theatre happened with more regularity.

Late one evening, Suzette found herself feeling sorely uncomfortable. She was busy working with her most challenging student—a talented little girl, but one who needed plenty of confidence boosting. Suzette felt as if her bladder was about to burst, and the pressure was more than she could handle. She looked around for Isaac, but he was down in the seating area speaking to a family about their son. His back was to her, and she didn't want to interrupt. She thought she could just run out back quickly and visit the privy without disrupting the rehearsal.

"You go over this passage a couple of times, Sally, and I

will be right back," she told the little girl. "You are doing very well. I am proud of you."

"Yes, ma'am," Sally replied in a tiny voice. She was a shy one, and her parents had hoped that music lessons would bolster her confidence a bit.

Suzette knew there were guards stationed by the doors and didn't give her safety any more thought. She grabbed a kerosene lantern and headed out. In her rush, she missed that the watchmen were not at their regular posts.

She took care of her needs in record time, and feeling much better, she swung open the outhouse door and stepped back out into the foggy night. Immediately a rough hand clapped over her mouth, and a wiry arm wrapped around her from behind. She tried to scream, but all that came out was a muffled cry of alarm.

"Do not make a sound, my naughty, naughty wife. I have a knife to your throat, and I will not hesitate to use it. And when I am done with you, I will use it on that big creature you live with and spread your legs for."

Suzette tried to swing the lantern at Gilles Dernier, but he avoided her aim and shook her so hard, she dropped it. Then he quickly dragged her away through the alley. As they left the area, she caught a glimpse of a man laying prostrate on the ground. She could not tell in the hazy darkness whether he was alive… or not. Tears filled her eyes, and terror filled her heart as she wondered, *Where is the other watchman?*

As he hauled her through the darkness, Gilles muttered and grumbled in a one-sided conversation about the hardships she'd been causing him. "I have lost so much waiting around for you. Some of my special possessions were stolen from me. Can you imagine? And just tonight, standing out here in the chill next to the stink of that outhouse was no royal ball. I thought I was about to gag from the smell. You owe me, my little troublemaking woman. I will make sure you pay me back with your flesh, and you will be so happy to know that we're heading home to France in the morning. Your father will be so happy to have us return. It will be beautiful, living in the chateau with him and his nice staff of servants again, will it not? My bags are already stowed on the ship, I was so sure you would be coming with me tonight."

Suzette tried to shake her head to loosen his grip over her mouth, but his strength was fueled by insanity, greed, and lust. So she just kept putting one foot in front of the other to keep from falling. She had no fear for herself, but she was afraid of what a tumble might do to her precious baby.

Eventually, his knife hand dropped from her throat to her abdomen so they could travel more efficiently. "One false move, and I will stab you and that nasty little bastard you have growing inside you. Did you think I would not notice, wife? You parade your infidelity around like a brazen whore. Do not worry; once you are delivered of that monstrous little burden, I will get rid of it, and we can have our own *real* children."

Suzette's heart felt like it was being ripped in two, and her stomach roiled.

"I HAVE JUST THE RIGHT INSTRUMENT IN MIND FOR YOUR SON," Isaac assured the parents he spoke to. "Thomas has been growing so quickly; I think he'll be a lot more comfortable with a larger size. We can trade, so there won't be any additional cost to you," he assured them.

"Thank you, Mr. Stark," the mother said. "He's been enjoying the lessons tremendously and he practices religiously. We're very proud of him. We've never had a musician in the family before." She reached over and stroked her son's hair lovingly. The boy avoided Isaac's eyes, clearly embarrassed by his mother's effusiveness, but pleased with himself at the same time.

"We're proud of him as well, aren't we, Suzette?" Isaac turned to speak to his wife and was shocked to see little Sally Anderson practicing a passage on the stage all by herself. "Sally? Where is Madame Suzette?"

Sally quickly stopped her playing and her face reddened. "I don't know. She just hurried offstage a while ago. She went that way." Sally pointed her bow. "She said that I was to practice this passage twice, and she'd be right back. But I've played it four times now."

A cold chill of worry trickled down Isaac's spine as he frowned. "Excuse me," he muttered distractedly, ascending the stage steps and heading out to the wings. "Suzette?" he called out.

No response. He proceeded toward the back door of the theater, figuring she had no reason to head into the dressing rooms. Opening the door, he was caught off-guard by a terrible sight. "Fire!" he hollered. "The outhouse is burning!" Rushing toward the flames, he could see that the door was ajar, and that gave him some relief. *At least no one is trapped inside*, he told himself. He quickly grabbed two of the several required buckets of water that all businesses had to keep on hand and tossed the water onto the flames. He could see an overturned lantern that had clearly been the cause of the fire, and his heart pounded with fear.

Turning around and quickly surveying what he could see in the close proximity of the privy, he realized there was a man lying on the ground to the side of the door he'd left through. As people began to rush out into the area, he told them all, "You need to evacuate from the front door and keep clear of the back of the theater. Get the children out of here right away! And someone, fetch a doctor!" Then he continued to yell at the top of his voice, "FIRE! FIRE!" until he could hear the shout being echoed by other voices throughout the streets. Finally, he heard the clanging of the nearest fire company's alarm bell.

The water he'd used to douse the outhouse had only slowed the progression of the fire; the flames had recovered and were burning more quickly. He grabbed another bucket and poured that on as well, but he was equally concerned with the watchman's health and terrified about the whereabouts of Suzette. Just then, he saw the guard move his legs and reach for the back of his head. Isaac let out a sigh of relief that the man was still alive. He searched around until he saw the shovel that was hanging at the back door and began to heave dirt onto the flames.

Torn between not letting this fire gain leverage and possibly burn down the city and running off to look for Suzette, he settled into what he could control himself. He had no idea where to look for her, and that thought was making him crazy. Faster and faster, he shoveled dirt, trying in vain to smother the growing flames.

Looking back toward the theater, Isaac saw Thomas' father emerging. "Can I do anything to help?"

Thinking quickly, Isaac answered, "Yes! This is very important. Please take Suzette's and my violins, and return them right away to Hart House, if you would. Let them know there that Suzette is missing, a watchman was injured, and the National Theatre is in danger of burning down. Tell them I am working on the fire. Thank you!"

The man nodded, clearly glad to be doing something useful, and ran back into the theater as Isaac wondered where the theater manager was and why he hadn't had more water on hand.

Shoveling in the searing heat, Isaac's muscles felt the burn, and his eyes watered from the smoke. Finally, he heard the men of the local fire company arrive with their equipment and more water. *Took them long enough*, he grumbled to himself. It had felt like ages. *The Aylesbury men are surely quicker than these fellows*. Nevertheless, he gladly let them take over as he turned his attention to the man on the ground.

"Can you stand?" Isaac asked as he helped the guard into

a sitting position. "We need to get away from the fire and out of their way."

"I think so."

Isaac helped him up, and they walked slowly around to the front of the building, where a crowd of curious onlookers was gathering.

"Did you see who did this?"

The guard put his hand up to the back of his head and grimaced when it came away bloody. "Nah. I was minding my own business when someone clobbered me on the back of my head with a rock or somethin', and I musta blacked out. I don't feel too good." The man retched and heaved, so Isaac helped him sit back down. "I kinda came to a little and have this faint recollection of seeing two people leaving down the alley, but that feels almost like more of a dream than a real memory."

"Which direction did they go?"

"Thataway." The guard gestured vaguely to the north. "Maybe."

Fighting the urge to drop everything and run in the direction the guard had indicated, Isaac asked, "Don't you men work in pairs? Where's your partner?"

"He was at the front door. Must be around here somewhere." He looked around. "There he is now." He jutted his chin at a man who was walking quickly, if a bit unsteadily, toward them.

As the other watchman approached, Isaac stood up to his full height and glared at him. "I'm sorry your partner was injured, but you're fired!" he snarled at the man. "You should have been working in pairs at *both* doors, especially when we had a building full of children along with the primary person you're supposed to be guarding! What's the matter with you men? And where have you been?" He took a whiff and detected the aroma of whiskey on the guard's breath. It was all Isaac could do not to flatten the man. His fists balled at his sides, and he practically shot flames from his eyes at him. "Your boss is going to hear about this. *Suzette is missing!*" he bellowed.

"I'm sorry, Mr. Stark. The other two men never showed up. We had to cover what we could."

"And does that job entail stepping out for a shot of whiskey?" Isaac hissed at him with venom in his voice. "You are *never* to leave your post when you're on the job!"

The watchman hung his head. "No, sir. I guess I just got bored, sir."

"Then clearly, this is the wrong career for you. When you were off getting drunk, did you happen to see an ugly little Frenchman dragging a woman down the street? She would have looked like… my wife!" The watchman stared stupidly at him, so Isaac gave him a shove. He wanted to rip the man's head off for falling down on his job, but violence wasn't going to help this situation.

Turning to the gathering crowd, Isaac yelled, "May I have your attention for a moment?" The crowd was too busy speculating about the cause of the fire and most of them didn't pay any attention to him.

Frustrated beyond measure, Isaac tried once again—this time at the top of his voice and losing control of his emotions, he begged, *"Listen to me, please!"* The crowd stilled finally and gaped at him. "My wife is missing. I am fairly certain she was kidnapped a little while ago by a Frenchman who calls himself Baron Gilles Dernier." Isaac grimaced. "He has long dark hair and he is not a tall man—maybe about yay-big." He indicated his shoulder height with his hand. "I assure you he is no baron and is nothing but a sneaky, conniving criminal. My wife is blonde and is wearing a blue gown. She is visibly with child."

The onlookers gave a collective gasp.

"I will pay you five hundred dollars if you can find out where he took her. They were seen leaving this area and were believed to be heading north. He is a terribly dangerous man, so do not try to apprehend him yourself. Just get the information to anyone at either the building company Roja Wais on Rincon Hill or the Aylesbury Fire Company. They will know where to find me. My name is Isaac Stark, and my wife is Suzette. She is French. Please, everyone," Isaac's voice finally broke. "I need to find her right away. Gilles Dernier is a madman."

Shaken by Isaac's distress and the thought that a pregnant woman was in danger, the crowd of onlookers all rallied themselves. One man seemed to immediately take control and commanded them, "Fan out and look everywhere!" He turned back to Isaac and hollered, "We'll find her, Mr. Stark!" They all stormed off.

"God, help them," Isaac prayed.

A man approached them just then who had not been among the onlookers. He had a satchel with him and a very concerned expression. "I'm a doctor. How many people are injured?"

"Just this one, as far as we know. He seems to have been knocked on the head with a rock or something." Isaac indicated the watchman sitting at his feet. "I'm going to leave you to it, however, and search for my missing wife." The doctor gave him an odd look, so Isaac explained, "She was abducted a little while ago."

"Sorry to hear that." The doc got to work looking at his new patient—who'd just vomited again and was swaying where he sat. "You don't look too good, young man," he added kindly.

Thirty-One

Isaac felt as vulnerable as can be heading off to find Suzette without anything for a weapon. He had nothing more lethal than his bare hands and his wits. He needed some men to back him up. *There must have been someone around who saw something. Anything!*

But then something potentially helpful happened. As he'd been speaking to the doctor, he realized that the men of Aylesbury Fire Company had shown up armed with buckets of water and their hooks and ladder equipment, but they were also armed with axes. And best of all, they knew Suzette.

Spotting Isaac, Richard called out, "How's the fire doing, Isaac? It doesn't look too bad. We heard the alarm, though, and thought we'd head over as well. You can't be too careful in this area where the buildings are so close together."

Quickly Isaac let Richard know the situation with Suzette.

Richard made a sickened face and shook his head. "Still having trouble with that awful little Frenchman? Sorry to hear that. How can we help?"

Isaac considered things for a second, then asked, "How about if you leave some of the men here to help the Number Four Company, and the rest of you come with me and look for her? We need to hurry. I can't let him have her!" He looked at the assembled men and asked, "Where's Walter?"

"Haven't seen him tonight," Richard answered. "Maybe he didn't hear the bell. Or maybe we left before he got to the firehouse. We got out of there pretty quickly and made good time getting here too, considering how far away we are."

Isaac looked down at the two polite Dalmatians sitting at Richard's feet. "Do your dogs know how to track a person?" he asked suddenly. He felt a glimmer of hope spread through him finally.

"I've actually just started playing a tracking game with them because they seemed to need a new challenge. These dogs may not be bloodhounds, but they're smart and have amazing noses, so it's definitely worth a try. They've tracked Alfonzo and me for a couple of blocks," Richard answered with a modest smile. He was ready to try anything to alleviate the haunted look in Isaac's eyes. "Do you have something of Suzette's here?"

Isaac brightened and cried, "Yes! Her cape! Wait here." He rushed back into the National Theatre and quickly returned with a blue velvet wrap. He'd always loved the way it looked on Suzette and hoped she wasn't too cold on this dank, foggy night—wherever she was. He handed over the garment, missing its softness and its association to Suzette as soon as he let go.

"Cinder! Ember! Smell this," Richard commanded the dogs. The two dogs went instantly alert, with their ears perked up and their tails wagging. They loved this game, so they gave the cape their undivided attention. "Find her!" he ordered. "Let's go find Suzette!"

The dogs began sniffing the ground and pawed in a couple of places near the front door.

"She stood right there talking to some parents," Isaac said excitedly. "Let's go around to the back where she was abducted. It's probably bedlam right now with the fire, but I'm pretty sure they took off in that direction," Isaac pointed north as they rounded the building.

Cinder and Ember looked lost for a moment, and then suddenly, their noses hit the ground once again. Cinder barked and Ember pawed at the dirt.

"Good dogs!" Richard exclaimed. "Here, smell it again, girls." He offered them the wrap once more and then led them away from all of the firefighters. Alfonzo and two other Aylesbury men fell in line with them then as they followed the dogs, racing up the alleyway.

"Now we're getting somewhere," Isaac sighed as they jogged along after the dogs. He just hoped they would get wherever this somewhere was before Suzette was harmed by that insane man.

Cinder and Ember made their way haltingly between what looked to Isaac like hiding places in the various alleys behind the downtown buildings. They sniffed behind crates, stuck their noses into lean-tos, and pawed around refuse dumps, only to take off again in the direction of the harbor. Richard was filled with praise for his dogs, telling them over and over, "Good girls! Keep going, Ember. Don't stop, Cinder! That's the way. Good dogs."

The dogs led them to the long pier that jutted way out into the harbor. They circled a spot on the dock and sat down. Staring at Richard with their tongues lolling out, they had pleased looks on their faces that clearly said, "Well, we did it. Now what?" Richard fished a chunk of jerky out of his pocket and broke it into two pieces while the dogs barked greedily. Then they happily snapped up their reward.

Isaac looked around and saw… fog. A dense wall of it had settled over the bay. There were a few lights on the water that gleamed eerily, but it was impossible to tell how far from shore they were or even what kind of boat they were on. The sky was starless, and the chilly gloom felt as if it were seeping into Isaac's bones. The bay water lapped at the pier, jiggling it and making soft splashing sounds. They could hear the creaking of timber from the pilings and the many ships floating in the bay. Some were seaworthy, and many had simply been abandoned during the gold rush. The harbor was a congested conglomeration of vessels of all shapes, sizes, and capabilities.

Isaac shook his head. "Obviously, she's been taken and put on a ship. I just have to hope the skipper isn't planning to go anywhere tonight in this soup. He'd no doubt crash into something if he tried." There was no ship moored to the dock where they stood, so he had to believe she'd been transported by a smaller skiff out to a ship. "I bet anything the ship she's on is bound for France. We need to find out who's heading in that direction and figure out some way to get out to the ship to get her back. We could try to grab a boat and row around from ship to ship, but it would be like searching for a needle in a haystack. There are hundreds of boats out there, and some of them have people who live on them permanently."

The men stood staring in different directions, hoping for a great idea to come to them. So far, nothing did. Clearly, the dogs could only get them this far. Hopelessness began to settle on their shoulders like the blanket of fog.

"If only we could see something!" Isaac complained bitterly, then he shouted at the top of his voice, "*Suzette, where are you?*" His ears strained, but he could only hear the panting dogs, the clank of metal against wood, and the creaking sounds of old timber. The water sloshed, and the fog grew thicker.

"Let's try that once again," Richard suggested. "Only this time, we'll all shout her name together. Ready? One, two, three!"

"*Suzeeeette!*" they shouted in unison and then listened carefully.

This time they heard something. It sounded like, "*Help m...*" but was smothered out before she could finish the last word.

"It sounded like it came from that direction," Isaac said excitedly. He pointed with his right hand.

"Really? I'd swear it came from over there," Richard protested, indicating with his left.

"You're both wrong," Alfonzo argued. "I distinctly heard it from that way," he explained, pointing somewhere in the middle.

"Damned fog!" Isaac cried, kicking at a pile of rotting rope at his feet. "This is ridiculous. The sound bounces off the water and echoes all over the harbor, but at least we know she's out there somewhere—and still alive."

"Should we shout again and let her know we're coming?" Alfonzo asked.

"I don't think so," Isaac replied. "She knows we're here, but if we holler that we're on our way, the men on the ship will be able to get ready for us, and that might just get us— and Suzette—killed."

"*Hey, mister!*" A man's voice—much louder than Suzette's —carried toward them on the dock. "Mr… ah… Stark! I have information!"

Isaac spun around so fast, he almost fell into the water. A wiry young man who looked to be barely out of boyhood was running down the dock toward them at breakneck speed. Catching his foot on a loose timber on the ratty old dock, he pitched forward. Isaac lunged to grab him before he hurt himself and just managed to right the young man before he gouged himself with some random bit of detritus laying around on the pier. The place was a disaster.

"Thank you, Mr. Stark," he gasped. "My name is Jonathan Marcus. I heard what you said tonight at the National Theatre. My wife 'n I was just passin' by on our way home. It struck me to the core when you said your wife was missin' and pregnant. Mine is too… pregnant, not missin'. So I sent her home straightaway and came over here to see if I could find out anything. I been working 'round the docks doin' whatever I can, and I thought maybe if I was to kidnap anyone—not that I ever would, a course—I'd want to get them outta town right away. And I thought how you must feel with your wife missin' and all, and I couldn't just stand around doing nothin'." He finally stopped speaking long enough to catch his breath.

"And?" Isaac prompted eagerly—wishing this character would get to the point.

"I come over here to see if anyone on the dock seen anything and talked to a fellow I know named Pete, and he said some odd lookin' man was draggin' a woman up the gangway of the *Ophelia*. She looked mighty perturbed at him, I guess—kickin' at 'im and the like. But he looked like he had a knife or sumpthin', Pete said. The ship took off right away from the dock, but the fog was getting' so thick, they'd be crazy to try to go very far. They'd crash into another ship fer sure in this crowded mess out here. Anyways, Pete says he's pretty sure they're waitin' out there for the fog to lift, and then the ship'll sail for France."

Isaac was both horrified and relieved in equal measure. The fog could lift at any moment, not that it looked like it would, and Suzette would sail away on the *Ophelia*. But, on the other hand, now he knew something. "Thank you, Jonathan. I'll make sure you get that reward. Come see me at Roja Wais—the building company on Rincon Hill."

"Thank you, Mr. Stark, but I don't expect no reward. I'm just doin' what I hope someone would do for me if the tables was turned. I just hope you get your wife off that ship before they leave. I know how I'd feel in that situation. My Edith is everythin' to me."

"Do you know where in the harbor the ship is moored now?"

"I don't, sir. I'm sorry. And Pete took off a while back. There's no one else around this late on the dock usually— unless it's a few drunks or whores. Um, excuse me. I don't even see any of those in this fog. I'm lucky I saw you. It was 'cause I heard them dogs bark that I found you, actually."

"Look, Jonathan. Stop by Roja Wais anyway. If you need steady work, we'll find you a good position. You're just the kind of man we like to hire, and once you prove you're a hard worker—which I suspect you will be—you'll be part of the family."

"Well, thank you, sir! I'll fer sure do that. I can't wait to tell Edith. She'll be so happy. You can count on me to work hard, sir, I promise."

"Yes, well, now we just need to figure out how to get aboard that ship and remove Suzette from the clutches of an insane individual before he harms her."

"From what I hear, the *Ophelia* is a ratty ol' brig, and she's past 'er prime," Jonathan offered. "If I had to catch 'er, I'd do it with a schooner. And I'm frankly confounded the skipper of the *Ophelia* was able to put a crew together to sail 'er. It takes an awful lotta men to do the job on a ship that size, and decent crewmen are as scarce as hen's teeth around here. I heard he'll take just about anyone."

"Do you know someone with a schooner?"

"Nah, but someone will when folks start showin' back up in the mornin'."

"Oh, lord. I don't know if I can stand to wait that long," Isaac said, gritting his teeth. "That man has a vile temper, and he's capable of anything."

Richard cut into Isaac's thoughts, "Isaac, we're all in agreement that we're here to help you, but we can't go anywhere near that Frenchman without at least a couple of pistols—if not a few rifles. If he is armed, he could shoot Suzette or one of us in an instant. We need protection. So, I recommend that we head back to the firehouse, where we can leave the dogs and arm ourselves. We can come right back and look for some help once we're armed."

Isaac let out a pained breath. "I guess you're right."

"Can I help?" Jonathan asked eagerly.

"Jonathan, I'd love more manpower, but you have a wife at home who needs you to stay safe. This isn't your battle. I'm eternally grateful for your help so far, but you go home and wrap your arms around your woman and tell her how much you love her." Isaac's voice cracked. "Do that for me, will you?"

"Yessir. I can do that. Good luck to you, Mr. Stark."

"Call me Isaac."

"Yessir, Isaac."

Thirty-Two

Walter James had had a long day. He was anxiously awaiting Isaac and Suzette's return so they could all go to bed. He'd had a meeting with a potential new client who'd been particularly ornery to deal with and was not satisfied with much that Walter offered. The man argued about everything. Walter didn't know how to please him and finally started over with his original idea, ready to offer to make changes to it, but suddenly that plan was the one the man had chosen, forgetting he'd seen it once already. That began a new round of questions and complaints.

After hours of dealing with this most trying customer, Walter was mentally exhausted and longed for a good dinner and a brandy followed by the loving arms of his two favorite people. But when he arrived home, it was to find he'd forgotten the rehearsal they had at the National Theatre. Delphine apologized profusely that she'd served them an early supper before they left. Walter assured Delphine, "My irritation has nothing to do with you. Thank you for the lovely meal you've prepared." He had to dine alone that night and read a book for company, thinking, *If I weren't so worn out, I'd head over to the theater and watch them rehearse.*

Dog-tired, he decided a long soak in the bathtub sounded good. So that's what he did, only to fall asleep in the water. A familiar noise crept into his dream, but he closed his mind to it. It was much better to stay warm and cozy than to spring into action and run out into the clammy night after a disaster. His subconscious knew it was the fire alarm, but his sleepiness overruled. He had not slept a lot the night before, and that was unusual for him, so it was all catching up to him now.

Eventually, the water cooled down, and the chill brought him to his senses. Shivering, he stood and began to dry himself off, trying to recall what was making him feel uneasy. Then it hit him. *It was the alarm! I'm shirking my responsibility to the city if I don't make it over to Aylesbury right away!* He grabbed up clothing he'd dumped on the floor and dragged it on over his damp skin. Nothing was fastened correctly, but he decided he was decent enough as he sprinted toward the front door. The house was still eerily quiet, making him certain that Isaac and Suzette were still out. Glancing at the clock in the foyer, he gasped. "Why aren't they home at this hour?" he asked out loud to no one. Still, he needed to hurry if he was going to help with a fire. Indeed, he could see the orange glow of flames in the distance, but the whereabouts were still a mystery in this fog.

Running flat out, he arrived at Aylesbury only to find everyone already gone. So he did the next best thing and hurried toward the flames. He ran into a few people on his way and tried to ask them if they knew anything about the fire. Everyone either ignored him or shrugged until, finally, one man said, "Yeah, it's the National Theatre." He started to elaborate, but Walter got the most horrified look on his face the man had ever seen.

Wishing he had a horse, Walter took off like a shot. *No, no, no, no, it cannot be. Not them. Not the children. Surely, they got everyone out. Isaac knows how to deal with fire. Oh, Suzette, all of that smoke cannot be a good thing for the baby! Why aren't you at home?*

Walter kept running until he had to stop to catch his breath—afraid he might faint. He sucked in great lungsful of air, holding onto the side of a building. He bent over and forced himself not to be sick. Once his heart stopped trying to pound its way out of his chest, he took off once again. The sheer terror of what he might discover once he got to the theater drove him on and on as fast as he could pound one foot in front of the other. And then, finally, the theater was just up ahead. Walter slowed as relief flooded his system. He could see some of the Aylesbury men arranging their equipment to go home, and the theater was still standing.

"Little late, Walter!" one of his friends called out to him. "Nice of you to show up finally." The man grinned at Walter, not perturbed, but ready to give him a hard time about it anyway. It was just friendly ribbing.

Ignoring the jab, Walter gasped haltingly, "Have you…

seen Isaac… and Suzette? Are they around anywhere?" He was still panting and out of breath.

As the firefighter shrugged, another one of the Aylesbury men stepped up to answer the question. He put a comforting hand on Walter's shoulder. "Maybe you need to sit down a moment, Walter," he said in a calming tone that Walter knew meant the man had something awful to impart. Firefighters sadly had to give out bad news frequently, and he knew "the voice."

Walter's knees gave out and he plunked to the ground. "What is it? Tell me!"

"We got here just as the fire in the outhouse was going out, but the wind picked up and caught the building across the alley on fire, so we've been here longer than we expected at first. It's all out now, but, anyway, when we got here, Isaac was all in a state because apparently Suzette has been kidnapped." Walter grabbed the man's arm and stared wildly into his eyes. "Isaac took off with Richard, Alfonzo, Grady, and Mick. They had the dogs with them, and Richard thought the dogs could track her. That's all I know. They took off that-away," he indicated with a jut of his chin. "But the rest of us had to stay and help with the fire."

"Oh, my God." Walter covered his face with his hands. "Now what?"

"Well, they could be just about anywhere. Maybe you ought to come back to the fire company with us. You don't look so good, Walter." He tried to give Walter a bolstering look and added, "Maybe they're all back home right now wondering where you went."

"I can't leave. I have to do something!" Walter protested. He felt like crying, he was so frustrated.

"Look, I'm sure you feel that way, but it's hard as hell to see anything in the fog that's rolled in, and you don't know where to go."

Sighing, Walter answered, "I know you're right. I just don't want to feel like I'm giving up on them." He craned his neck around as his eyes went wild. "Where are the watchmen? Did they go with Isaac too? The theater was supposed to be guarded while Suzette was inside! How could she have been abducted?"

"I can't help you there. When we got here, there were two men who looked like guards. Isaac yelled at one of them that he was fired, and the other one went off with a doctor. He had a bloody head. The one who got the boot smelled like whiskey."

"Oh, lord," Walter moaned and struggled to his feet. "This is a disaster. Was anyone hurt in the fire?"

"No. No casualties or injuries except for the guard who'd been clobbered with a rock to the head. We found the bloody rock behind the theater, so he must have been guarding that door. He looked to be in pretty bad shape, but he could walk with help. And just as we arrived, I heard a man shouting to the other onlookers to fan out and look for Suzette. I don't think they had a clue what to do, but they meant well."

Walter hung his head and covered his face with his hands. "What am I going to do? I have to find them."

"Why don't you come back to the firehouse, and we can ditch the fire equipment and form a search party to go out with you. How does that sound? You know the men will help a fellow Aylesbury brother."

Reluctantly, Walter saw the good sense in the fellow's reasoning. He shook his head in resignation and answered, "I guess that sounds like a good enough start. Let's go."

As they trudged back to the fire company, Walter's legs felt heavy—but not nearly as heavy as his heart.

Thirty-Three

When Isaac arrived back at Aylesbury company and discovered Walter already there, they rushed to greet each other with a strong embrace. "I have bad news," Isaac said almost immediately as they let go of one another. "He has her."

"I heard. What can we do?" Walter asked in a frantic tone. "Why are you here?"

"We came to get weapons and to formulate a plan to get her off of the *Ophelia* where he's taken her. It's a large brig out in the harbor. Why are you here and not at home, and why do you look like you've been through a war?"

"Long story. Not important now. The important thing is that all of the men here are willing to help get Suzette back. We just had to rally and figure out how to find her, but if you already know where she is, we're half the way there."

"Well, I don't know exactly. We know the name of the

ship, but the docks were so foggy, we couldn't see a thing. And no one knows where the ship is moored out there in all of those hundreds of vessels. We just have to get to it before they take off for France. Apparently, the skipper is in a big rush or something."

Walter shook his head. "Poor Suzette must be scared to death, and that can't be good for her or the baby."

Once they stowed their equipment, the men convened in the dining hall. Isaac, with Walter at his side, filled them all in on what he knew and thanked them for their willingness to help. The men grumbled lots of, "Of course!" and "We're brothers!" kinds of statements that warmed his heart.

Walter voiced his thanks as well and then asked, "Does anyone know anything about ships? Or where we can locate a vessel to get us out to the *Ophelia*? Speed is paramount."

"My pa and brother did some repair work on that ship just the other day!" one of the youngest firefighters exclaimed. "They complained about the skipper who tried to weasel out of paying them for the job. Then he tried to get them to stay aboard and join his crew. He's a real jackal, that one."

Looking excited, Walter said, "Please, take us to them. Do you think they'd help us?

"Well, sure they would. They're decent men. Let's go get 'em!"

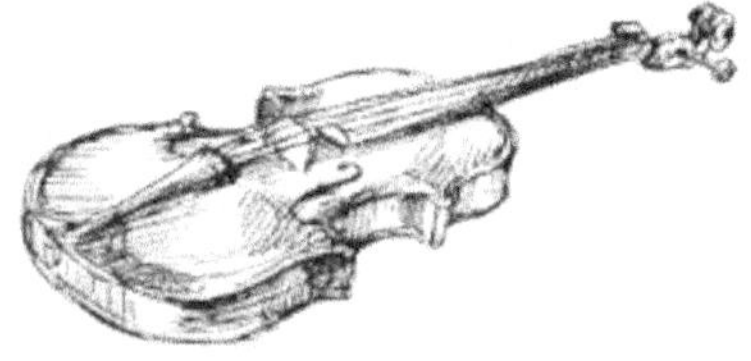

Thirty~Four

S uzette was freezing, miserable, and furious. She could not believe the hideous luck of being abducted by her self-proclaimed husband, to whom she was absolutely, legally, *not* married. She desperately tried to explain her plight to the skipper as soon as her feet hit the deck of the *Ophelia*.

"I demand that you release me immediately. I have been kidnapped by this charlatan!"

Apparently, that was the wrong tactic to take. The captain just smirked at her knowingly, then rolled his eyes at Dernier, saying, "I see what you mean, Baron. She is a bit irrational. I've heard that women in her condition can get to be over-wrought. You can tuck her away in the nice stateroom I've assigned you two, and we'll give her some rum to calm her down." To her, he said, "Now, why would a man pay good money to transport a woman all the way back to France if she weren't his wife? It's not like there ain't any good females left in that whole country, you know?" He laughed in her face, showing her the gaps where teeth used to be, and stomped away before she could answer.

Dernier punctuated his devotion by patting her conde-scendingly on the arm. She slapped him away and glared at him. "You will pay for this one way or another," she growled. "Even if it is only when you rot in hell." To herself, she thought, *Oh, lord. He has bamboozled the captain. Now, what can I do?* She tried not to cry at the thought of never seeing Walter and Isaac again, and she was worried sick about Dernier's threat to hurt her precious baby. Her arms went protectively around her middle. She knew the baby had no chance of survival if it was born with Dernier nearby. He'd likely toss the babe overboard if she delivered before they reached France. She began to think about what life would be like with Dernier as her husband and decided she would rather plunge into the sea.

The blackness in her mind began to intensify as Dernier sneakily poked her side with a knife. He began to drag her toward the stateroom that she was condemned to share with him. *There is only one way out. Once we leave the confines of San Francisco Bay, I will jump. Better to feed the sharks than to live with this insane man. I cannot comprehend a life like that.*

But then, just as Dernier was getting ready to propel her below deck and shove her into their quarters, she heard something beautiful. A chorus of male voices shouting her name! Immediately, she hauled in a deep breath and screamed, "HELP M—" but Dernier's reflexes were quick enough to snuff out her response. He clamped his hand over her mouth, and she almost choked with fury. All she managed to do was stomp on his instep before he dragged her below.

Standing in the passageway, Dernier roughly shoved her through an open door, snarling, "Ungrateful slut! I am doing all of this for you and your happiness! You belong in France in that wonderful chateau with your own kind. And me!" After yanking and pulling the warped door to get it to close properly, he jiggled the key around in the lock several times. Finally, the lock engaged with a dull thud that made Suzette's stomach roil.

Leaving his wife behind in the darkness, Dernier went back above deck to have some of that rum with the captain. After the night he'd had, he could use a draught of the good stuff.

Dernier knew he had to stay on the skipper's good side. He planned to tell him some more fancy stories about the beautiful land he would deed over to him as soon as they arrived on French soil. The way he'd tell it, the property was not vast, but it was full of plentiful game, and it included a vineyard that produced fabulous wines. It was just the right amount of acreage for a gentleman.

In truth, Dernier planned to dispatch the skipper by slitting his throat as soon as they were safely delivered to France.

Back below deck, Suzette blew out a calming breath. Hearing her name shouted by multiple men had done wonders for her morale. Someone knew she was in the harbor, and it was going to be fine once they located her. She smiled her first true smile since she'd been dragged away from her students and Isaac. *Oh, Isaac, you must be worried sick. And what of Walter? We had not seen him for hours. Does he even know?* She had not been able to discern the different voices or even where they came from, but they did know her name. That was something. *Hopefully, they heard my cry for help.*

Unfortunately, her immediate rescue did not seem to be forthcoming. Nor was the promised rum. A crewman was dispatched to her quarters with it, but when he discovered her locked door, he quickly ducked out of sight and drank it himself.

Inside the stateroom, Suzette heard the crewman's approaching footsteps and the jangling of the door handle and her smile faded. She was sure it was Dernier, coming back into the room to claim her. Terror as she'd never known gripped her, and she braced herself for a fight. Only when the footsteps retreated harmlessly did she relax enough to think straight.

Minutes stretched into hours. At least after their original quick departure from the dock, the ship seemed to be anchored—they had not set sail. Having sailed to San Francisco from France originally, Suzette knew the difference in how it felt to be on a ship on open waters as compared to being moored in a bay. They were definitely not moving. That lifted her spirits somewhat.

But she both feared for her men's safety as well as continued to worry that her vile "husband" would return to the stateroom and rape her. She also remembered the hideous one-sided conversations he'd had with her back in France. He said the most disgusting things to her as she pretended not to understand German.

From what little she could see, the stateroom was fairly decent, she supposed, but the entire ship had a worn-out, beaten-down appearance. There had been some repairs done recently, she noted. When they came aboard, she saw unmistakable new timbers showing here and there amongst the rattier seasoned ones. *At least we are not full of holes*, she told herself grimly. It was cold, though, and she still shivered in the damp. In the gloomy, barely-there moonlight that shone through the porthole, she squinted at the bed and saw that it had a coverlet she could use for warmth—though she was convinced she would *never* lie down on it. Hoping that it was not infested with fleas, she tore the blanket from the bed and wrapped herself in it. She plopped herself down in the one and only chair. It had to do. Gradually, she began to thaw somewhat. It was a bit better, at least for now.

Too nervous and uncomfortable to fall asleep, she listened to every sound that wafted into her consciousness. There were a few bells tolling in the distance and waves slapped at the sides of the ship. Timbers creaked everywhere, and footsteps scurried around above her, scraping and stomping. She could hear the muffled sounds of several men's voices.

Oh, how she longed to hear the voices of her dear Walter and Isaac. She prayed over and over that she would see them again.

The best part of that night aboard the *Ophelia* was that Dernier did not come back to the stateroom. Suzette hoped he was dead drunk somewhere, or better yet… dead.

FINALLY, HOWEVER, IN THE EARLY HOURS OF THE MORNING, when the sun had just broken and burned off the night fog, a key rattled in the stateroom lock. Suzette realized she'd dozed off and felt a sharp pain in her neck as she straightened up. She had an immediate and terrible need to use the chamber pot, so she discarded the blanket and set it aside.

"Do not come in!"

"Why not?" Dernier's unmistakable nasal voice grumbled at her.

"Please, give me a moment of privacy. I will finish quickly."

"Oh. I do not care about that. I find I have a need for my *wife* just now."

Suzette could hear the leer in his voice, and her skin crawled, but she took care of her needs, hoping she had the time to finish and maintain some dignity.

The key twisted in the lock, and he had to shove the door three times with his shoulder before he could heave it open. It creaked on its rusty hinges. Each sound was like an arrow piercing her heart. This was the moment she'd feared above all others—being truly alone with this madman. For a crazy half second, she contemplated heaving the chamber pot at him but then decided against further inflaming his ill temper. If he was going to rape her, she didn't want him furious at the same time.

She cast her gaze about the chamber in a futile attempt to locate a possible weapon and came up empty-handed.

With bloodshot eyes and a drunken swagger, he stepped into the room and repeated the process of attempting to get the ill-fitting door to close again. With each passing moment, Suzette's heart rate sped up until she felt she was ready to scream. She noticed he did not take the time to lock them inside—perhaps not wanting to waste the effort. Turning to her, he slowly began to remove his coat. His eyes never left her bosom, and he licked his lips.

As Dernier continued his repulsive striptease, the miracle she'd prayed for all night happened. She heard Walter's clear voice ring out, "Ahoy, Captain! We request permission to come aboard and retrieve Suzette de Massey. We are here to return her to her rightful home!"

He must have found us and is alongside in a boat! Suzette spun around and screamed out the porthole, "Walter! I am here!" Then she gave a bloodcurdling screech as Dernier grabbed her from behind. She hoped Walter and whoever was with him had been able to hear her.

"Captain!" Walter shouted. "You have a hostage aboard your ship who is being held against her wishes. That scream sounded like a cry in pain to me. You must let her go now before she is harmed!"

There were some scurrying noises above and some indecipherable voices.

Dernier was much more intent on having Suzette than anything else, so he ignored what was happening outside. He rushed to untie the laces on Suzette's gown, but she deftly swatted him away over and over. Frustrated by his lack of progress, he bent over instead to lift her skirts—he was so desperate to have her. *Maybe I do not have the time to prep her with my flogger, but I want to be inside this juicy peach now!* Her fighting back simply stirred the fire within him. *She has spirit!*

Suzette felt her disgust for Dernier creep over her skin like slimy moss. He was still bent over, trying to pull up her skirts, so she kneed him in the nose. He cried out and fell back, landing on his skinny derrière.

A sense of pride and accomplishment filled her as Suzette noted a bright streak of blood pouring from his left nostril.

Dernier jumped up with fire in his beady eyes. *Maybe she has a bit too much spirit. I shall have such a wonderful time taming her!* He cursed as he said, "You will pay for that, *wife!*" Then he wiped his bloody nose on his sleeve, but the blood continued to dribble down his face.

A large sailor, who was at least twice the size of Dernier, flung open the door without the slightest trouble. "Cap'n says to come up on deck and bring the woman," he ordered in a gravelly voice. "And do it *now.*"

Breathing a sigh of relief, Suzette tried to flounce her way past Dernier, but he grabbed her hard enough to bruise her arm. "Not so fast, you little slut. One wrong word out of you, and you know what will happen." She felt the poke of a blade in her ribs and cried out as its point tore her skin.

To her surprise, the sailor pointed a pistol at Dernier's face and said, "Better let her go. You can have her back if this is all settled, but Cap'n wants a word or two with you."

Dernier blanched and let go of Suzette's arm. She whimpered and clutched her side where he'd stabbed her. It stung something fierce.

If ever he had to make his case, now was the time. Dernier's mind was in a whirl as they made their way up to the deck.

As soon as Suzette saw the men standing in their small boat, she cried out to them, "Isaac! Walter! *Please* get me off this ship! They are leaving for France, and I do not want to leave you and go back." Finally, Suzette broke down. She had not yet shed any tears, but seeing the worried expressions on her beloved men's faces nearly broke her.

"*Let her go*!" Isaac cried. His plea seemed to fall on deaf ears, unfortunately.

The captain stood there gaping at Suzette and then staring at the men in the skiff. He furrowed his brow. "Why would a woman of your caliber want to stay here in this awful city instead of returning to your family and the grandeur of a chateau where you can live with your husband?" he asked her.

"I love them!" she shouted in his face. "This man," she pointed to Dernier, "is nothing but a fraud. He is no baron, and he lies about everything."

Still in his cups from the copious amount of rum the two men had drunk during the night, the skipper frowned and asked, "Are you not married to him?"

"I went through an illegal ceremony with him. He is not the person he professes to be, so I cannot be married to him. I am legally married to the men over there." She pointed to Isaac and Walter. "I love them!"

"Them, eh? I'm not sure how that can be." The skipper regarded her waistline and snickered. "Did one of your lovers put that in there?"

"Yes, I am proud to say."

Dernier spoke up then, "She is lying, of course. It was my tender loving that put the babe in her before she lost her mind and began her infidelity. I am being as generous as a man can be by accepting her back into my home in France."

Suzette looked ill and spat, "You mean my *father's* home to which you have no claim!"

The skipper narrowed his eyes. "What about my land?"

"What land?" asked Suzette.

Ignoring her, Dernier said to the captain in a placating voice, "We should not discuss financial matters with a woman present. She is not aware of our agreement. Do not forget the lovely vineyard, though. You will love living there."

Almost sobbing now, Suzette cried, "If you try to take me back to France, I will throw myself overboard! I will not go!"

"Then perhaps I will have to confine you to your stateroom to keep you safe," Dernier said. To the captain, he said, "You see what I have to contend with? She becomes completely irrational at times. She forgets her station in life as the wife of a baron and consorts behind my back with ruffians such as these men in the boats over there." He shook his head sadly. "She even struck me when I tried to bring her up here to speak with you." He wiped his nose with the back of his hand.

Suzette gasped, "That is not exactly what happened!" She

grabbed her frock and tried to show the captain her sliced skin by opening the gash in her bodice. "He stabbed me with his knife. Look!" she ordered.

"*Wife*, stop trying to expose yourself to the captain! Keep yourself covered, woman! Have you no modesty whatsoever?" Turning to the captain again, he said, "She tore her gown on the doorway to the stateroom. There is a rough piece of timber sticking out that needs repair. Do not succumb to her nonsense, sir. She is simply a hysterical woman in need of a cure from a French physician. Perhaps a trip to the spa will help her find her good humor once again when she is delivered of my heir."

The captain had an expression on his face that indicated that he was experiencing a pounding headache. He thought for a few moments and then bellowed out orders to his crew to lift the anchor and set the sails. They were leaving. He'd had enough of this city and this drama and wanted to retire to a beautiful French vineyard where he could drink his fill and hunt for game—when and if he felt like it. It sounded like such a wonderful, quiet life. He was tired of this ship and his crew. He wanted to relax.

Frantically, the men in the smaller surrounding boats began shouting at the captain. "You cannot take her!" "She is our wife!" "Do not trust that man; he does nothing but tell lies!" and on and on. But the captain was resolved and too muddy-headed to care about these men who claimed things that sounded like nonsense. He knew they'd never catch him in their little rowboats, and he wanted to get back to France as quickly as his rotting old brig could get him there.

Soon the huge sails filled with wind, propelling the ship toward the opening of the harbor.

"NO!" cried Walter and Isaac in unison.

"NO!" screamed Suzette as she clutched her belly and sobbed.

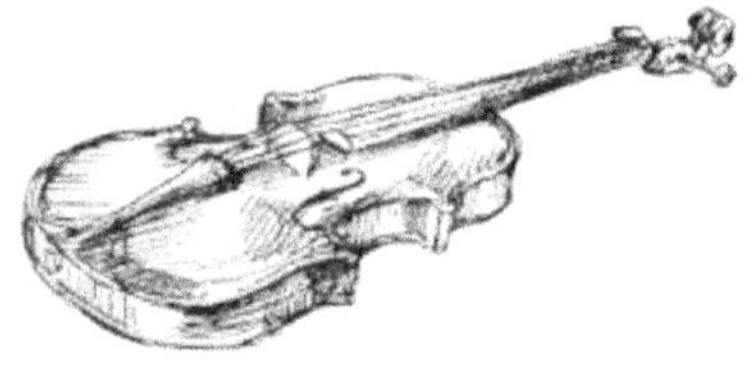

Walter and Isaac stood in the skiff along with Richard, Alfonzo, Royal, and Jasper. Four other boats filled with Aylesbury firefighters flanked them. Each man had a rifle or a pistol trained at the *Ophelia*. No one was taking this mission lightly, but they all understood that opening fire on the ship would potentially be an act of murder and would endanger everyone's lives. As the ship pulled away, they lowered their guns. Their intimidation hadn't helped, and now no one knew what to say.

Isaac sat down and began to row. He did it with such ferocity the others in the boat fell over into their seats.

"Isaac," Jasper said soothingly after righting himself, "I know this is the worst possible outcome, but slow down, man. You can't out-row a ship of that size, and you can't row all the way to France." Isaac ignored him and kept rowing like a furious automaton.

Royal looked as concerned as Jasper and suggested, "Perhaps we can book you passage on another ship, and you can sail to France and retrieve Suzette from her family's estate. Surely, they know that Derrière is a fraud. Walter has papers now to prove it."

Walter removed his glasses and wiped his eyes. His shoulders were slumped like a man who'd already lost everything. But then Richard poked him, asking, "Hey, look! What's going on out there?" Walter smashed his glasses back on, and his head popped up.

The wind suddenly seemed nonexistent. The sails on the *Ophelia* drooped and sagged. They had almost reached the mouth of the harbor, where the opening was narrow. Huge rocks lay on either side of the opening, making entry and departure a tricky business of piloting even on a good day.

Fearing a crash if they couldn't steer the ship, the captain bellowed, *"Lower the anchor! We need to stop drifting!"*

A brig typically needs twenty-two crewmen to handle the work of sailing it, but the *Ophelia* was considerably understaffed and with several poorly trained men at that. After raising the anchor, no one stayed anywhere near it, so they wasted precious time figuring out who was supposed to lower it into the water. As they shouted and swore, the ship drifted in the heavy ebb current, moving perilously close to a huge rock formation.

Finally, someone lowered the anchor. But the anchor's chain skittered across the deck like a snake and disappeared into the bay. It had become detached from the ship. Now they were completely adrift with no hope.

Richard hollered to the Aylesbury men, "They're going to crash on Mile Rocks! This is just like the *Caroline Amelia*!" That ship had crashed in this very spot in 1850 in similar conditions.

And sure enough, as they all watched, helplessly horrified, the *Ophelia* ran smack into Mile Rocks. The ancient timbers of her hull shattered, leaving a gaping hole, and the ship immediately began to take on water. It would not be long before the ship disappeared below the water's surface. The current bounced it against the rocks over and over, making the monstrous hole grow larger.

In the surrounding skiffs, everyone with a set of oars rowed as if their life depended on it toward the wreck, hoping to save whomever they could… especially Suzette. Harder and harder they rowed, straining their muscles to catch up to the disaster before it got to be any worse.

Aboard the ship, chaos had taken hold. The captain ran to his quarters to retrieve what he deemed most important—his money—and rushed back up to the deck as the ship listed precariously to one side. His pockets were full of heavy gold, nearly dragging his pants down, so he clutched the waistband of his trousers with one hand and grabbed for things to hold onto for stability with the other.

Dernier stood on the deck with a death grip on Suzette. He covered her mouth with his hand, as if it was important to keep her quiet for some unfathomable reason. She fought and kicked him with all of her might, but he held on as hard as he could.

Dernier was so terrified of plunging into the churning

water that he lost what was left of his mind. His eyes were glazed over with insanity, rolling around in his skull without firm focus. His body curled around Suzette as if he hoped she might protect him from the crashing waves. He thought to himself that at least he could control Suzette—if nothing else.

The large sailor who'd summoned them to go speak to the captain gaped at what Dernier was doing. It did not seem to him that the Frenchman was in any way trying to protect his beloved wife. Knowing that he'd cut her with a knife and judging by the way she was thrashing, it seemed as if she might fear Dernier more than the sinking of the ship. Making a split-second decision, the sailor leapt forward and grabbed Dernier from behind, prying him off of Suzette as he flailed and squealed curses in French. Without hesitating, the big sailor threw the little weasel overboard.

Suzette stared at him with wide eyes. "Th-thank you," she said, more than a little dazed by the sudden change in luck.

The sailor shrugged. If death was coming for them, he had decided to make sure his last act was one of bravery.

Suzette looked around wild-eyed, seeing the water pouring into the gaping hole in the side of the ship. "Now, what should we do?"

"We have rescuers coming. Take a look." He gestured at the small fleet of skiffs heading their way. "If we sink before they make it to us, just hang onto me. I'm a good swimmer. I'll keep you safe."

Suzette liked his confidence and his willingness to help. She tried to maintain a level of optimism, but their predicament was terrifying. She had to hold onto the railing for dear life, and her feet kept slipping out from under her.

The noises were unbelievable. Men hollered everywhere, and the ship sounded like she was screaming as she cracked and heaved. Timbers continued to shatter, and cargo spilled out of the hole below the deck. Lower and lower they sank as the water rushed in. Everything that wasn't secured slid around and crashed into something else.

It was bedlam.

But then the deck itself heaved, and one of the huge masts split. "Look out!" Suzette cried as it toppled over.

As the enormous timber rolled toward them, the sailor snatched her up and jumped backward. Overboard. The two of them flew through the air, wind rushing around them as they fell. The sailor lost his grip on Suzette. His body twisted to the side in the fall, and he hit his head on a protruding piece of wood on the side of the ship.

Suzette heard a sickening thud, followed by his dull cry of pain. Then he splashed into the water of the tumultuous bay.

Suzette struck the water only a moment behind him. It felt as if she were suddenly submerged in a pool of ice. The cold was incredible—nothing like the beautiful, tiled swimming pool she'd enjoyed as a child at her family's chateau. This was the rolling, frigid Pacific Ocean, and it took her breath away.

The fall itself was not that bad; her landing had been cushioned by the large body of the sailor, and they hadn't dropped all that far because the ship was so low in the water to begin with. But the strong arms that grasped her slipped away all too quickly.

Suzette began to tread water, seriously impeded by her petticoats and frock. She turned around to look at her protector and saw that his head was bleeding, and his eyes were closed. Clinging to him with all her might, Suzette kicked her legs to keep them both afloat, but the heaviness of her skirts frustrated her efforts.

A large piece of wood drifted nearby, and she tried to grab it to keep them buoyant, but it stayed just out of her reach. She couldn't swim to it and hold up the sailor at the same time, so she just tried to keep them both from drowning.

Other sailors were floating in the water around them. The skipper was among those men. He seemed to drift farther from the boat, and Suzette watched, completely appalled, as the man made some awkward, flailing attempts to float but slowly sunk into the bay. He did not resurface, so she assumed he was either not a swimmer or was weighed down too much to stay afloat.

In fact, the gold in his pockets pulled the captain down; he ended up at the bottom of the harbor and was never seen again.

Some of the men had managed to swim over to the rocks and were climbing up onto them. No one seemed very interested in helping Suzette, and she could not see Dernier anywhere. *Please, God, get Isaac and Walter here soon. I am so tired. I do not know how much longer I can stay afloat,* she prayed over and over.

Something stuck Suzette on the back and she craned her

neck to see a piece of lumber roughly the size of a door. It looked sturdy, and she thought maybe she could get the sailor on top of it. She grabbed it, almost losing her grip on him in the process. Shoving his arm onto the wood plank without any help from him nearly sent her to a watery grave. She would have to get onto it herself and pull him up. *How do I do that? I cannot let go of him.*

She tried to hoist one leg up onto the wood and discovered that was also nearly impossible in skirts that seemed to be intent on either strangling her or dragging her to the bottom of the harbor. Finally, she just held onto the man with one arm and grasped the wood with the other. It wasn't a lot of help, but it made her feel a little better to have it anyway. Hanging onto both of them taxed her endurance terribly.

It was only about twenty minutes, but to Suzette, it felt as if several painful hours before Isaac rowed his boat right up to her. He was drenched in sweat from his exertion but didn't slow down one bit. As soon as they came alongside her, Walter and Royal grabbed her arms and hoisted her inside the boat. This caused her to let go of the sailor, and she cried out, "Help him! He saved me! Do not let him drown!"

Without thinking twice, Walter tore off his glasses and dove overboard. The water was murky and sixty feet deep. Looking around, he could barely see a thing. Surfacing again, he sucked in a huge gulp of air and dove back down. The current was strong, and he felt himself getting shoved away from Isaac and the others in the boat.

"Find him, find him, Walter. But do not get hurt!" Suzette was shaking from head to toe, but she watched the water anxiously, praying for Walter's safe return. Isaac grabbed her and wrapped her in his heated embrace as his breath heaved from his exertion. He was so hot and sweaty from rowing he warmed her instantly. She sagged against him. "Oh, Isaac," she sobbed. "I was so afraid I would never see you again. Thank you for following the ship and getting to us before I sank into the sea!"

Isaac was gasping for breath too hard to reply.

Below the skiff, Walter tried desperately to find the sailor. When he didn't surface with the sailor in his grip immediately, Royal also dove overboard. The strongest swimmer in the group—and with better eyesight than Walter—Royal sped downward past Walter and, with a stroke of luck, managed to grab the sinking man's hand. Kicking with all of his might, he rose up to where Walter was almost out of breath. Walter grabbed for the man's shirt and helped propel him the last ten feet up to the surface.

When they broke the surface, they realized that the current had separated them from the skiff, so they had to swim the painstaking distance back to the boat, hauling dead weight between them. When they finally reached the small skiff, Richard, Alfonzo, and Jasper each grabbed part of the sailor and hauled him gracelessly over the gunwale and into the boat. As he landed with a bump, he expelled a gush of water from his mouth.

"He's a big one," Jasper pointed out. "And he doesn't look too good. Do you think he's still alive?"

"Oh, please let him be alive," Suzette whimpered as she clung to Isaac.

The men of Aylesbury Fire Company were well-trained in emergency situations, so Richard dropped to his knees and turned the man to his side. He pressed steadily on the sailor's abdomen. Another flood of seawater escaped his mouth, so then Richard began mouth-to-mouth resuscitation. After about thirty seconds of this, the man's eyelids fluttered, and Suzette cried, "*Merci, mon Dieu!* He lives!"

When the sailor noisily sucked in a massive breath of air, everyone in the boat cheered.

Walter and Royal were helped back into the boat by Alfonzo, who had a massive grin on his face. Walter went immediately to Suzette and Isaac and wrapped his arms around them. "Thank God," he whispered. Then he asked, "How do you feel, Suzette? Is the baby alright?"

"We are fine, I promise. And now that we are together, everything is perfect." She kissed him sweetly. "This will be quite the story to tell our child."

Isaac surveyed the harbor and saw that some larger boats were headed out to the wreck, presumably to rescue the rest of the crew who were still perched on the rocks and to salvage whatever they could of what was floating on the surface of the bay. The other Aylesbury men in the accompanying boats had already scooped up as many of the sailors as they could fit in their boats without capsizing, and they were heading back to the dock.

Jasper sat down and picked up the oars. "You can take a rest, Isaac, after all of your rowing. The rest of us can take turns getting us back."

As they all took seats and got as comfortable as possible,

shivering in soaking wet clothes, Suzette asked the sailor they'd rescued, "What is your name, sir? I need to know whom to thank for keeping me alive."

His gravelly voice sounded even rougher than before when he answered, "And I need to thank you all as well for not letting me drown. My name is Hawkins, ma'am. Jeb Hawkins."

"Have you always been a sailor, Mr. Hawkins?"

"Jeb is fine, ma'am. No, I used to be a shipwright in Boston, but then one day I got the urge to go to sea instead of building ships. I made a mistake. Turns out I like being on land a lot more than sailing. I was planning to make some money sailing home on this voyage by working on a few different ships until I made it to Boston."

"Oh, so do you have a family to go back to?"

"No, not really. I was just hoping to get my old job back. I missed building things and working with my hands."

Isaac, Walter, Royal, and Jasper all began to chuckle then, and Jeb looked at them questioningly.

"This may be your lucky day in more ways than one, Jeb," Walter explained. "The four of us own a building company. We don't build boats, but if you're interested in houses and furniture, we'd be obliged to offer you a position."

Jeb looked pleased, shook their hands, and then coughed up some more of the San Francisco Bay before he could thank them.

"I think first we need to have Doc Louis take a look at you before we put you to work," Royal said. "You'll like him."

Just then, Walter squeezed Suzette's side a little too energetically, and she gave a small cry.

"What's wrong?" Walter pulled back like he'd been burned.

"Oh, it is nothing. Just a little scratch."

Jeb grumbled, "Don't be so brave, ma'am." To Walter, he said, "That miserable scum stabbed her with his knife. I think your doc needs to look at her first."

"He *stabbed* you?" Isaac bellowed at her. "Let us see." He carefully peeled back the torn portion of her clothing and eyed her wound. "Doc Louis needs to see this, but it doesn't actually look too bad."

"That's a relief," Walter sighed. "I'm sorry if I hurt you by touching it, though, dearest."

"I will be fine. I am so happy to be rid of Dernier and together with you, I cannot think of anything that could be wrong."

Isaac grimaced. "I could kill that miserable bastard for doing this to you and putting you through such awful turmoil."

"I am not sure you need to. I did not see him anywhere after we crashed on the rocks. He made a quick exit into the water, thanks to Jeb, and that may have been the end of him. Dernier was nearly strangling me when Jeb tossed him overboard."

Walter thought a moment and said, "It's highly likely he was caught in the current and became trapped. If he couldn't swim away from it, he probably went down with the ship."

Regarding Jeb, he added, "We all owe you a great debt of gratitude, sir."

WHEN THEY GOT BACK TO SHORE AND TO THE AYLESBURY FIRE Company, everyone who was in another boat agreed that they had not fished an angry little Frenchman out of the bay, and no one remembered having seen anyone like that stranded on the rocks.

Doc Louis was on hand to check out all of the survivors, and he was delighted to report that everyone was healthy, including Suzette and Jeb. He prescribed a few days rest in bed for Suzette, however.

The sailors all happily dispersed—some back to their homes and others back to the dock where they knew they could be hired onto another ship. Only Jeb remained, and he was given quarters in the Fire Company. "I would love to join your ranks as a volunteer," he declared happily. "This is wonderful. I have a new job and a fine place to live, all because I was saved by this beautiful woman here."

Suzette's laugh sounded like tinkling bells when she responded, "You are far too modest, Jeb. Thank you for the compliment, but let us agree that without each other's interference, neither of us would be standing here alive. I owe my life to you."

Isaac wrapped his arms around her tightly. "Let's get you

home, my love." Regarding Jeb, he added, "We'll see you at work on Monday morning. Take care of yourself and let us know if you need anything."

Jasper and Royal had already invited Jeb to Friday supper at Hart House.

Walter solemnly shook Jeb's hand, and they all left for home, but not before Isaac had a short, whispered conversation with Doc Louis.

D elphine and Fabienne were beside themselves with joy when the men returned with Suzette.

"I will fix you a nice bath immediately, madame," Fabienne declared.

"And as soon as you are comfortable in your bed, I will bring you a nice hot meal."

"I would prefer to have breakfast with the men first, and then I will go to bed," Suzette announced. "I find that after my ordeal and having had no sleep last night, I am rather exhausted." She looked at Isaac and Walter. "I imagine both of you feel the same since you were up running around all night as well. And we all need baths."

After they were all clean, warm, and fed, the three lovers made their way to the bed. After kissing one other soundly, they slept the rest of the day away wrapped in each other's embrace. When they awoke hours later with rumbling bellies, it was time for dinner. Suzette wanted to get up, but Isaac had other things to say about that.

"We'll help Delphine bring our food up here, and you will stay in bed as Doc Louis said to do. We don't want to take any chances, my love."

"He is right, dearest," Walter agreed. They left the room.

Suzette was not very keen on lying about in bed, but she agreed to it. However, after the men left, she could hear them laughing and exclaiming over something from downstairs. Curiosity got the better of her, so she pulled on a dressing gown and followed the sound of their voices down the stairs.

The house was filled with bouquets and lovely cakes and confections from their friends and neighbors. Note after note proclaimed their relief that all was well. Apparently, word traveled quickly around here. Suzette was touched to the core to realize how many people cared. There were also sweet notes and drawings from the children she taught.

Wiping her eyes, Suzette read every last message. "My heart is so full right now. I never expected to find love in my life. And now I have it from the two best men in the world and from friends all over the city. How did I become so blessed?"

Walter took her hand and said, "We're the ones who are blessed. When you arrived here, our lives changed for the better. And soon, our love will increase even more." He bent to kiss her belly.

"Now that you've seen this, it's back to bed for you," Isaac ordered. He scooped Suzette up into his arms and carried her up the stairs again. He made sure she was comfortable and then checked the fire to see that it was just right, and he climbed in next to her. "Walter and the girls ought to be back with our food soon, but I wanted to tell you privately how much I love you and how terrifying this experience has been for Walter and me. I don't know what we'd have done if you'd sailed back to France with that madman." He closed his eyes and leaned his head against hers. "Our love is perfect, Suzette. Thank you."

When Walter, Delphine, and Fabienne arrived with the food, they decided it would be more practical to dine in front of the fire, but as soon as they finished, they all climbed back into their enormous bed.

Isaac announced, "I checked with Doc Louis, and he said that as long as the cut on Suzette's side doesn't bother her too much, we should be able to make love with no problems. The baby seems just fine to him, so we have no worries." He grinned. "Maybe we'll have an excellent swimmer on our hands."

"That's just grand news," Walter exclaimed with a huge smile. "Suzette, how do you feel about it?" As he said this, he kissed gently down her neck from ear to collarbone.

"Oh, yes, please," she whispered. She grasped Isaac's hand and tilted her neck to give Walter better access. "I was so afraid we would never have this again."

"Only happy thoughts now." Isaac freed his hand and undid her dressing gown, exposing her full breasts and rounded belly. He bent to play with her nipple, kissing and nibbling at it and then sucking it into his hot mouth. Walter mirrored Isaac's attention on Suzette's other breast, and she groaned contentedly as she felt her arousal awaken. The men played like that until she squirmed. When they pulled off of her chest, they leaned forward and kissed each other. Suzette stroked her fingers through their hair as they showed their love for one another. It always heightened her excitement when they did that. She knew she was growing wetter by the moment.

And that fact was confirmed when, still kissing Walter, Isaac spread her legs with one hand and slipped the finger of the other hand inside her. He moaned as he felt her readiness. At almost the same time, Walter's hand sought out her clit, and he massaged it as Isaac stroked one and then two fingers in and out of her. They set up an orchestrated rhythm of prodding in and out and swirling round and round, then pulled back from each other and attacked her nipples again with their mouths. This time the men flicked with their tongues and nibbled with teeth, urging Suzette onward, closer and closer to release.

Rather than stiffening with pent-up sexual tension, Suzette surprised herself as an orgasm whooshed through her like a wave. A soft moan escaped her lips, and then she whispered words of love and devotion in French. The waves continued over and over as she rode out spasms of pleasure, each one making her gasp and twitch. Finally, she said, "Please, I need you inside me. Both of you."

Isaac was closest to the bedside table that held their bottle of oil, so he reached for it and applied it liberally to his erection. Raising Suzette's legs and spreading them further, he also massaged her backside with the oil, rubbing and prodding with an oily finger. All the while, he and Walter crooned loving words to her, and Walter kissed her body from top to bottom, nipping and licking his favorite parts as he went. Suzette shivered with desire as the men readied her in such a loving manner. "Now, Isaac," she pleaded.

Suzette turned to face away from Isaac, and he gently lifted her up over himself. Walter grabbed Isaac's steely member and sucked on it for a moment before applying more oil, causing Isaac to sigh with pleasure. Walter then held it firmly in place while Isaac positioned Suzette over it. Gradually, Isaac let Suzette slide down onto him. She groaned when he was seated deeply inside her body. "Now you, Walter. Join us," she said with a hitch in her voice. Walter bent and sucked her clit into his hot mouth, causing her to shake and cry out with pleasure.

Walter was terribly excited when he took himself in hand and realized he'd been leaking precum all over. So, with an oily hand, he rubbed the liquid up and down his shaft. He scooted closer to Suzette and kissed her deeply as he carefully fed himself into her wet heat.

The three of them relaxed a moment to enjoy the magic of their connection. Each realized privately how close they'd come to losing this, but not one of them wished to break the spell by voicing that thought.

Gradually, they began to move, perhaps a tad more gently than usual. Suzette wanted to urge them to pound in and out of her, proving that she was in no way delicate, but she knew the men could not do that to her on this day. *Perhaps soon,* she told herself. *Once they see that I am completely fine.* She merely loved them all the more for it. She let them set a gentle pace for once.

On and on they demonstrated their passion to her, and she rode the tender tide of love to an exquisite climax. The men reached release at the same time—eyes closed as if in prayer.

Later, as they lay together in bed, holding one another, Suzette proclaimed out of the blue, "Ondine!"

"Dearest?" Walter asked.

"What or who is Ondine?" Isaac questioned her.

"This is a girl. I feel it in my very bones, and we will call her Ondine. It means 'little wave.' I feel that she has felt many waves today. It is a suitable name for her."

"It's a beautiful name," Isaac agreed.

"Yes," said Walter and kissed Suzette's belly. "We can't wait to meet you, Ondine. Now don't go disappointing your mother by turning out to be a boy."

Isaac laughed. "If it's a boy, we can call him Bay."

"That works as well," Walter agreed with a grin.

Epilogue

They delayed their concert so Suzette could rest and recuperate. And then they had to delay it a bit longer.

Two months after her harrowing adventure aboard the *Ophelia*, Suzette safely brought Ondine de Massey Stark-James into the world. Blue-eyed with curly blonde hair, Ondine looked like a tiny miniature copy of her mama. Her two papas would never be the same as their hearts nearly burst with love for Suzette, Ondine, and each other.

Eventually, they had their concert, and it was a grand success.

Over the next few years, Ondine was joined by her siblings, Bay—whose name had become a favorite of theirs—and then Martha and Warren, named for Isaac's late parents. A few years went by, and the family had accepted that they were probably done having children when they were surprised to find Suzette in the family way once more. They named this one Nicolo to honor Paganini. Fortunately or unfortunately, according to your point of view, Nicolo was not an ideal music student. He would prove that he had his own talents.

One day when Ondine was a toddler and Bay was still a baby, Suzette came downstairs to breakfast to hear her daughter giggling amongst a lot of grown male laughter. Entering the dining room, she gasped at the sight in front of her. Sunburnt with shaggy locks and a very uncharacteristic costume of casual clothing, between her husbands, sat… "Pascal? What are you doing here? Where have you been?" Her brother sat bouncing his niece on his knee, looking happier than she'd ever seen him.

Rising to kiss her cheeks, Pascal exclaimed, "Suzette, you look wonderful. I have so much to tell you of my adventures. Life at sea has been the education I always needed."

It seemed that Pascal had flourished when required to complete tasks. The sense of accomplishment motivated him to set aside his gambling and drinking. He learned to take orders well and enjoyed working so hard that his muscles burned by the end of the day. He loved visiting ports of call all over the world, and his ability to speak multiple languages came in handy and made him a favorite with his skipper. So, he rose in the ranks and learned all he could about ships.

Although he did not stay long, Pascal's arrival caused a shift in the men of Roja Wais. He spoke endlessly of the beautiful land to the south of San Francisco, adding that vast acreage could be bought up easily from the government. He talked about ranching opportunities that he'd seen and men he'd met who'd built homesteads. The climate was nice, he assured them, and opportunity was everywhere.

There was no doubt that San Francisco was still a boom town, but the men of Roja Wais loved a challenge. Night after night, they would stay up, discussing the possibilities of moving their business south. Life would lack the sophistication of an established city, but there were opportunities calling to them, just as once they had felt called to move west. Their biggest concerns were their wives.

So, during one Friday night supper at Hart House, they broached the subject with Adeline and Suzette. Adeline merely smiled and said, "We wondered when you would get around to asking our opinion." It seemed the women were completely on board with the idea of moving south to a new frontier. "Just so long as I get to bring my piano," Addie laughed.

"My violin is more portable, so I am not concerned," Suzette said with a nod. "As long as I have my men and my babies, I will be happy anywhere."

Not expecting an affirmative answer, they asked Doc Louis and Marguerite to move south with them. They were delighted to find that the couple also saw moving south as an opportunity for some adventure. Marguerite had created a successful business, but she was willing to retire from it, and Doc Louis thought the people in the south just might need a good physician. So, in 1860, they all sold their houses and businesses and took off for the south.

It was the start of a grand new adventure, but they were used to that.

. . .

The End

Have you read The Golden Rush?

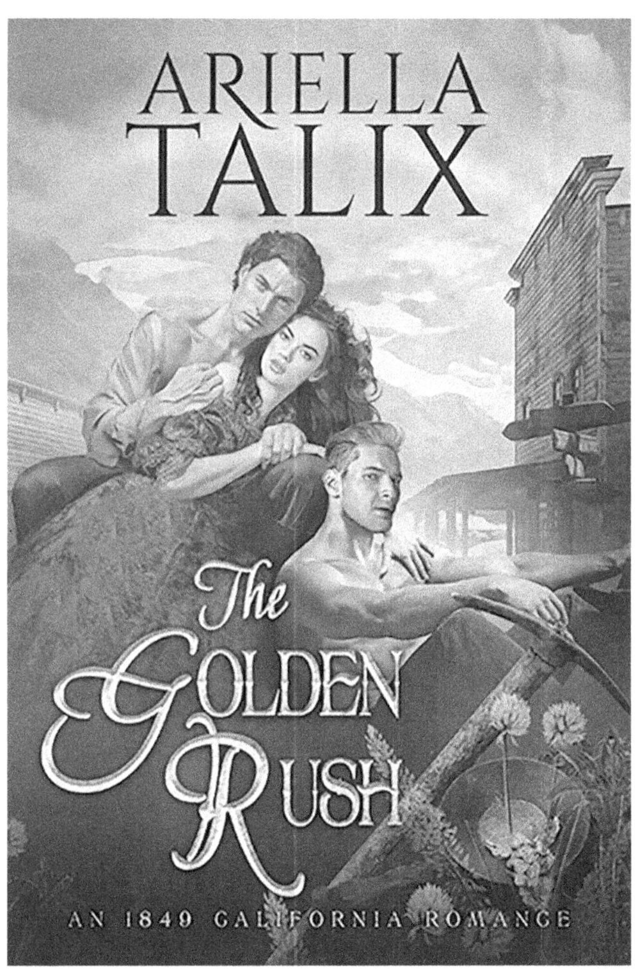

Musings and Acknowledgements

I have never taken so long to write a book. I originally started this one right after finishing *The Golden Rush*, but had a few doubts about moving forward. After a few chapters, another sequel kept pounding away at my head, and I found myself writing *The Passion of 3* instead of *Fiddle and Fire*. Once *The Passion of 3* was out in the world (and I was completely in love with the story), only then was I able to get back to this one. I am so glad I completed it this time.

My apologies to the readers who've patiently awaited this installment in the story. Things happened in my life (like surgery) that just made progress difficult. Thank you for sticking with me!

If you've read *The Golden Rush*, you may be aware that some of the story parallels my own family's background as early California citizens. That was partially the reason I was so drawn to the history of that time. I actually allowed my family's patriarch a one-line cameo appearance in this book.

Something I wanted to be sure to do, however, was to get my beloved characters out of San Francisco before the many upcoming disasters happened. I couldn't even bear the thought of having their children involved in what was to come in San Francisco. So, I moved them south, the same way my family migrated. The terrible earthquake and subsequent fires completely destroyed Rincon Hill, and it never regained its residential grandeur. Eventually, it became an industrial area. San Francisco has been a resilient city that has rebuilt countless times, but Rincon Hill did not return to glory.

There were also social changes in the wind that would have precluded the acceptance of these characters' lifestyles, and I didn't want them to be subjected to that. It was time to move on. It's just my personal opinion, but I think that moving them to a less populated area—one that was still a frontier—may have kept them away from the prejudice that began to infiltrate San Francisco. Without making up tales or pointing fingers at my ancestors, I have reason to believe that there was some ménage activity going on. It was certainly hinted at broadly by my mother and aunt who typically got the giggles about it.

I cannot stress enough the debt of gratitude we owe the courageous forty-niners who founded San Francisco and shaped California. But also those pioneers who came before them and trekked across the country only to be barricaded from the promised land by the Sierra Nevada. The grit those people exemplified is beyond humbling. They met with tremendous, frightening challenges that we can't even comprehend today. The trip to southern California must have felt like a lovely Sunday drive in comparison, but it took an adventurous spirit to contemplate that move. It was still very much the wild west. I am so proud of my ancestors.

When I mention "ancestors" in this context, I refer to my mother's family. Half of my father's family preceded the white man. They were Native American, as I explained in *The Golden Rush*. The other half arrived in California more like the characters in *Grapes of Wrath*. But in all cases, my family has been in this country for a long, long time.

I owe thanks to several people who nominated the dogs' names in a contest. Apparently, Ember and Cinder were fated as they showed up from multiple sources. Thank you to everyone who participated. I hope you all had fun coming up with names. Free books went to the winners—Judy, Laurie, and Susan.

Always big thanks go to Amy Maranville, my editor (who was self-proclaimed #teamisaac). I've been so all over the place with a date for when I could send her this book, it's positively embarrassing. She graciously said not to worry, and for that, I am tremendously thankful. No one needs stress on top of surgery, that's for sure.

Likewise, my lovely proofreader Mattie Davenport (solidly in the #teamwalter camp) has been able to accommodate my lack of timeliness, so many thanks go to both of these wonderful, talented ladies. As the author, it was fascinating to read Mattie and Amy's reactions to parts of the book. They both responded emotionally to the same sections and various characters, but often with opposite opinions. None of this was negative in any way, but it made me feel good to know that I could stir up emotion before I let this story go out into the world.

Dar Albert of Wicked Smart Designs also outdid herself once again by designing the beautiful cover for the book. It is my great pleasure to have her work grace my books even if Amazon thinks the cover is too sexy to advertise.

Thank you once again to my terrific beta reader Susan. Her input is always such an important part of the process of writing. I couldn't do it without her. Her friendship is very special to me. Another great perk that comes with writing is meeting great people. Susan was so excited when I named Suzette loosely after her. I couldn't resist.

It's rather amazing where and when inspiration strikes. I was at physical therapy when a fellow patient mentioned a young woman he'd met years ago named Fabienne. I thanked him profusely and grabbed that great name for my character.

Once again, my husband stepped up and not only listened to me but offered some great suggestions. He also pitched in admirably when I couldn't do much other than recuperate. A very fine husband.

What's next? As of this writing, I'm not completely sure. A new series sounds good… we'll see… I've started experimenting with something, but I'll decide soon whether to turn it into a book or a short story.

Thank you, dear reader, for spending time soaking up the stories that I conjure up in my head. Each time someone reads a book, it's a compliment.

I'll try to be faster with the next one.

Love,
Ariella Talix

Please sign up for my newsletter if you'd like to stay in touch. https://landing.mailerlite.com/webforms/landing/m6f3i7 I generally mail one out once a month.

Also, I love to hear from readers. info@ariellatalix.com

Just Curious

Compelling Urges

HISTORICAL ROMANCE

<u>Hearts of Gold</u>

The Golden Rush

Fiddle and Fire

www.ingramcontent.com/pod-product-compliance
Lightning Source LLC
Chambersburg PA
CBHW071238300726

48975CB00002B/461